NEW DIMENSIONS 6

New Dimensions

SCIENCE FICTION

NUMBER 6

Edited by ROBERT SILVERBERG

HARPER & ROW, PUBLISHERS

NEW YORK

HAGERSTOWN

SAN FRANCISCO

LONDON

FIRST EDITION

LIBRARY OF CONGRESS CATALOG CARD NUMBER: 75–25103

ISBN: 0–06–013864–5

Designed by Sidney Feinberg

Drawings by Raccoona Sheldon

76 77 78 79 10 9 8 7 6 5 4 3 2 1

CONTENTS

INTRODUCTION

This is the sixth in a series of annual collections dedicated to presenting the most original and significant science fiction being written today. All stories in *New Dimensions* are being published here for the first time. The contributors range from long-established professionals to brilliant beginners; the one thing they have in common is a desire to explore new territory, to discover new ways of approaching the ideas, images, and assumptions of classic science fiction. Old formulas and exhausted clichés are unwelcome here; *New Dimensions* seeks writers whose visions are exciting and unique.

The editor of *New Dimensions* is Robert Silverberg, himself one of science fiction's best-known writers, whose novels and stories include *Dying Inside, The Book of Skulls, Nightwings, Born with the Dead, A Time of Changes, Tower of Glass, Son of Man,* and many others. Mr. Silverberg, who lives in California, has won science fiction's prized Hugo and Nebula awards for literary excellence many times, is a past president of the Science Fiction Writers of America, and was American Guest of Honor at the World Science Fiction Convention held in Heidelberg, Germany, in 1970.

NEW DIMENSIONS 6

The vein that GEORGE ALEC EFFINGER *seems to be mining within science fiction is that of surrealism—which, it is important to remember, has never been quite as self-indulgent a mode as it seems to its detractors, for its effect depends chiefly on extraordinary realism, on realism carried to a lunatic extreme. (The teacup may have fur on it, sure, but the fur is meticulously rendered by painstaking strokes of the brush.) Here we have a delectable and many-leveled vision of the other World War II, the one that broke out in 1974, the one that was fought with armadas of Toyotas and Volkswagens, the war we didn't know about until Effinger thoughtfully set down this account of it for our benefit.*

■

George Alec Effinger

■

TARGET: BERLIN!
The Role of the Air Force Four-Door Hardtop

PREFACE

Feeling neglected, my wife left me during those terrible months. I also lost the friendship of several colleagues, but we succeeded in modifying a Lincoln Continental four-door sedan into our first great bomber of the war, the B-17 Flying Fortress. It was a trying time, but I'll tell you about it if you care to listen.

Effinger WWII Book Gossipy, Rambling

Reviewed for the Rusty Brook, N. J., *Sun* by Louis J. Arphouse

The opening words of Effinger's memoir, the very first paragraph of his preface, give the flavor of the remainder of the book. After a chapter or two, it is not a pleasant flavor. This is the first eye-witness document we have gotten from the war, at least from so notorious a participant. One could have hoped for a more disciplined, less discursive book. Effinger was personally involved in many of the tactical decisions and technical inventions that shaped the Second World War. He has seen fit in his history of those years to give us instead his meager snapshots of great figures, mere glimpses of elbows and coats rushing out of the frame while momentous consequences remain hinted at in the background.

One might even think that Effinger's book was written well

3

before the end of the war, as a kind of hedging of his bets. In places it seems like the author is placating his former enemies, smoothing over their errors in the hopes that, had they emerged victorious, they might have gone easier on Effinger in whatever hypothetical war crimes trials that might have ensued. It's unlikely that the book would have had even that effect. Instead, it is too stilted to be read with any pleasure as a personal memoir, and not strict enough to be of value as a history text. It is fortunate for Effinger, and for the free world, that his talents during the war were used in other directions.

PREFACE *(Continued)*

The decision not to hold the Second World War in the nineteen-forties was made by mutual consent of all combatant parties, and a general agreement was signed in Geneva. Simply speaking, most nations felt it would just be better to wait. But there were often more probing reasons, situations which reflected sophisticated and convoluted paths of national policy. The Japanese, for example, at the Maryknoll conference, were rankled at the oil embargo a suspicious United States had placed on that island empire. A Japanese delegate rose from his seat at one point and abandoned his polite but false diplomatic manner. "What's the matter?" he said in a loud voice. "I can't understand it. Your own Admiral Perry opened us up to trade. Now you won't sell us what we want. That's stupid." And the irate delegate walked out of the conference room, blushing at his own brazenness.

There was a stunned silence, and then a great deal of muttering from the American side of the table. One of the American delegates cleared his throat. "You know," he said, "we never looked at it that way. He has a point."

The conference went on more smoothly from there and eventually achieved a compromise that both sides could accept enthusiastically. Japan no longer felt threatened economically, and war with the United States was averted. However, there were other causes for the sudden mending of political fences, many of which might have seemed laughable at the time but which cannot be underestimated in the light of successive events. One of the emperor's younger nephews, a member of the Imperial War Office, was a great baseball fan, as were many of his countrymen; this influential person believed that it would be a shame to interrupt the career of such a star as Joe Di-Maggio. The emperor's nephew, too, was a voice that counseled patience.

In Nazi Germany, the citizens were made aware of the activities of Heinrich Himmler and Reinhard Heydrich. These men, chiefs of the SS and the Security Police, were assembling vast dossiers on millions upon millions of people: Nazis, anti-Nazis, politicians, common people, rich, poor, old, young. No one in the Reich could escape their scrutiny. Of course, this news made the people of Germany nervous; at the first opportunity, the Nazis were removed from office. "Thank God for the American news services," said many German citizens afterward, for it was through the American newspapers and radio broadcasts that the Germans were alerted to the shenanigans of the Nazis. "The Americans are the sentinels of liberty. Once again they have had to save our necks." The political structure of Germany reformed, moving from the extreme right, stopping comfortably just left of middle; the new rulers in Berlin made it embarrassingly clear to Washington that there was no further reason to seek war. Italy, her trains humming along on schedule, followed suit a few months later. The trains got all fouled up, but tourists in Italy reported that otherwise things had changed for the better, except around Venice during July and August, and even Mussolini hadn't been able to do anything about that.

AT LAST, THE WAR AS IT WAS!

TARGET: BERLIN!
BY GEORGE ALEC EFFINGER
OFERMOD PRESS, $12.95
ILLUSTRATED

At long last, Ofermod Press is proud to announce the publication of the first genuine firsthand documentary to come out of the war. A searing indictment of the conservative voices in

President Roosevelt's cabinet and of the timid liberal partisans, both groups which almost led the United States to ruin. MORE! A caustic attack on the fearful counselors who would allow other nations in this postwar world to maintain a superiority in number and type of bombing weapon. MORE! A vital book for all thoughtful citizens, a shocking, sometimes amusing glimpse into the world of high-pressure politics and top-level decision-making. MORE! This book is much more because it was written by one of the most influential men of the Second World War, and it contains an urgent message for all Americans.

NATIONAL ADVERTISING,
PROMOTION, AND TWENTY-FOUR-CITY
AUTHOR TOUR

$12.95, Pub Date Sept. 9, 1981

PREFACE (Continued)

I could see how the war was going to go, even at the very beginning. I know that isn't the kind of thing one should say about oneself, especially in a book like this. But in this case there isn't anyone else around to say it and, after all, my opinion was later seconded by President Roosevelt himself, in addition to a handful of lesser dignitaries. "Well, George," said the President, "you guessed which turn this war would take quite a while ago, didn't you?" I had to agree. And, in the same way, I can see which way this book is going, too, not that it does me any more good. Because during the war I had what I came to call a Cassandra complex. I'll discuss that in more detail later; let me just say now that I had a sense of the magnitude of the war's climax, but I never felt certain of the moral implications.

It must be made clear, prefatorily, that international disagreements had not been completely resolved without open conflict. No, rather, the war had merely been shelved. The more bloodthirsty members of Japan's Imperial War Office went underground for some years, as did their counterparts in France and Great Britain, in the Soviet Union, the war-seekers in the United States, Hitler's colleagues and Mussolini's. The world at large slumbered in three decades of what the Twenties and Thirties had been—a mixed bag of peace, prosperity, anxiety, and depression. Franklin Delano Roosevelt, relieved of many of his heaviest political worries, continued in office, as hearty as ever, a visual reminder, along with Winston Churchill, of a nostalgic time. The Forties passed, and the Fifties, and the frenetic Sixties. Then the Seventies began, and it looked once more as if the world were edging closer to that irrevocable stumble into total war. In Germany the populace, tired of thirty years of liberal politics and the rowdiness it induced in the younger generation, began a slow retreat toward fascism. Adolf Hitler, now eighty-five years old, came out of retirement to lead his country. Himmler dusted off his old dossiers. The people of Germany who recalled the old days smiled and nudged their neighbors. Hitler was something they could understand, not like the glittery transvestite singing stars of their children's generation. Hitler would show those guys something. The older people settled back to watch.

In Japan, the emperor's nephew no longer followed American baseball. He had taken up golf. With a worldwide fuel shortage in 1974, Japan found herself back in the same situation that she had been in the early Forties. "What the hell," muttered the Imperial War Office. "What the hell," muttered the emperor. Secret plans were made.

France watched nervously, Great Britain watched confidently, the Soviet Union watched slyly. The United States didn't seem to be watching at all, but it was difficult to be sure.

Events moved quickly thereafter, resuming their inexorable march to war along the very same lines that had been abandoned three decades before. But there were a few alterations, thanks to the progress of both technology and human relations.

Hermann Goering, leader of Hitler's Luftwaffe, studied detailed maps of Poland and France. Goering, now eighty-one years old, looked somewhat ridiculous in his refurbished uniforms. His fat face was masked by broad striations of wrinkles. His hands wavered noticeably as he lifted small replicas of aircraft, moving them from bases within the Reich to proposed targets all over the mapboard. He beamed happily as he set an airplane down in Paris, another in London, a third in Prague. An aide moved still another airplane to Moscow, too far for Goering to reach by himself. The air marshal's aides whispered behind his back. Some one would have to tell the Führer's trusted lieutenant about the Luftwaffe's weak point. The young men, fearful of the senile yet powerful man, contested among themselves. Eventually the least assertive and most vulnerable of them presented Goering with a special file, one which had been placed on his desk several times before and which Goering had chosen to ignore. He could ignore it no longer.

FROM THE DESK OF . . .
                                    . . .HERMANN GOERING
                                    Reich Master of the Hunt

                                                    June 10, 1974

Dear George:

It's been a long time since I've seen you. How are things in the Free World? Things are moving along at a rapid pace here, under the banner of National Socialism. I'm sure you're keeping up with events, but I'll bet we still surprise you. The next few years will be momentous ones in the history of the world. Isn't it kind of exciting, being on the inside?

Talk of war is heard on all sides. I'm sure you're keeping up to date on our air force, its size and capabilities, just as I receive reports on you and the others. I wonder if your reports are any better than mine. You must know that the Luftwaffe is in no shape to face a long, drawn-out war now. But there's no talking to Adolf these days. He has this timetable, he keeps telling us. Ah, well, we do our best. You know just how difficult this job is.

You probably also know that we've scrapped the idea of long-range heavy bombers. I don't suppose I'm giving away any secrets in saying that. We'd have to restructure our entire automotive industry. You've already beaten us there. But don't count us out altogether! You might wake up some morning to the sound of Volkswagen six-passenger luxury bombers driving by under your window. You know us. We have more Situation Contingency Plans than anyone even knows about—including me, Adolf, the OKW, or anybody. If we could just get everything indexed and sorted, we'd be in great shape. Too many personalities clashing for that, though, I'm afraid. . . .

Tell Diana that my Emmy tried her recipe for Mad Dog Chili last week. Emmy saw it in the New York *Post*. It was so good that I was in bed recovering for three days. That was a very nice profile on Diana, too. She must be happy. Emmy can't get anything like it here, in the *Beobachter*. I think Emmy's jealous.

If there isn't war by then, I'll see you in the fall in Milan for the air show. I wish I had your youth; nowadays, a few days away from Emmy means only that I'll end up with diarrhea. Regards to your . . . President (I almost wrote you-know-what).

Best,
H.

Preface *(Continued)*

In Tokyo, the War Office studied a photographed copy of Goering's file. The Japanese conclusions were the same as the German: the Imperial Air Force would also have to be drastically restructured. As things turned out, that did not prove to be so large an obstacle.

Finally, here in the United States, the clamor to arms did not sound so loudly. Nevertheless, President Roosevelt was aware of what the potential belligerent nations were doing and spurred production. The Air Force followed in the footsteps of Germany and Japan and turned from the development of aircraft to the exploration of the motorcar as a tactical weapon, both as long-range bomber and as fighter escort. The reasons were the same; the Air Force generals were astonished by the statistics concerning the vast amounts of petroleum products that an all-out war would demand. Oil was scarce, and supplies were dangerously low. There was no guarantee that overseas oil-producing nations would remain friendly. Automobiles could bring about the same results as aircraft and with much greater economy. All that was necessary was a certain basic alteration in military thinking. Naturally enough, because of the conservative outlook of the military mind, this change met some resistance. But when the facts were made clear and the economic and political ramifications were explained, the real business of realigning the Air Force began, in Washington as well as Berlin, Tokyo, Moscow, Paris, and London.

It was against this background, then, that I began my work. I was given a suite of offices in the Pentagon; that was on February 18, 1974. Across the United States, huge lines of cars waited at service stations, unable to purchase gasoline with the freedom the American motorist had come to enjoy. On the way home each day I saw hundreds of automobiles still queued up hopefully; I remember thinking that it was ironic that the same gasoline shortage that paralyzed these motorists had made an all-out air war equally impractical and that the common solution of all the leading nations had been to replace their aircraft with automobiles. Billions of gallons of gasoline would be saved in this way—involuntarily, of course, as the gasoline was not actually available to be saved in the first place; still, I wondered if the man in the street would react as we hoped, would rise up in patriotic sacrifice and curtail his pleasure driving for the war effort, should hostilities become official.

CHAPTER TWO

George Alec Effinger, *Special Assistant to President Roosevelt:* Then you were involved with the early Luftwaffe attacks on Poland?

Oberleutnant Rolf Mulp, *pilot of the German Nazi Luftwaffe:* Yes, indeed, certainly so. I commanded a *kette* in an attack—

Effinger: *"Kette"?*

Mulp: Yes. I'm sorry. It's a German word. Don't worry about it. Anyway, we were taking these three Stukas against a bridge just across the Polish border. This was September 1, 1974. The first day of the war.

Effinger: And the Stuka, the old terror bomber—

Mulp: Was now the 1973 Opel 53 four-door sedan. We had made the change in strategy and procedures very quickly, thanks to our basic German love of discipline. We practiced a lot, driving around shopping centers, aiming our fingers at people—

Effinger: And with Hitler and Goering and everybody back in power, it was like old times.

Mulp: I wouldn't know first-hand, of course. I was too young in the Thirties to remember them. But my parents told me stories of what it had been like. And we all joined in, and we all settled down quickly. It was so comfortable to have those familiar faces back, now grown so old, but still so familiar. Comfortable, like an old boot.

Effinger: A high black one, no doubt.

Mulp: It comes just below the knee. Ah, I see that you understand, do you not? Ha, ha, ha.

Effinger: Ha, ha, ha. We can laugh, now that the war's over.

Mulp: Ha, ha, ha. Indeed, yes. But those were terrible years. Me, driving the Opel at top speed. My tail gunner sitting in the back seat, worried, nervous, chattering nonsense while I was trying to keep my mind on the road. We had a constant fear of enemy fighters screaming toward us around the next bend in the road. And then the business of having to pitch bombs at bridges or whatever, or stopping the car and getting out to toss the things. It took a lot of skill and a lot of luck.

Effinger: And a lot of daring.

Mulp: I'm glad that you can appreciate that now. I'd like to ask you a question, if I may.

Effinger: Certainly. I'll bet I know which one, too.

Mulp: You were almost single-handedly responsible—

Effinger: No, for crying out loud, I don't want to hear it. I'm tired of hearing it already.

From the Cormorant, Indiana, *Flash-Comet*

ON THE TOWNE

by Craig Towne

This column's reporter went to an unusual promo party last week. In town for a few days pushing a new book was a former aide of the late President Roosevelt. The author, George Effinger, visited our little city once several years ago, before the war. I recall meeting him then, shaking his hand, and hearing him say that he was "glad I could make it." This reporter was very gratified that Mr. Effinger, too, remembered that brief acquaintanceship. Also, his book seems very handsome. But remember when books cost five bucks?

CHAPTER FOUR

Effinger: What was it like?

Maginna: It was awful, what do you think? Really awful. Anybody who lived through it would tell you the same thing. About how awful it was. We were all thinking such idiotic things while it was happening. And now, looking back, it's kind of hard to straighten it all out in my mind. I remember thinking, "God, they're all going to think we were idiots here." I was afraid that people would laugh or something, because we let it happen. That Pearl Harbor would go down in history as our fault.

Effinger: Of course, there was a certain lack of communication.

Maginna: Things seemed worse at the time. I've read about the attack since, many times. I'm glad, of course, that the whole thing wasn't as bad as it looked to me then. But the accounts never convey the real feeling we had, the loud awfulness. I thought, "There goes the shortest war in the world." I thought the Navy was sunk.

Effinger: Can you describe what it looked like?

Maginna: Sure. Nothing easier. It was mostly these Honda Civics—we called them Kates during the war—that did most of the bombing. And these Toyota Corolla 1200 coupes, what we called Zeroes, were the fighter escorts. It was such a quiet morning. I don't know, I can't remember what I had planned for the afternoon. Anyway, these Jap cars started driving up in long lines from Honolulu, a couple of hundred of them at least. They roared through the sentry posts, the Zeroes shooting down soldiers, sailors, a lot of civilians, even. The Kates screeched their brakes at the end of the piers, threw their bombs, and drove away. All the time their Zeroes, those Toyota coupes, were demolishing our planes before our pilots could get them started. Most of the damage was done real quick. We never knew what hit us.

Effinger: And you have no trouble recalling your feelings.

Maginna: No trouble at all. That's something I'll remember until the day I die. That's the reason I don't like to read about Pearl Harbor, because the accounts just don't capture it.

Effinger: I'm giving you the chance to correct that.

Maginna: Sure. A lot of us that saw the *Arizona* get hit—some of us had friends on her—were glad of what you did at the end of the war. We would have voted for you for President. And you're right these days, about not letting other countries do that to us all over again. Sure. We ought to screw them down while we have the chance.

Effinger: That's not exactly what I—

Maginna: I wouldn't want that to happen all over again.

Effinger: Me, neither.

Maginna: Right. Right. *(Pause)* Are you okay?

Dear Mr. Effinger:

I recently borrowed your book *Target: Berlin!* from the library. It isn't such a big library, here in Springfield, not so big as you'd think with a college right in town, but then the college has its own, of course, but we had your book, and since my husband was a pilot in the war I thought I'd read your book. My husband was killed in one of the raids over Germany that you talk about in Chapter Eight late in the war. We were married only a little while before Pearl Harbor, and when my husband was killed, it was a tremendous loss, but I have learned to live with it and accept it as God's will, something that a lot of us wives have trouble doing but I don't. That's just the way I was raised, I guess.

I liked your book a lot. A lot of us wives had trouble understanding just why our husbands were dying, dropping bombs on tiny towns that didn't look like they'd be worth anything to anybody. I liked your book because it made me understand for the first time that my husband was actually contributing and doing something important instead of just throwing his life away which is what we all thought for so long. I'm glad at last that somebody told us something. We all are, though a lot of us wives have trouble believing it, even still.

But I know that if Lawrence was alive today, he'd like your book too, on account of he was a part of what you describe so well. And the fact that it was you, personally, that did so much to help our country win the war, not only coming up with the idea of the big bombing missions but also making the decision to go ahead with the A-bomb, I know that would have impressed him no end. Of course, I didn't know who you were then, during the war I mean, and I doubt that Lawrence did, either, but I know that if he wasn't dead, he'd know who you are now and be grateful. I know that I am.

God bless you. I hope things work out all right for you.

Very truly yours,
Mrs. Catherine M. Tuposky

CHAPTER SEVEN

Dr. Nelson: I walked into the project director's office that first Monday, I recall it very clearly, and I was mad as a drowning hornet. I said, "Who is this jerk?" I figured I'd worked for twenty years, and now was no time for some idiot with no experience and a lot of nerve to come and tell me what to do, war or no war. It was the wrong way for the President to go about things, I thought. Roosevelt was always like that, even in his first five or six terms, if you'll remember. But, like I say, the matter was settled, and I didn't have anything to say about it. We were at war. We needed another heavy bomber to fill in on certain kinds of missions on which the B-17 had demonstrated a kind of vulnerability. The project director said to me, "This guy Effinger wants you to make something out of this." He tossed me a picture of a 1974 Chrysler Imperial Le Baron four-door hardtop. A beauty of a car. Well, I didn't know as much about the situation as the President or you did. I thought about all the work we did to rig up a heavy bomber out of the Lincoln Continental. I didn't want to have to go through all of that again. But what could I say?

Dr. Johnson: This was my first big project. I was very excited about it. I can still picture Dr. Nelson fuming and raging at his desk, but I never shared that feeling. I was still very much impressed by your development of the long-range bombing attacks against the enemies' industrial complexes. That showed a certain sophistication that I admired. Up until that point, the bomber was used only to support troops and armored attacks—in short, limited raids. But both Germany and Japan were learning the hard way that we meant business.

Dr. Nelson: It was a kind of perverse rebellion that forced me to include many of the Le Baron's luxury extras as standard equipment on what eventually came to be the B-24 Liberator. It was only later that I learned from B-24 crew members that these things which I intended as a harmless slap at the government, hitting it in the budget so to speak, actually saved many lives and greatly added to the crews' driving pleasure.

Dr. Green: The B-24 had certain advantages over the B-17, although some B-17 pilots say the same about their own bombers. Still, the Liberator was fitted out better in some respects, particularly the leather trim inside, rear radio speaker, glove compartment vanity mirror, carpeted luggage space in the trunk, and an interior gas cap lock release. These things had been left off the B-17 for monetary reasons, but they showed up on the B-24 as Dr. Nelson's little joke.

Dr. Nelson: Still, they saved many lives and undoubtedly shortened the war.

Dr. Johnson: And you, Mr. Effinger, you were with us through all of it, with the B-17, the B-24, and, later, with the B-29. I'll never forget how much I hated your guts.

Dr. Green: Still, our country will always be grateful.

Dr. Nelson: Still.

FROM THE OFFICE OF THE PRESIDENT

Feb. 7, 1981

Dear George:

It's been a long time, I know, since we've last had the time to talk. Well, after all, I'm President now, you know. I sometimes miss the old days, before FDR died and I accepted the burden that so wears me down these days. I miss the pinball contests in the Executive Mansion. I miss the table-tennis matches with the Senate Majority Leader whose name I've forgotten, he's dead now. I miss being able to sneak out for some miniature golf and not being recognized.

It's silly to live in the past. They all tell me that, every day. Even Miss Brant says the same thing. Am I living in the past? That's a kind of mental illness, isn't it? I suspect that they're trying to convince me that I'm unstable. Sometimes I'm thankful that we don't have the vote of confidence in this country.

What brought all this on was I found the enclosed while moving a file cabinet this morning. Thought you'd like to have it. We *all* live in the past, just a little.

> Regards,
> Bob
>
> Robert L. Jennings
> President of the United States

RLJ/eb
Enc.

FROM THE OFFICE OF THE PRESIDENT

August 21, 1979

Dear George:

How are things going with the you-know-what? Have you heard from the Manhattan District boys lately? Are you working on the delivery vehicle for the you-know-what? I suppose you are, but I can't help worrying that Uncle Adolf will beat us to it. Hitler is an even ninety years old this year. He dodders when he speaks these days, you can see it in the newscasts. I'm ninety-seven, but at least I have an excuse not to have to stand up. I do all my doddering with a shawl on my lap.

War is hell, did you know that? It's also futile. And inhuman, if you listen to the right people. But it can be glorious, and no one can deny that marvelous things come out of war. For instance, if you recall your history, the elimination of a lot of odd little Balkan states (a wonderful thing, I wish they'd thought of that in my childhood) and, of course, the you-know-what. Hurry it up, will you?

I hope you're not feeling the weight of responsibility for the you-know-what. I mean, it'll shorten the war, won't it? Try to think of it like that.

I remember when it looked like this war was going to be fought forty years ago. I thought about all the wonderful patriotic movies that could have been made: Fred MacMurray as a pilot, Pat O'Brien as a tough old naval officer, John Wayne in the Marines, James Stewart as a bashful hero. Who do we have today? Robert Redford? O'Toole? Newman? Gatelin? I miss radio.

Eleanor tried Diana's recipe for chicken in honey sauce. In fact, she tried it on some Englishman over here for something or other. He said he knew for a fact that it was a dish that Rudolf Hess asks for a lot in prison. Hess calls it Poulet au Roehm; he always gets a laugh from ordering it, poor man.

So. Keep up the good work. Push on with the you-know-what, keep me posted, and let's have you over for supper some evening when I'm back on solid food.

Hello to Diana.

> *Best,*
> *F.*
>
> *Franklin Delano Roosevelt*
> *President of the United States*

FDR/sf

CHAPTER NINE

Major Erich von Locher, *German fighter pilot:* I am frequently . . . Can you hear me? I am frequently . . . How is that?

Effinger: Fine. Fine.

Von Locher: All right, I suppose. I am frequently asked these days to comment on what I feel to be the reasons for the sudden deterioration of the Luftwaffe after the Battle of Britain. I generally avoid that question. It is too complex. I would be doing my former comrades an injustice by trying to answer.

Instead, let me speculate on the relative strengths of our "aircraft," such as they were. I feel I have more experience and more confidence to discuss such a concrete problem.

The chief workhorses of our fighter-interceptor arm were the Me 109, which the Messerschmitt people had built from the beautiful little Porsche 911-T, and the FW 190, which came later, a development of the ungainly Volkswagen Beetle. With the introduction of disposable fuel tanks, these two fighters had great range, great mobility. They were unmatched in the air during the early part of the war. However, it was not long before the Allies came up with planes that equaled and, finally, surpassed them. Much has been made of the supposed even match between our Porsche and the English Triumph Spitfire "Spitfire." As far as I'm concerned, it was an even match only when neither was destroyed. That did not happen often.

I piloted a Volkswagen during most of the war, first in the west, then on the Russian front. Is that all right?

Effinger: You're doing fine.

Von Locher: You don't think I'm being too pedantic? I don't want to sound like a professor or something.

Effinger: No, no. Just keep going like you were. It's fine.

Von Locher: Where was I?

Effinger: Here, I'll play it back.

Von Locher: *Was destroyed. That did not happen often. I piloted a Volkswagen during most of the war, first in the west, then on the Russian front. Is that all—*
Oh, yes. Well. I remember one particular battle. A whole gang of American bombers was coming east, along the northern route. Our spotters along the way had counted over five hundred bombers, all Lincoln Continentals and Chrysler Imperials, the big ones. They had landed in France and driven across Belgium, then southeast toward Augsburg. This was '79, when

the Allied bombing missions were going on night and day, without much resistance from the weakened Luftwaffe. Anyway, our Operations people had the facts on this wave, but all we could do was wait. That was the hard part, sitting in our Volkswagens with the engines revving, waiting.

Suddenly we got the call: The bombers had taken the freeway to Berlin. I felt a cold chill; this was the first actual attack on our capital. It had a tremendous symbolic meaning for us. We all gritted our teeth and swore to defend Berlin. Still, even then, all we could do was wait. The drive from France to Berlin was very long, even on the good roads. The Allied crews would have to stop in motels along the way. Our nerves were worn thin, if that is possible with nerves. At last our group leaders ordered us to pull out. We drove in squadrons, spaced out over all four lanes of the divided highway. We did not anticipate running into any civilian traffic, so we drove on both sides of the median strip. The civilians were mostly taking the trains at the end of the war, leaving the highways to the Luftwaffe.

We met the Allied bombers about one hundred and seventy miles from Berlin. There we got the greatest and most horrifying surprise of the war. The bombers were escorted by fighter planes, the Ford Mustang "Mustang." Until this time the bombers were escorted by Plymouth Duster "Thunderbolts" and Chevy Vega "Tomahawks," which could not carry enough fuel to make a long journey into Germany and then return. The bombers were usually on their own during the last stages of their missions. That's when we had our greatest success. But the "Mustangs" changed that. Even Goering realized this fact. That's when he finally admitted that the end had come. And besides their range, the "Mustangs" were our superior in most offensive categories as well.

We did our best, weary and low in morale as we were. We were defending Berlin. I ignored the "Mustangs" and went straight for the bombers. I drove at about eighty-five miles per hour, approaching at a right angle to the path of a Lincoln ahead of me. The bomber's gunner began firing, but my Volkswagen made a small target. I also could turn quicker than he could; it was shortly after dawn, and the sun was rising in the

Lincoln pilot's eyes. I drove out of the sun, swung in to him, and raked the side of the car with my 20-mm cannons. The bomber exploded, then swerved off the road and through the guardrail. The battle was less than five minutes old, and already I had a confirmed kill. My squadron leader congratulated me over the radio. I did not take time to relax. A "Mustang" was trying to position itself on my tail. All around me the battle raged; tires screamed as evasive maneuvers were made; burned cars, American and German, littered the highway, making tactics and strategy more difficult. By the end of the morning I had six kills. The Americans lost hundreds of planes, but enough got through to Berlin to shock our leaders into an awareness of just how defenseless the Reich had become.

We drove back to our base in a subdued—

Effinger: I'm sorry, I think the tape's running out. Let me change . . . no, doggone it, that's the last one.

Von Locher: I wanted to talk about the time I held off three Ford Pintos while my machine guns were jammed.

Effinger: Tomorrow. As soon as I g—

June 18, 1980

Dear George:

I hope you understand. I just can't take it any more, that's all. I suppose people will think I'm unpatriotic, but they don't know how much I've given to the war effort. I sit home every night alone, watching television, wondering what you're doing. And you're always saying that you're with those scientists of yours, trying to come up with a better airplane. Well, we're supposed to be married. Germany surrendered already, remember? Japan isn't going to last much longer, either, as far as I can see. Still, you have to go have "meetings." I'm beginning to wonder.

Last Monday you said you were going to have a meeting with the President. But did you know that at just the time you were supposed to be huddling with him in the Oval Office he was on

TV addressing the nation? Did you know that? I won't even bother to ask you where you were. It doesn't matter any more. I've left you before, and the Secret Service boys always convinced me to come back, for reasons of national security. But what about *my* security? Nobody seems to worry about that.

You spend all day tinkering with Imperials and things, and what does the government give us to drive? A Mercury Comet. I think it's ridiculous.

Don't think that I don't love you, because I still do. But it's just gotten to be too much. I really mean it.

What's-her-name, that old bag secretary of yours, can take care of you. She can learn to make macaroni and cheese, and after that you won't miss me at all. That's about all you needed me for, anyway. And don't worry about money or things like that. I'm not going to bleed you. I think I'll go back to Matamoras for a while, and then I think I'll go into the theater. I've already got an offer of a job from Mickey.

All good wishes,

Your wife,
Diana

CHAPTER TWELVE

Tanora Keigi, *Japanese fighter pilot:* Now here's an interesting point. Today in America many people believe that the kamikaze pilots were religious fanatics or superpatriotic men hypnotized by their devotion to the emperor. As I recall it, this was not the case. We were merely defending our homeland and our families. The B-29 bases in the South Pacific were too numerous and too well defended to be destroyed. With the fall of Iwo Jima to the Americans, the long-range "Mustang" fighters could be based close enough to the Japanese home islands to accompany the bombers on their missions. All that the dwindling Japanese air force could accomplish were attacks against the aircraft carriers that ferried bombers and fighters from the more distant American bases. And ammunition production was down, and fuel was scarce. We suicide pilots took our inspiration from several high-ranking officers who crashed their planes against American craft in demonstration of their love for their countrymen. It was not long before suicide squadrons were organized on a regular basis.

It was very difficult to crash an automobile against a ship, especially if the ship were still at sea. Therefore, our tactics called for waiting until the American ships dropped anchor near our shores, and the bomber cars and the fighter cars were landed on the beach. We could attack these enemy cars, or the landing craft, or, with the aid of the navy and our own motorized rafts, we might be able to crash into the American ships themselves. Few of us were that lucky.

We had very strange procedures, once these decisions to give our lives in suicidal attacks were made. A friend of mine who drove a Toyota Corolla "Zero" was given a large bomb to throw. The idea was that he would toss the bomb, the bomb would damage his target, and a few seconds later he would crash his Toyota into the same target. Of course, he had to throw the bomb from very short range. The odds were that the target would be shooting back at my friend. As it turned out, he threw the bomb too soon, the bomb hit the ground and bounced up, my friend's "Zero" hit the bomb, which exploded. My friend was already dead when the flaming mass of his car struck his target. He was a hero, and we praised his name from a position of safety about a half mile away.

I had my opportunity to emulate my friend the next day, but bad luck caused me to overshoot my target and waste my precious bomb. Three days later I was ordered to drive my Datsun into a flight of Cadillac Fleetwood "Superfortresses." Again, the gods willed otherwise. Although I weaved through the American bombers for nearly an hour, I did not hit a single target. The bombers passed me by, and I was left out of gas on a highway seven miles from the small town of Gogura.

I kept trying. My commanding officers were very sympathetic. One by one my comrades met glorious death, while I found only frustration. At last the war ended before I found my own moment of honorable sacrifice.

Today I am a moderately successful and prosperous automobile dealer, with a Toyota showroom in San Diego, California. I bear no ill will toward the people who slew so many of my friends and relatives. They seem to harbor no resentment toward me, at the same time. Years have passed, and old disagreements are forgotten. A group of fellow businessmen from Japan have joined me in forming a syndicate, and we are currently buying golf courses in America, athletic teams, and opening franchised fast-food stands. Everything is fine. Everyone is happy. The emperor must have been right, after all. My service mates did not die in vain.

December 10, 1983

Mr. George Alec Effinger
c/o Ofermod Press
409 E. 147th Street
Cleveland, Ohio
      44010

Dear Mr. Effinger:

I recently had the pleasure of reading your book, *Target: Berlin!*, which was published a few years ago. I don't exactly know why I picked it up, except for the fact that I enjoy reading memoirs of famous people. Sort of like high-class gossip. Also, I've had acquaintances with several people mentioned in your book. I liked your book very much, though much of it was way over my head. I learned a lot from it.

This letter is being written for more than one reason. I don't know if you'll recall, but a couple of years ago I prosecuted a paternity suit against then White House aide Arthur Whitewater, who figures often in your work. Because of governmental pressure, the case was eventually dismissed. Another typical example of administrative self-preservation at the expense of the common man. In the following year I brought L. Daniel

Dresser, former presidential press secretary to President Jennings during the close of the war, to court on similar grounds. Again, the case was thrown out before I ever had a fair chance to prove my charges. But I've learned to accept the facts that high-up officials can do just about anything these days. That's why I really liked your book, because it shows these people in everyday life, fallible and slightly stupid.

I saw you on a late-night talk show with Don McCarey, and I thought you were terrific, even if you only had four minutes. Just think, a few years ago you were one of the most influential men in the country. Now you're lucky to get four minutes of time at one o'clock in the morning. Still, that's more than I'll ever get.

Did you have any trouble publishing your book? I mean, did the government censors hassle you or threaten you at all? I bet they did. You have a lot of integrity, and I admire that. That's why I'm sure you'll behave with more honor than either Whitewater or Dresser. I can't say anything for certain as yet, but I go to the doctor the day after tomorrow, and I may have some important news for you then.

Keep up the good work. I know that in the years since the war you've had a constant guilt thing about being responsible for the dropping of the A-bombs on Japan. It shows up all the time in your book. I just want to say that we all have things to be guilty about, and we just have to learn to stifle those feelings before they interfere with regular life. So your situation is a little more extreme than most everyone else's. In a way, we're all responsible for those tragedies. Did you ever think of it like that? It probably doesn't make any difference to you, but I wish I could make you happier. I'd like to meet you in person some day.

Like I said, you'll get the results of the doctor's examination, and we can proceed from there. Surely the royalties on your book would be more than enough to cover the minor expenses that I might cost you. It's no big thing. It happens to people all the time. I don't hold any personal grudge. After all, you never really did anything; we've never been in the same state together. Still, you must admit that, as a famous celebrity, you're a target. This is just part of the circumstances you agreed to accept along with your notoriety. So there isn't any personal animosity between us. I want you to understand that.

Anyway, I'm looking forward to your new book. I saw an ad for it in the *Plain Dealer. The Lighter Side of Hiroshima.* Lots of humorous anecdotes collected in the years since 1980. That takes a little nerve, too, you know. I'm impressed. The wild, wacky world of nuclear holocaust. Perhaps it's good therapy for you, though. Who am I to say?

Hoping to hear from you soon (I enclosed a self-addressed, stamped envelope for your convenience),

Heather Oroszco

CHAPTER FOURTEEN

Colonel Holbrook Leaf, *pilot of the B-29 Enola Gay:* I think that I was the only man in the entire 509th Composite Group that knew of the existence of the atomic bomb. I was the commanding officer of the Group, of course, and we had been assembled specially for the purpose of delivering the bomb on certain selected targets in Japan. We went through what seemed to the regular crews unusual training procedures and special treatment. I imagine that it must have been a hard time for the three other members of my crew.

Major Charles W. Bartz, *co-pilot of the Enola Gay:* It sure was. The other men on the base on Tinian laughed at us and called us names. They couldn't understand what we were contributing to the war effort. We weren't going on regular bombing runs. We were contributing, but even we, except for Colonel Leaf, were unaware of just how. But everybody suspected that something special was in preparation. We never guessed that it was on the order of the A-bomb, though.

Major Andrew Douglas Swayne, *bombardier:* The B-29 was a beautiful car. The Cadillac Fleetwood. After flying B-17s during the early part of the war, it was like a vacation to be transferred to the 509. But we had to take a lot of ribbing from the guys. It's funny. When you meet those fellows today, they never remember all of that that happened before the dropping of the bomb. They just remember the awe and the pride.

Bartz: I've had to describe that moment to my kid at least a hundred times.

Leaf: Me, too. Your kid never gets tired of hearing about it.

Swayne: As bombardier, and with just the single bomb, I took over the job of navigator. They put us ashore in some God-forsaken rural area of Japan. I didn't even know where we were. It was Colonel Leaf and Major Bartz in the front seat, and me and Captain Ealywine in the large, comfortable back seat. We drove for nearly an hour before we saw a sign. It put us on the road to the main road to Hiroshima. We were really afraid that we'd run out of gas before we got there. The *Enola Gay* wasn't going to make the return trip with us, but it still had to get us to the target.

Captain Solomon Ealywine, *gunner:* The back seat wasn't as comfortable as in most B-29s, because the A-bomb itself was nearly ten feet long, and a hole had been cut to allow the nose of the thing to extend out from the trunk and across the seat. It separated Swayne and me. It was an eerie feeling, driving along with that thing under my right arm.

Swayne: And it made navigation more difficult. I had to sit in the back seat with the road maps spread out on my lap, and I didn't really have room to operate. In those days in Japan, the road-map markings and the routes they represented bore little relation to each other. Just finding our way to Hiroshima was a tough job. No divided highways with large green overhead signs.

Bartz: Still, we got there. I didn't have much to do, as it turned out. We weren't bothered the whole time. No enemy fighters to meet us or anything. It was like a weekend drive in the country. It seemed like a shame to abandon such a nice car, but we left the Cadillac in the parking lot of a largish shopping center in Hiroshima, where it would blend in with a lot of other cars, many of them pre-war American.

Swayne: I had been trained to operate the bomb, although during the instruction drills I never had any idea of the magnitude of the bomb I'd be working with. I set it to explode in ninety minutes. ConComOp had worked out the schedule with almost split-second precision. That was their thing, even though it rarely worked in practice. Still, we kept amazingly to the schedule. We got out of the car, keeping our eyes on the ground, trying to be inconspicuous in enemy territory. We said goodbye to the faithful *Enola Gay*, slammed and locked the doors, and walked across the parking lot to where we could catch the bus back to the village of Horoshiga. There would be a submarine waiting for us offshore. That's the last we saw of the plane, but ninety minutes later, many miles away, riding on the bus, we saw the sky turn pinkish-white. It happened with a suddenness like a bolt of lightning. We turned and shook hands all around. We knew that stroke would crumble the Japanese will to continue the war.

Effinger: Do you ever feel the least bit guilty about killing and maiming so many thousands of innocent Japanese civilians?

(Pause)

Swayne: Guilty? Innocent?

Ealywine: We had the weapon. We had the Cadillac to deliver it. Our soldiers and marines, not to mention our fellow aircraft crews, were still dying in large numbers. For four years the Japanese had mercilessly waged war against us. Here we had the chance to end it all, with one shot, tie it up neatly with one hit.

Bartz: There were civilians killed at Pearl Harbor. There were civilians killed everywhere.

Effinger: But the numbers—

Ealywine: All right. According to your thinking there are numbers of civilian dead that ought to make us feel bad, like at Hiroshima. That implies that there are numbers of civilian dead that ought not to make us feel bad, that we ought to accept. Somewhere in the middle those feelings change. Say, if we kill five thousand civilians, it's all right, but if we kill five thousand and five hundred, we'll be haunted for the rest of our lives. You just can't analyze it like that.

Leaf: You may regret heading up the Manhattan Project, and you may regret encouraging President Jennings to drop the bomb, but I can tell you for a fact that none of the United States Air Force fliers, and none of the rest of the wartime servicemen, and, most likely, truthfully, none of the Japanese people regret the dropping of the bomb. They all appreciate how many lives it saved by avoiding a longer, more protracted war.

Effinger: You know, I've never been able to visualize it like that. But now I think I can begin to learn to live with it.

Swayne: That's the first step.

Effinger: Thank you all very much.

Leaf: Not at all. That's what we're here for. Don't give the dead Japanese another thought. After all, they started it, didn't they? It's not often that we get involved in a situation with so clearly marked good and bad sides.

Ealywine: I'm glad we were on the right side.

Effinger: I'm sure that makes it unanimous. Good night, my friends, good night.

NOW, FOR THE FIRST TIME IN PAPERBACK!

SKIES FULL OF DEATH (Original title: TARGET:BERLIN!)
The fascinating story of World War II as told by one of the most influential leaders of America's struggle for freedom.

SKIES FULL OF DEATH, by George Alec Effinger, a Gemsbok Book.

"The taste of truth pervades each page in a way that simply can't be found in works by mere observers. Effinger was there, and he tells it all the way it happened."
                                            —The Destrehan *Sun-Star*

SKIES FULL OF DEATH is an amazing account of Effinger's efforts to hold Germany and Japan at bay, and the relationships he endured with less far-sighted members of our nation's leadership.

SKIES FULL OF DEATH will be published March 2, 1983. $1.95, wherever good books are sold. A Gemsbok Book.

TARGET: BERLIN! An eyewitness account of the sometimes madcap goings-on at the top of the executive heap during the Second World War, written by a member of President Roosevelt's inner circle. A must for hobbyists and collectors.
PUB. ED. $12.95   Our remainder price: **ONLY $2.95**

This is JAMES TIPTREE*'s third contribution to* New Dimensions. *(His last, "The Girl Who Was Plugged In," won a Hugo in 1974, to go with the Nebula he had collected earlier that year for a story published elsewhere.) No Tiptree story is quite like any other, except in the quality of its prose and the sharpness of the human perceptions, so it is futile to compare this one to its two predecessors except to say, perhaps, that it is less flamboyant in style, quietly told, Tiptree without the pyrotechnics—but Tiptree all the same.*

■

James Tiptree, Jr.
∎

THE PSYCHOLOGIST WHO WOULDN'T DO AWFUL THINGS TO RATS

He comes shyly hopeful into the lab. He is unable to suppress this childishness which has deviled him all his life, this tendency to wake up smiling, believing for an instant that today will be different.

But it isn't; is not.

He is walking into the converted cellars which are now called animal laboratories by this nationally respected university, this university which is still somehow unable to transmute its nationwide reputation into adequate funding for research. He squeezes past a pile of galvanized Skinner boxes and sees Smith at the sinks, engaged in cutting off the heads of infant rats. Piercing squeals; the headless body is flipped onto a wet furry pile on a hunk of newspaper. In the holding cage beside Smith the baby rats shiver in a heap, occasionally thrusting up a delicate muzzle and then burrowing convulsively under their friends, seeking to shut out Smith. They have previously been selectively shocked, starved, subjected to air blasts and plunged in ice water; Smith is about to search the corpses for appropriate neuroglandular effects of stress. He'll find them, undoubtedly. *Eeeeeeee—Ssskrick!* Smith's knife grates, drinking life.

"Hello, Tilly."

"Hi." He hates his nickname, hates his whole stupid name: Tilman Lipsitz. He would go nameless through the world if he

33

could. If it even could be something simple, Moo or Urg—
anything but the absurd high-pitched syllables that have followed him through life: Tilly Lipsitz. He has suffered from it.
Ah well. He makes his way around the pile of Purina Lab Chow
bags, bracing for the fierce clamor of the rhesus. Their Primate
Room is the ex-boiler room, really; these are tenements the
university took over. The rhesus scream like sirens. Thud! Feces
have hit the grill again; the stench is as strong as the sound.
Lipsitz peers in reluctantly, mentally apologizing for being unable to like monkeys. Two of them are not screaming, huddled
on the steel with puffy pink bald heads studded with electrode
jacks. Why can't they house the creatures better, he wonders
irritably for the nth time. In the trees they're clean. Well,
cleaner, anyway, he amends, ducking around a stand of
somebody's breadboard circuits awaiting solder.

On the far side is Jones, bending over a brightly lighted
bench, two students watching mesmerized. He can see Jones's
fingers tenderly roll the verniers that drive the probes down
through the skull of the dog strapped underneath. Another of
his terrifying stereotaxes. The aisle of cages is packed with animals with wasted fur and bloody heads. Jones swears they're all
right, they eat; Lipsitz doubts this. He has tried to feed them
tidbits as they lean or lie blear-eyed, jerking with wire terrors.
The blood is because they rub their heads on the mesh; Jones,
seeking a way to stop this, has put stiff plastic collars on several.

Lipsitz gets past them and has his eye rejoiced by the lovely
hourglass-shaped ass of Sheila, the brilliant Israeli. Her back is
turned. He observes with love the lily waist, the heart-lobed
hips that radiate desire. But it's his desire, not hers; he knows
that. Sheila, wicked Sheila; she desires only Jones, or perhaps
Smith, or even Brown or White—the muscular large hairy ones
bubbling with professionalism, with cheery shop talk. Lipsitz
would gladly talk shop with her. But somehow his talk is different, uninteresting, is not in the mode. Yet he too believes in
"the organism," believes in the miraculous wiring diagram of
life; he is naïvely impressed by the complexity, the intricate
interrelated delicacies of living matter. Why is he so reluctant
to push metal into it, produce lesions with acids or shock? He

has this unfashionable yearning to learn by appreciation, to tease out the secrets with only his eyes and mind. He has even the treasonable suspicion that other procedures might be more efficient, more instructive. But what other means are there? Probably none, he tells himself firmly. Grow up. Look at all they've discovered with the knife. The cryptic but potent centers of the amygdalas, for example. The subtle limbic homeostats—would we ever have known about these? It is a great knowledge. Never mind that its main use seems to be to push more metal into human heads, my way is obsolete.

"Hi, Sheila."

"Hello, Tilly."

She does not turn from the hamsters she is efficiently shaving. He takes himself away around the mop stand to the coal-cellar dungeon where he keeps his rats—sorry, his experimental subjects. His experimental subjects are nocturnal rodents, evolved in friendly dark warm burrows. Lipsitz has sensed their misery, suspended in bright metal and plexiglas cubes in the glare. So he has salvaged and repaired for them a stack of big old rabbit cages and put them in this dark alcove nobody wanted, provoking mirth among his colleagues.

He has done worse than that, too. Grinning secretly, he approaches and observes what has been made of his latest offering. On the bottom row are the cages of parturient females, birthing what are expected to be his experimental and control groups. Yesterday those cages were bare wire mesh, when he distributed to them the classified section of the Sunday *Post*. Now he sees with amazement that they are solid cubic volumes of artfully crumpled and plastered paper strips. Fantastic, the labor! Nests; and all identical. Why has no one mentioned that rats as well as birds can build nests? How wrong, how painful it must have been, giving birth on the bare wire. The little mothers have worked all night, skillfully constructing complete environments beneficient to their needs.

A small white muzzle is pointing watchfully at him from a paper crevice; he fumbles in his pocket for a carrot chunk. He is, of course, unbalancing the treatment, his conscience remonstrates. But he has an answer; he has carrots for them all. Get down, conscience. Carefully he unlatches a cage. The white head stretches, bright-eyed, revealing sleek black shoulders. They are the hooded strain.

"Have a carrot," he says absurdly to the small being. And she does, so quickly that he can barely feel it, can barely feel also the tiny razor slash she has instantaneously, shyly given his thumb before she whisks back inside to her babies. He grins, rubbing the thumb, leaving carrots in the other cages. A mother's monitory bite, administered to an ogre thirty times her length. Vitamins, he thinks, enriched environments, that's the respectable word. Enriched? No, goddam it. What it is is something approaching sane unstressed animals—experimental subjects, I mean. Even if they're so genetically selected for tameness they can't survive in the feral state, they're still rats. He sees he must wrap something on his thumb; he is ridiculously full of blood.

Wrapping, he tries not to notice that his hands are crisscrossed with old bites. He is a steady patron of the antitetanus clinic. But he is sure that they don't really mean ill, that he is somehow accepted by them. His colleagues think so too, somewhat scornfully. In fact Smith often calls him to help get some agonized creature out and bring it to his electrodes. Judas-Lipsitz does, trying to convey by the warmth of his holding hands that somebody is sorry, is uselessly sorry. Smith explains that his particular strain of rats is bad; a bad rat is one that bites psychologists; there is a constant effort to breed out this trait.

Lipsitz has tried to explain to them about animals with curved incisors, that one must press the hand into the biter's teeth. "It can't let go," he tells them. "You're biting yourself on the rat. It's the same with cats's claws. Push, they'll let go. Wouldn't you if somebody pushed his hand in your mouth?"

For a while he thought Sheila at least had understood him, but it turned out she thought he was making a dirty joke.

He is giving a rotted Safeway apple to an old male named Snedecor whom he has salvaged from Smith when he hears them call.

"Li-i-ipsitz!"

"Tilly? R. D. wants to see you."

"Yo."

R. D. is Professor R. D. Welch, his department head and supervisor of his grant. He washes up, makes his way out and around to the front entrance stairs. A myriad guilts are swirling emptily inside him; he has violated some norm, there is something wrong with his funding, above all he is too slow, too slow. No results yet, no columns of data. Frail justifying sentences revolve in his head as he steps into the clean bright upper reaches of the department. Because he is, he feels sure, learning. Doing something, something appropriate to what he thinks of as science. But what? In this glare he (like his rats) cannot recall. Ah, maybe it's only another hassle about parking space, he thinks as he goes bravely in past R. D.'s high-status male secretary. I can give mine up. I'll never be able to afford that transmission job anyway.

But it is not about parking space.

Doctor Welch has a fat file folder on his desk in Exhibit A position. He taps it expressionlessly, staring at Lipsitz.

"You are doing a study of, ah, genetic influences on, ah, tolerance of perceptual novelty."

"Well, yes . . ." He decides not to insist on precision. "You remember, Doctor Welch, I'm going to work in a relation to emotionalism too."

Emotionalism, in rats, is (a) defecating and (b) biting psychologists. Professor Welch exhales troubledly through his lower teeth, which Lipsitz notes are slightly incurved. Mustn't pull back.

"It's so unspecific," he sighs. "It's not integrated with the overall department program."

"I know," Lipsitz says humbly. "But I do think it has relevance to problems of human learning. I mean, why some kids seem to shy away from new things." He jacks up his technical vocabulary. "The failure of the exploration motive."

"Motives don't *fail*, Lipsitz."

"I mean, conditions for low or high expression. Neophobia. Look, Doctor Welch. If one of the conditions turns out to be genetic we could spot kids who need help."

"Um'mmm."

"I could work in some real learning programs in the high tolerants, too," Lipsitz adds hopefully. "Contingent rewards, that sort of thing."

"Rat learning . . ." Welch lets his voice trail off. "If this sort of thing is to have any relevance it should involve primates. Your grant scarcely extends to that."

"Rats can learn quite a lot, sir. How about if I taught them word cues?"

"Doctor Lipsitz, rats do not acquire meaningful responses to words."

"Yes, sir." Lipsitz is forcibly preventing himself from bringing up the totally unqualified Scotswoman whose rat knew nine words.

"I do wish you'd go on with your brain studies," Welch says in his nice voice, giving Lipsitz a glowing scientific look. Am I biting myself on him? Lipsitz wonders. Involuntarily he feels himself emphathize with the chairman's unknown problems. As he gazes back, Welch says encouragingly, "You could use Brown's preparations; they're perfectly viable with the kind of care you give."

Lipsitz shudders awake; he knows Brown's preparations. A "preparation" is an animal spread-eagled on a rack for vivisection, dosed with reserpine so it cannot cry or struggle but merely endures for days or weeks of pain. Guiltily he wonders if Brown knows who killed the bitch he had left half dissected and staring over Easter. Pull yourself together, Lipsitz.

"I am so deeply interested in working with the intact animal, the whole organism," he says earnestly. That is his magic phrase; he has discovered that "the whole organism" has some fetish quality for them, from some far-off line of work; very fashionable in the abstract.

"Yes." Balked, Welch wreathes his lips, revealing the teeth again. "Well. Doctor Lipsitz, I'll be blunt. When you came on board we felt you had a great deal of promise. *I* felt that, I really did. And your teaching seem to be going well, in the main. In the main. But your research; no. You seem to be frittering away your time and funds—and our space—on these irrelevancies. To put it succinctly, our laboratory is not a zoo."

"Oh, no, sir!" cries Lipsitz, horrified.

"What are you actually doing with those rats? I hear all kinds of idiotic rumors."

"Well, I'm working up the genetic strains, sir. The coefficient of homozygosity is still very low for meaningful results. I'm cutting it as fine as I can. What you're probably hearing about is that I am giving them a certain amount of enrichment. That's necessary so I can differentiate the lines." What I'm really doing is multiplying them, he thinks queasily; he hasn't had the heart to deprive any yet.

Welch sighs again; he *is* worried, Lipsitz thinks, and finding himself smiling sympathetically stops at once.

"How long before you wind this up? A week?"

"A week!" Lipsitz almost bleats, recovers his voice. "Sir, my test generation is just neonate. They have to be weaned, you know. I'm afraid it's more like a month."

"And what do you intend to do after this?"

"After this!" Lipsitz is suddenly fecklessly happy. So many, so wondrous are the things he wants to learn. "Well, to begin with I've seen a number of behaviors nobody seems to have done much with—I mean, watching my animals under more . . . more naturalistic conditions. They, ah, they emit very interesting responses. I'm struck by the species-specific aspect—I mean, as the Brelands said, we may be using quite unproductive situations. For example, there's an enormous difference between the way Rattus and Cricetus—that's hamsters—behave in the open field, and they're both *rodents.* Even as simple a thing as edge behavior—"

"*What* behavior?" Welch's tone should warn him, but he plunges on, unhappily aware that he has chosen an insignificant example. But he loves it.

"Edges. I mean the way the animal responds to edges and the shape of the environment. I mean it's basic to living and nobody seems to have explored it. They used to call it thigmotaxis. Here, I sketched a few." He pulls out a folded sheet,* pushes it at Welch. "Doesn't it raise interesting questions of arboreal descent?"

Welch barely glances at the drawings, pushes it away.

*See illustration.

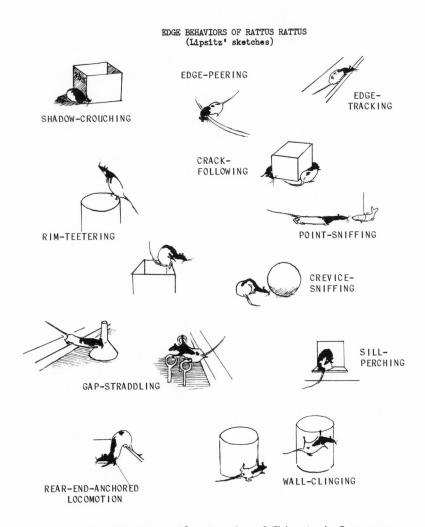

EDGE BEHAVIORS OF RATTUS RATTUS
(Lipsitz' sketches)

SHADOW-CROUCHING

EDGE-PEERING

EDGE-TRACKING

CRACK-FOLLOWING

RIM-TEETERING

POINT-SNIFFING

CREVICE-SNIFFING

GAP-STRADDLING

SILL-PERCHING

REAR-END-ANCHORED LOCOMOTION

WALL-CLINGING

Appendix III, Figure 18.   Examples of Thigmotaxic Responses
Drawings by Raccoona Sheldon

"Doctor Lipsitz. You don't appear to grasp the seriousness of this interview. All right. In words of one syllable, you will submit a major project outline that we can justify in terms of this department's program. If you can't come up with one such, regretfully we have no place for you here."

Lipsitz stares at him, appalled.

"A major project . . . I see. But . . ." And then something comes awake, something is rising in him. Yes. Yes, yes, of course there are bigger things he can tackle. Bigger questions—that means people. He's full of such questions. All it takes is courage.

"Yes, sir," he says slowly, "There are some major problems I have thought of investigating."

"Good," Welch says neutrally. "What are they?"

"Well, to start with . . ." And to his utter horror his mind has emptied itself, emptied itself of everything except the one fatal sentence which he now hears himself helplessly launched toward. "Take us here. I mean, it's a good principle to attack problems to which one has easy access, which are so to speak under our noses, right? So. For example, we're psychologists. Supposedly dedicated to some kind of understanding, helpful attitude toward the organism, toward life. And yet all of us down here—and in all the labs I've heard about—we seem to be doing such hostile and rather redundant work. Testing animals to destruction, that fellow at Princeton. Proving how damaged organisms are damaged, that kind of engineering thing. Letting students cut or shock or starve animals to replicate experiments that have been done umpteen times. What I'm trying to say is, why don't we look into why psychological research seems to involve so much cruelty—I mean, aggression? We might even . . ."

He runs down then, and there is a silence in which he becomes increasingly aware of Welch's breathing.

"Doctor Lipsitz," the older man says hoarsely, *"are you a member of the SPCA?"*

"No, sir, I'm not."

Welch stares at him unblinkingly and then clears his throat.

"Psychology is not a field for people with emotional problems." He pushes the file away. "You have two weeks."

Lipsitz takes himself out, momentarily preoccupied by his lie. True, he is not a *member* of the SPCA. But that ten dollars he sent in last Christmas, surely they have his name. That had been during the business with the dogs. He flinches now, recalling the black Labrador puppy, its vocal cords cut out, dragging itself around on its raw denervated haunches.

Oh God, why doesn't he just quit?

He wanders out onto the scruffy grass of the main campus, going over and over it again. These people. These . . . people.

And yet behind them loom the great golden mists, the reality of Life itself and the questions he has earned the right to ask. He will never outgrow the thrill of it. The excitement of *actually asking*, after all the careful work of framing terms that can be answered. The act of putting a real question to Life. And watching, reverently, excited out of his skin as Life condescends to tell him yes or no. My animals, my living works of art (of which you are one), do thus and so. Yes, in this small aspect you have understood Me.

The privilege of knowing how, painfully, to frame answerable questions, answers which will lead him to more, insights and better questions as far as his mind can manage and his own life lasts. It is what he wants more than anything in the world to do, always has.

And these people stand in his way. Somehow, some way, he must pacify them. He must frame a project they will buy.

He plods back toward the laboratory cellars, nodding absently at students, revolving various quasi-respectable schemes. What he really wants to do is too foggy to explain yet; he wants to explore the capacity of animals to *anticipate*, to gain some knowledge of the wave-front of expectations that they must build up, even in the tiniest heads. He thinks it might even be useful, might illuminate the labors of the human infant learning its world. But that will have to wait. Welch wouldn't tolerate the idea that animals have mental maps. Only old crazy Tolman had been allowed to think that, and he's dead.

He will have to think of something with Welch's favorite drive variables. What are they? And lots of statistics, he thinks, realizing he is grinning at a really pretty girl walking with that cow Polinski. Yes, why not use students? Something complicated with students—that doesn't cost much. And maybe sex differentials, say, in perception—or is that too far out?

A wailing sound alerts him to the fact that he has arrived at the areaway. A truck is offloading crates of cats, strays from the pound.

"Give a hand, Tilly! Hurry up!"

It's Sheila, holding the door for Jones and Smith. They want to get these out of sight quickly, he knows, before some student sees them. Those innocent in the rites of pain. He hauls a crate from the tailboard.

"There's a female in here giving birth," he tells Sheila. "Look." The female is at the bottom of a mess of twenty emaciated struggling brutes. One of them has a red collar.

"Hurry up, for Christ's sake." Sheila waves him on.

"But . . ."

When the crates have disappeared inside he does not follow the others in but leans on the railing, lighting a cigarette. The kittens have been eaten, there's nothing he can do. Funny, he always thought that females would be sympathetic to other females. Shows how much he knows about Life. Or is it that only certain types of people empathize? Or does it have to be trained in, or was it trained out of her? Mysteries, mysteries. Maybe she is really compassionate somewhere inside, toward something. He hopes so, resolutely putting away a fantasy of injecting Sheila with reserpine and applying experimental stimuli.

He becomes aware that the door has been locked from the inside; they have all left through the front. It's getting late. He moves away too, remembering that this is the long holiday weekend. Armistice Day. Would it were—he scoffs at himself for the bathos. But he frowns, too; long weekends usually mean nobody goes near the lab. Nothing gets fed or watered. Well, three days—not as bad as Christmas week.

Last Christmas week he had roused up from much-needed sleep beside a sky-high mound of term papers and hitchhiked into town to check the labs. It had been so bad, so needless. The poor brutes dying in their thirst and hunger, eating metal, each other. Great way to celebrate Christmas.

But he will have to stop that kind of thing, he knows. Stop it. Preferably starting now. He throws down the cigarette stub, quickens his stride to purposefulness. He will collect his brief-case of exam papers from the library where he keeps it to avoid the lab smell and get on home and get at it. The bus is bound to be jammed.

Home is an efficiency in a suburban high-rise. He roots in his moldy fridge, carries a sandwich and ale to the dinette that is his desk. He has eighty-one exams to grade; junior department members get the monster classes. It's a standard multiple-choice thing, and he has a help—a theatrically guarded manila template he can lay over the sheets with slots giving the correct response. By just running down them he sums an arithmetical grade. Good. Munching, he lays out the first mimeoed wad.

But as he starts to lay it on the top page he sees—oh, no!— somebody has scrawled instead of answering Number 6. It's that fat girl, that bright bum Polinsky. And she hasn't marked answers by 7 or 8 either. Damn her fat female glands; he squints at the infantile uncials: "I wont mark this because its smucky! Read it, Dr. Lipshitz." She even has his name wrong.

Cursing himself, he scrutinizes the question. "Fixed versus variable reinforcement is called a—" Oh yes, he remembers that one. Bad grammar on top of bad psychology. Why can't they dump these damn obsolete things? Because the office wants grade intercomparability for their records, that's why. Is Polinsky criticizing the language or the thought? Who knows. He leafs through the others, sees more scribbles. Oh, shit, they know I read them. They all know I don't mark them like I should. Sucker.

Grimly masticating the dry sandwich, he starts to read. At this rate he is working, he has figured out, for seventy-five cents an hour.

By midnight he isn't half through, but he knows he ought to break off and start serious thought about Welch's ultimatum. Next week all his classes start Statistical Methods; he won't have time to blow his nose, let alone think creatively.

He gets up for another ale, thinking, Statistical Methods, brrr. He respects them, he guesses. But he is incurably sloppy-

minded, congenitally averse to ignoring any data that don't fit
the curve. Factor analysis, multivariate techniques—all beautiful; why is he troubled by this primitive visceral suspicion that
somehow it ends up proving what the experimenter wanted to
show? No, not that, really. Something about qualities as opposed
to quantities, maybe? That some statistically insignificant results *are* significant, and some significant ones . . . aren't? Or just
basically that we don't know enough yet to use such ultrapre-
cise weapons. That we should watch more, maybe. Watch and
learn more and figure less. All right, call me St. Lipsitz.

Heating up a frozen egg roll, he jeers at himself for supersti-
tion. Face facts, Lipsitz. Deep down you don't really believe
dice throws are independent. Psychology is not a field for people with personality problems.

Ignoring the TV yattering through the wall from next door,
he sits down by the window to think. Do it, brain. Come up with
the big one. Take some good testable hypothesis from somebody in the department, preferably something that involves
electronic counting of food pellets, bar presses, latencies, defe-
cations. And crank it all into printed score sheets with a good
Fortran program. But what the hell are they all working on?
Reinforcement schedules, cerebral deficits, split brain, God
knows only that it seems to produce a lot of dead animals. "The
subjects were sacrificed." They insist on saying that. He has
been given a lecture when he called it "killing." Sacrificed, like
to a god. Lord of the Flies, maybe.

He stares out at the midnight streets, thinking of his small
black-and-white friends, his cozy community in the alcove.
Nursing their offspring, sniffing the monkeys, munching apples,
dreaming ratly dreams. He likes rats, which surprises him. Even
the feral form, Rattus rattus itself; he would like to work with
wild ones. Rats are vicious, they say. But people know only
starving rats. Anything starving is "vicious." Beloved beagle
eats owner on fourth day.

And his rats are, he blushingly muses, affectionate. They nes-
tle in his hands, teeteringly ride his shoulder, display humor. If
only they had fluffy tails, he thinks. The tail is the problem.
People think squirrels are cute. They're only overdressed rats.

Maybe I could do something with the perceptual elements of "cuteness," carry on old Tinbergen's work?

Stop it.

He pulls himself up; this isn't getting anywhere. A terrible panorama unrolls before his inner eye. On the one hand the clean bright professional work he should be doing, he with those thousands of government dollars invested in his doctorate, his grant—and on the other, what he is really doing. His cluttered alcove full of irregular rodents, his tiny, doomed effort to . . . what? To live amicably and observantly with another species? To understand trivial behaviors? Crazy. Spending all his own money, saving everybody's cripples—God, half his cages aren't even experimentally justifiable!

His folly. Suddenly it sickens him. He stands up, thinking, It's a stage you go through. I'm a delayed adolescent. Wake up, grow up. They're only animals. Get with it.

Resolve starts to form in him. Opening another ale can, he lets it grow. This whole thing is no good, he knows that. So what if he does prove that animals learn better if they're treated differently—what earthly use is that? Don't we all know it anyway? Insane. Time I braced up. All right. Ale in hand, he lets the resolve bloom.

He will go down there and clean out the whole mess, right now.

Kill all his rats, wipe the whole thing off. Clear the decks. That done, he'll be able to think; he won't be locked into the past.

The department will be delighted, Doctor Welsh will be delighted. Nobody believed his thing was anything but a waste of time. All right, Lipsitz. Do it. Now, tonight.

Yes.

But first he will have something analgesic, strengthening. Not ale, not a toke. That bottle of—what is it, absinthe?—that crazy girl gave him last year. Yes, here it is back of the roach-killer he never used either. God knows what it's supposed to do, it's wormwood, something weird.

"Fix me," he tells it, sucking down a long liquorice-flavored draft. And goes out, bottle in pocket.

It has, he thinks, helped. He is striding across the campus

now; all the long bus ride his resolve hasn't wavered. A quiet rain is falling. It must be two in the morning, but he's used to the spooky empty squares. He has often sneaked down here at odd hours to water and feed the brutes. The rain is moving strange sheens of shadow on the old tenement block, hissing echoes of the lives that swirled here once. At the cellar entrance he stops for another drink, finds the bottle clabbered with carrot chunks. Wormwood and Vitamin C, very good.

He dodges down and unlocks, bracing for the stench. The waste cans are full—cats that didn't make it, no doubt. Inside is a warm rustling reek.

When he finds the light, a monkey lets out one eerie whoop and all sounds stop. Sunrise at midnight; most of these experimental subjects are nocturnal.

He goes in past the crowded racks, his eye automatically checking levels in the hundreds of water bottles. Okay, okay, all okay . . . What's this? He stops by Sheila's hamster tier. A bottle is full to the top. But there's a corpse by the wire, and the live ones look bedraggled. Why? He jerks up the bottle. Nothing comes out of the tube. It's blocked. Nobody has checked it for who knows how long. Perishing of thirst in there, with the bottle full.

He unblocks it, fishes out the dead, watches the little beasts crowd around. How does Sheila report this? Part of an experimental group was, uh, curtailed. On impulse he inserts some carrots too, inserts more absinthe into himself. He knows he is putting off what he has come here to do.

All right, get at it.

He stomps past a cage of baby rabbits with their eyes epoxyed shut, somebody's undergraduate demonstration of perceptual learning, and turns on the light over the sinks. All dirty with hanks of skin and dog offal. Why the hell can't they clean up after themselves? We are scientists. Too lofty. He whooshes with the power hose, which leaks. Nobody cares enough even to bring a washer. He will bring one. No, he won't! He's going to be doing something different from here on in.

But first of all he has to get rid of all this. Sacrifice his subjects. His ex-subjects. Where's my ether?

He finds it back of the mops, has another snort of the cloudy liquor to fortify himself while he sets up his killing jars. He has evolved what he thinks is the decentest way: an ether pad under a grill to keep their feet from being burned by the stuff.

The eight jars are in a row on the sink. He lifts down a cage of elderly females, the grandmothers of his present group. They cluster at the front, trustfully expectant. Oh God; he postpones murder long enough to give them some carrot, deals out more to every cage in the rack so they'll have time to eat. Tumult of rustling, hopping, munching.

All right. He goes back to the sink and pours in the ether, keeping the lids tight. Then he reaches in the holding cage and scoops up a soft female in each hand. Quick: He pops them both in one jar, rescrews the lid. He has this fatuous belief that the companionship helps a little. They convulse frantically, are going limp before he has the next pair in theirs. Next. Next. Next . . . It takes five minutes to be sure of death.

This will be, he realizes, a long night.

He lifts down another cage, lifts up his bottle, leaning with his back to the jars to look at his rack, his little city of rats. My troops. My pathetic troops. An absinthe trip flashes through his head of himself leading his beasts against his colleagues, against the laughing pain-givers. Jones having his brain reamed by a Dachshund pup. A kitten in a surgical smock shaving Sheila, wow. Stop it!

His eye has been wandering over the bottom cages. The mothers have taken the goodies in to their young; interesting to see what goes on in there, maybe if he used infra-red—stop that, too. A lab is not a zoo. Down in one dark back cage he can see the carrot is still there. Where's Snedecor, the old brain-damaged male? Why hasn't he come for it? Is the light bothering him?

Lipsitz turns off the top lights, goes around to the side to check. Stooping, he peers into the gloom. Something funny down there—good grief, the damn cage is busted, it's rotted through the bottom. Where's old Sneddles?

The ancient cage rack has wheels. Lipsitz drags one end forward, revealing Stygian darkness behind. In prehistoric times there was a coal chute there. And there's something back here now, on the heap of bags by the old intake.

Lipsitz frowns, squints; the lab lights behind him seem to be growing dim and gaseous. The thing—the thing has black and white patches. Is it moving?

He retreats to the drainboard, finds his hand on the bottle. Yes. Another short one. What's wrong with the lights? The fluorescents have developed filmy ectoplasm, must be chow dust. This place is a powder keg. The monkeys are still as death too. That's unusual. In fact everything is dead quiet except for an odd kind of faint clicking, which he realizes is coming from the dark behind the rack. An animal. Some animal has got out and been living back there, that's all it is.

All right, Lipsitz: Go see.

But he delays, aware that the absinthe has replaced his limbs with vaguer, dreamlike extensions. The old females on the drainboard watch him alertly; the dead ones in the jars watch nothing. All his little city of rats has stopped moving, is watching him. Their priest of pain. This is a temple of pain, he thinks. A small shabby dirty one. Maybe its dirt and squalor are better so, more honest. A charnel house shouldn't look pretty, like a clean kitchen. All over the country, the world, the spotless knives are slicing, the trained minds devising casual torments in labs so bright and fair you could eat off their floors. Auschwitz, Belsen were neat. With flowers. Only the reek of pain going up to the sky, the empty sky. But people don't think animals' pain matters. They didn't think my people's pain mattered either, in the death camps a generation back. It's all the same, endless agonies going up unheard from helpless things. And all for what?

Maybe somewhere there is a reservoir of pain, he muses. Waiting to be filled. When it is full, will something rise from it? Something created and summoned by torment? Inhuman, an alien superthing . . . He knows he is indulging drunkenness. The clicking has grown louder.

Go and look at the animal, Lipsitz.

He goes, advances on the dark alcove, peering down, hearing the click-click-click. Suddenly he recognizes it: the tooth-click a rat makes in certain states of mind. Not threatening at all, it must be old Sneddles in there. Heartened, he pulls a dim light bulb forward on its string—and sees the thing plain, while the lab goes unreal around him.

What's lying back there among the Purina bags is an incredible whorl—a tangle of rat legs, rat heads, rat bodies, rat tails intertwined in a great wheellike formation, *joined* somehow abnormally rat to rat—a huge rat pie, heaving, pulsing, eyes reflecting stress and pain. Quite horrible, really; the shock of it is making him fight for breath. And it is not all laboratory animals; he can see the agouti coats of feral rats mixed in among it. Have wild rats come in here to help form this gruesome thing?

And at that moment, hanging to the light bulb, he knows what he is seeing. He has read in the old lore, the ancient grotesque legends of rat and man.

He is looking at a Rat King.

Medieval records were full of them, he recalls dimly. Was it Württemberg? *"They are monstrously Joynt, yet Living . . . It can by no way be Separated, and screamed much in the Fyre."* Apparitions that occurred at times of great attack on the rats. Some believed that the rat armies had each their king of this sort, who directed them. And they were sometimes connected to or confused with King Rats of still another kind: gigantic animals with eyes of fire and gold chains on their necks.

Lipsitz stares, swaying on the light cord. The tangled mass of the Rat King remains there clicking faintly, pulsing, ambiguously agonized among the sacks. His other hand seems to the holding the bottle; good. He takes a deep pull, his eyes rolling to fix the ghastliness, wondering what on earth he will do. "I can't," he mumbles aloud, meaning the whole thing, the whole bloody thing. *"I can't . . ."*

He can do his own little business, kill his animals, wind up his foolishness, get out. But he cannot—can not—be expected to cope with this, to abolish this revenant from time, this perhaps supernatural horror. For which he feels obscurely, hideously to blame. It's my fault, I . . .

He realizes he is weeping thinly, his eyes are running.

Whether it's for the animals or himself he doesn't know; he knows only that he can't stand it, can't take any of it any more. And now *this*.

"No!" Meaning, really, the whole human world. Dizzily he blinks around at the jumbled darkness, trying to regain his wits, feeling himself a random mote of protesting life in an insignificant fool-killer. Slowly his eyes come back to the monstrous, pitiable rat pie. It seems to be weakening; the click has lost direction. His gaze drifts upward, into the dark shadows.

—And he is quite unsurprised, really, to meet eyes looking back. Two large round animal eyes deep in the darkness, at about the level of his waist, the tapetums reflecting pale vermilion fire.

He stares; the eyes shift right, left, calmly in silence, and then the head advances. He sees the long wise muzzle, the vibrissae, the tuned shells of the ears. Is there a gold collar? He can't tell; but he can make out the creature's forelimbs now, lightly palping the bodies or body of the Rat King. And the tangled thing is fading, shrinking away. It was perhaps its conjoined forces which strove and suffered to give birth to this other—the King himself.

"Hello," Lipsitz whispers idiotically, feeling no horror any more but emotion of a quite other kind. The big warm presence before him surveys him. Will he be found innocent? He licks his lips; they have come at last, he thinks. They have risen; they are going to wipe all this out. Me, too? But he does not care; a joy he can't possibly control rises in him as he sees gold glinting on the broad chest fur. He licks his dry lips again, swallows.

"Welcome. Your Majesty."

The Beast-King makes no response; the eyes leave him and go gravely toward the aisles beyond. Involuntarily Lipsitz backs aside. The King's vibrissae are fanning steadily, bringing the olfactory news, the quiet tooth-click starts. When the apparition comes forward a pace Lipsitz is deeply touched to see the typical half hop, the ratly carriage. The King's coat is lustrous gray-brown, feral pelage. Of course. It is a natural male, too; he smiles timidly, seeing that the giant body has the familiar long hump, the heavy rear-axle loading. Is old Snedecor translated into some particle of this wonder? The cellar is unbreathing, hushed except for the meditative click-click from the King.

"You, you are going to . . ." Lipsitz tries but is struck dumb by the sense of something happening all around him. Invisible, inaudible—but tangible as day. An emergence, yes! In the rooms beyond they are emerging, coming out from the score upon score of cages, boxes, pens, racks, shackles and wires—all of them emerging, coming to the King. All of them, blinded rabbits, mutilated hamsters, damaged cats and rats and brain-holed rhesus quietly knuckling along, even the paralyzed dogs moving somehow, coming toward their King.

And at this moment Lipsitz realizes the King is turning too, the big brown body is wheeling, quite normally away from him, going away toward the deeper darkness in the end of the coal bay. They are leaving him!

"Wait!" He stumbles forward over the dead rat pie; he cannot bear to lose this. "Please . . ."

Daring all, he reaches out and touches the flank of the magical beast, expecting he knows not what. The flank is warm, is solid! The King glances briefly back at him, still moving away. Boldly Lipsitz strides closer, comes alongside, his hand now resting firmly on the withers as they go.

But they are headed straight at what he knows is only wall, though he can see nothing. The cellar ends there. No matter— he will not let go of the magic, no, and he steps out beside the moving King, thinking, I am an animal too! —And finds at the last instant that his averted, flinching head is moving through dark nothing, through a blacker emptiness where the King is leading—they are going, going out.

Perhaps an old sewer, he thinks, lurching along beside the big benign presence, remembering tales of forgotten tunnels under this old city, into which the new subway has bored. Yes, that's what it must be. He is finding he can see again in a pale ghostly way, can now walk upright. His left hand is tight on the shoulders of the calmly pacing beast, feeling the living muscles play beneath the fur, bringing him joy and healing. Where are the others?

He dares a quick look back and sees them. They are coming.

The dim way behind is filled with quiet beasts, moving together rank on rank as far as he can sense, animals large and small. He can hear their peaceful rustling now. And they are not only the beasts of his miserable lab, he realizes, but a torrent of others —he has glimpsed goats, turtles, a cow, raccoons, skunks, an opossum and what appeared as a small monkey riding on a limping spaniel. Even birds are there, hopping and fluttering above!

My God, it is everything, he thinks. It is Hamlin in reverse; all the abused ones, the gentle ones, are leaving the world. He risks another glance back and thinks he can see a human child too and maybe an old person among the throng, all measuredly, silently moving together in the dimness. An endless host going, going out at last, going away. And he is feeling their emanation, the gentleness of it, the unspeaking warmth. He is happier than he has been ever in his life.

"You're taking us away," he says to the King-Beast beside him. "The ones who can't cut it. We're all leaving for good, isn't that it?"

There is no verbal answer; only a big-stemmed ear swivels to him briefly as the King goes gravely on. Lipsitz needs no speech, no explanation. He simply walks alongside letting the joy rise in him. Why had it always been forbidden to be gentle? he wonders. Did they really see it as a threat, to have hated us so? But that is all over now, all over and gone, he is sure, although he has no slightest idea where this may be leading, this procession into chthonian infinity. For this moment it is enough to feel the silent communion, the reassurance rising through him from his hand on the flank of the great spirit-beast. The flank is totally solid; he can feel all the workings of life; it is the body of a real animal. But it is also friendship beyond imagining; he has never known anything as wonderful as this communion, not sex or sunsets or even the magic hour on his first bike. It is as if everything is all right now, will be all right forever—griefs he did not even know he carried are falling from him, leaving him light as smoke.

Crippled, he had been; crippled from the years of bearing it, not just the lab, the whole thing. Everything. He can hardly believe the relief. A vagrant thought brushes him: Who will remain? If there is anything to care for, to be comforted, who will care? He floats it away, concentrating on the comfort that emanates from the strange life at his side, the myth-beast ambling in the most ordinary way through this dark conduit, which is now winding down, or perhaps up and down, he cannot tell.

The paving under his feet looks quite commonplace, damp and cracked. Beside him the great rat's muscles bunch and stretch as each hind leg comes under; he glances back and smiles to see the King's long ring-scaled tail curve right, curve left, carried in the relaxed-alert mode. No need for fluffy fur now. He is, he realizes, going into mysteries. Inhuman mysteries, perhaps. He doesn't care. He is among his kind. Where they are going he will go. Even to inhumanity, even alone.

But he is not, he realizes as his eyes adapt more and more, alone after all! A human figure is behind him on the far side of the King, quietly threading its way forward, overtaking him. A girl—is it a girl? Yes. He can scarcely make her out, but as she comes closer still he sees with growing alarm that it is a familiar body—it could be, oh God, it is! Sheila.

Not *Sheila*, here! No, no.

But light-footed, she has reached him, is walking even with him, stretching out her hand, too, to touch the moving King.

And then to his immense, unspeakable relief he sees that she is of course not Sheila—how could it be? Not Sheila at all, only a girl of the same height, with the same dove-breasted close-coupled curves that speak to his desire, the same heavy dark mane. Her head turns toward him across the broad back of the King, and he sees that although her features are like Sheila's, the face is wholly different, open, informed with innocence. An Eve in this second morning of the world. Sheila's younger sister, perhaps, he wonders dazedly, seeing that she is looking at him now, that her lips form a gentle smile.

"Hello," he cannot help whispering, fearful to break the spell, to inject harsh human sound into his progress. But the spell does not break; indeed, the girl's face comes clearer. She puts up a hand to push her hair back, the other firmly on the flank of the King.

"Hello." Her voice is very soft but in no way fragile. She is looking at him with the eyes of Sheila, but eyes so differently warmed and luminous that he wants only to gaze delighted as they pass to whatever destination; he is so overwhelmed to meet a vulnerable human soul in those lambent brown eyes. A soul? he thinks, feeling his unbodied feet step casually, firmly on the way to eternity, perhaps. What an unfashionable word. He is not religious, he does not believe there are any gods or souls, except as a shorthand term denoting—what?—compassion or responsibility, all that. And so much argument about it all, too; his mind is momentarily invaded by a spectral horde of old debating scholars, to whom he had paid less than no attention in his classroom days. But he is oddly prepared now to hear the girl recite conversationally, "There is no error more powerful in leading feeble minds astray from the straight path of virtue than the supposition that the soul of brutes is of the same nature as our own."

"Descartes," he guesses.

She nods, smiling across the big brown shape between them. The King's great leaflike ears have flickered to their interchange, returned to forward hold.

"He started it all, didn't he?" Lipsitz says, or perhaps only thinks. "That they're robots, you can do anything to them. Their pain doesn't count. But we're animals too," he added somberly, unwilling to let even a long-dead philosopher separate him from the flow of this joyous River. Or was it that? A faint disquiet flicks him, is abolished.

She nods again; the sweet earnest woman-face of her almost kills him with love. But as he stares the disquiet flutters again; is there beneath her smile a transparency, a failure of substance —even a sadness, as though she was moving to some inexorable loss? No; it is all right. It is.

"Where are we going, do you know?" he asks, against some better judgment. The King-Beast flicks an ear; but Lipsitz must know, now.

She smiles, unmistakably mischievous, considering him.

"To where all the lost things go," she says. "It's very beautiful. Only . . ." She falls silent.

"Only what?" He is uneasy again, seeing she has turned away, is walking with her small chin resolute. Dread grows in him, cannot be dislodged. The moments of simple joy are past now; he fears that he still has some burden. Is it perhaps a choice? Whatever it is, it's looming around him or in him as they go— an impending significance he wishes desperately to avoid. It is not a thinning out nor an awakening; he clutches hard at the strong shoulders of the King, the magical leader, feels his reassuring warmth. All things are in the lotus . . . But loss impends.

"Only what?" he asks again, knowing he must and must not. Yes; he is still there, is moving with them to the final refuge. The bond holds. "The place where lost things go is very beautiful, only what?"

"Do you really want to know?" she asks him with the light of the world in her face.

It *is* a choice, he realizes, trembling now. It is not for free, it's not that simple. But can't I just stop this, just go on? Yes, he can —he knows it. Maybe. But he hears his human voice persist.

"Only *what?*"

"Only it isn't real," she says. And his heart breaks.

And suddenly it is all breaking too—a fearful thin wave of emptiness slides through him, sends him stumbling, his handhold lost. "No! Wait!" He reaches desperately; he can feel them still near him, feel their passage all around. "Wait . . ." He understand now, understands with searing grief that it really is the souls of things, and perhaps himself that are passing, going away forever. They have stood it as long as they can and now they are leaving. The pain has culminated in this, that they leave us—leave me, leave me behind in a clockwork Cartesian world in which nothing will mean anything forever.

"Oh, wait," he cries in dark nowhere, unable to bear the loss, the still-living comfort, passing away. *Only it isn't real,* what does that mean? Is it the choice, that the reality is that I must stay behind and try, and try?

He doesn't know, but can only cry, "No, please take me! Let me come too!" staggering after them through unreality, feeling them still there, still possible, ahead, around. It is wrong; he is terrified somewhere that he is failing, doing wrong. But his human heart can only yearn for the sweetness, for the great benevolent King-Beast so surely leading, to feel again their joy. "Please, I want to go with you—"

—And yes! For a last instant he has it; he touches again the warmth and life, sees the beautiful lost face that was and wasn't Sheila—they are there! And he tries with all his force crazily to send himself after them, to burst from his skin, his life if need be—only to share again that gentleness. *"Take* me!"

But it is no good—he can't; they have vanished and he has fallen kneeling on dank concrete, nursing his head in empty shaking hands. It was in vain, and it was wrong. Or was it? his fading thought wonders as he feels himself black out. Did something of myself go too, fly to its selfish joy? He does not know.

. . . And will never know, as he returns to sodden consciousness, makes out that he is sprawled like a fool in the dirt behind his rat cages with the acid taste of wormwood sickly in his mouth and an odd dryness and lightness in his heart.

What the hell had he been playing at? That absinthe is a bummer, he thinks, picking himself up and slapping his clothes disgustedly. This filthy place, what a fool he'd been to think he could work here. And these filthy rats. There's something revolting back here on the floor, too. Leave it for posterity; he drags the rack back in place.

All right, get this over. Humming to himself, he turns the power hose on the messy floor, gives the stupid rats in their cages a blast too for good measure. There are his jars—but whatever had possessed him, trying to kill them individually like that? Hours it would take. He knows a simpler way if he can find a spare garbage can.

Good, here it is. He brings it over and starts pulling out cage after cage, dumping them all in together. Nests, babies, carrots, crap and all. Shrieks, struggling. Tough tit, friends. The ether can is almost full; he pours the whole thing over the crying mess and jams on the lid, humming louder. The can walls reverberate with teeth. Not quite enough gas, no matter.

He sits down on it and notices that a baby rat has run away hiding behind his shoe. Mechanical mouse, a stupid automaton. He stamps on its back and kicks it neatly under Sheila's hamster rack, wondering why Descartes has popped into his thoughts. There is no error more powerful—Shit with old D., let's think about Sheila. There is no error more powerful than the belief that some cunt can't be had. Somehow he feels sure that he will find that particular pussy-patch wide open to him any day now. As soon as his project gets under way.

Because he has an idea. (That absinthe wasn't all bad.) Oh yes. An idea that'll pin old Welch's ears back. In fact it may be too much for old Welch, too, quotes, commercial. Well, fuck old Welch, this is one project somebody will buy, that's for sure. Does the Mafia have labs? Ho ho, far out.

And fuck students too, he think genially, wrestling the can to the entrance, ignoring sounds from within. No more Polinskis, no more shit, teaching is for suckers. My new project will take care of that. Will there be a problem getting subjects? No—look at all the old walking carcasses they sell for dogfood. And there's a slaughterhouse right by the freeway, no problem at all. But he *will* need a larger lab.

He locks up, and briskly humming the rock version of "Anitra's Dance," he goes out into the warm rainy dawnlight, reviewing in his head the new findings on the mid-brain determinants of motor intensity.

It should be no trick at all to seat some electrodes that will make an animal increase the intensity of whatever it's doing. Like say, *running*. Speed it right up to max, run like it never ran before regardless of broken legs or what. What a natural! Surprising someone else hasn't started already.

And just as a cute hypothesis, he's pretty sure he could seal the implants damn near invisibly; he has a smooth hand with flesh. Purely hypothetical, of course. But suppose you used synthetics with, say, acid-release. That would be hard to pick up on X rays. H'mmm.

Of course, he doesn't know much about horses, but he learns fast. Grinning, he breaks into a jog to catch the lucky bus that has appeared down the deserted street. He has just recalled a friend who has a farm not fifty miles away. Wouldn't it be neat to run the pilot project using surplus Shetland ponies?

RACHEL POLLACK *is a young American writer currently living in Amsterdam, where, she reports, "I ride my bicycle around the canals, attempt to speak Dutch, and sit on sunny afternoons in a sidewalk café that serves American-style hamburgers—thereby combining the best of two worlds." She has had several stories published in the British speculative-fiction quarterly* New Worlds *and some political satires in the London underground press. This sly little story marks her first sale to an American publication. She is presently working on a novel.*

■

IS YOUR CHILD USING DRUGS? SEVEN WAYS TO RECOGNIZE A DRUG ADDICT

SPEECH: Does your child's speech pattern conform with his customary actions? Look for slurring, difficulty of speech, as if drunk.

◆

Allan and Gloria Rumsilver looked at their son standing in the doorway. The moonlight, bright to excess as it had been for nine nights, flared about Dominiq's head like an unstable aura, causing Allan to squint his eyes, then look away. "Since when do you ring the bell?" he asked. "You lose your key again?" Dominiq's mouth twisted. His facial muscles pushed up his nostrils to give his contorted lips, his bare teeth more room. His tongue curled and stretched with seeming indolence, experimenting in a private sexuality as it sought a proper cavity or surface to make a proper sound. He coughed, then jerked back his head. Allan and Gloria could see tremors ripple his skin's exposed areas. A moment later Dominiq squeezed between his parents and lurched upstairs (his arm muscles alone under reasonable control), only to stop at the landing and say, his back to them, "You must know. You must find out. Something must be done."

◆

CHEMICAL AROMAS: Do you smell strange aromas, like glue, Carbona, Magic Marker? Does your child's breath smell of any strange chemical odor?

◆

Dominiq's mother decided that before Dominiq came home from school she should clean out his room. For the last few days he'd denied her entrance, and this closeness, joined to his other strange behavior, had so aggravated Allan and Gloria that for the first time since Dominiq's early puberty they had considered invading his privacy for his own good. But now Gloria decided that she could enter her son's room as a gesture of aid rather than to spy, and so she labored upstairs with the vacuum cleaner. At the closed door she paused, her attention momentarily snagged by howling wind; earlier the day had felt calm and warm, though of course with cleaning she had not left the house in hours. A faint glow between the door and the frame further distracted her. As her hand touched the knob this glow flared up, then died, while the wind rose in pitch and volume till she felt her ears turn red trying to contain the noise. When the door did not open she thought, "Maybe God doesn't want me in there," but then embarrassment at such a juvenile notion strengthened her arm enough to force the door.

A smell, unbearably sweet—exotic fruit left to rot—smothered her like a great bear. Her sinuses in flames, she stumbled backward from the room. But before she slammed the door (and in confusion kicked the vacuum cleaner down the thirteen steps) she saw, through the closed window, the trees, motionless from the windless day.

◆

EATING HABITS: IS THERE EVIDENCE OF LOSS OF APPETITE? IS THERE UNUSUAL USE OF SWEETS, SODA, SUGAR, ETC.?

◆

To counteract Dominiq's several days' refusal to eat dinner Gloria had spent three hours preparing an elaborate Hunter's

Soup, her son's favorite. But now, once again, the boy just stared embarrassed at the final wisps of smoke from the cooling food. After ten minutes Allan said, "Are you planning to eat anything?" Pause. "You know, your mother worked all day on that." He waited only a moment more, then wiped off his spoon, laid it on the tablecloth, and, crossing behind his son, said, "You'll eat some all right." He pried open Dominiq's mouth—the boy did not struggle—lifted a spoonful and poured it down Dominiq's throat. An archetypal revulsion jerked Dominiq's muscles, as if a hand had rapped the motor centers in the cortex. His arms flung off his father, his legs kicked back his chair as he pitched forward, spitting out his soup. Gloria saw that the clear brown liquid had turned a muddy yellow in her son's mouth.

◆

PILLS: Are your prescription pills disappearing? Are strange colored pills found on clothing, dressers, or on person?

◆

Allan and Gloria first used the terms "drugs" and "narcotics" when they partially viewed Dominiq swallow a pill, then bury a plastic vial in the backyard—"partially" because Dominiq stood behind a willow tree so that his parents saw only specks, spots, blotches rather than a unified form. When the boy had gone his parents scooted forward and, digging like dogs, uncovered the vial, which indeed contained some twenty pills, all black and large, about three times the size of aspirin. When Allan tried to crush one he found it harder than the carborundum it vaguely resembled. This hardness, its inappropriateness to internal medication, so fascinated Allan he did not notice immediately the pill's extreme weight, at least two ounces. Allan wished to test it, see what tools would smash it, but Gloria insisted they rebury the batch before Dominiq could discover them.

◆

HALLUCINATIONS: User senses distortion, there may be intensification of sensory perception. There may be a loss of reality or unexplainable psychotic or antisocial behavior. User when on LSD or hallucinogenic drug might also want to destroy himself.

◆

Dominiq leaned his right shoulder against the garage and lifted his head toward the northeast. Twenty feet to the left Allan and Gloria watched him, certain he didn't notice them or didn't care, yet still embarrassed. Allan said, "He seems calm." Gloria watched Dominiq's left hand; the fingers flexed constantly, smoothly rippling the air. Just after moonrise (the moon that night appeared immense, yet dim, as if caution at close proximity shrouded its light) Dominiq collapsed their assumption of his obliviousness. With his arm pointed toward the moon he called to them, "See them? Gathering? They're putting everything together for the trip. Just like we used to do before we went away for fishing. But they don't need boats, you know. All they need's a place to put themselves together."

Allan shouted across the twenty feet, "There's no one there."

Now Dominiq turned to look directly at them. "When you stop me," he said, "please do it—" he shrugged—"softly."

"No one wants to hurt you," said Gloria, feeling in her voice insufficient reassurance.

"Yes, you must. But softly."

◆

CHANGE OF PERSONALITY: Is the child acting contrary to his known personality makeup? Is there unexplained elation? Is there erratic behavior or unusual physical activity?

◆

When Dominiq ran from the house at 3:00 A.M. his parents, awake to discuss his problem, decided to follow. By the time they'd put on their robes and slippers, grabbed the car keys, and got outside, the boy was heading, several hundred yards down the road, for the great rock field beyond the housing development. The station wagon followed quietly, lights off, but Dominiq loped so smoothly, his head thrown back snorting the wind, that they might have cruised alongside and not penetrated his elation. At the rock field the moon, even brighter there than over their house, provided sufficient light to watch from a safe distance as their son pushed uprooted tree trunks, two feet around and eight feet high, with little more effort than if he'd handled balsa wood or cardboard. (These petrified trunks, so round and flat, like stone pillars, had always intrigued them. Gloria had once investigated scientific studies of their origin, but unsatisfactorily.) Dominiq, his superhuman strength oddly normal in the moon glare, formed with the pillars a circle two hundred yards across. After he'd set the last trunk in place he stepped to the center, where he slowly rotated his body. "There," he called loudly, as if to awaken sentience in the wood, "I've set it up for you. Just like the picture. It's all ready, so now you can let me go."

◆

EYES: Is there a glassy look? Are the pupils pinpointed? Do the eyes look strange to you?

◆

Nearly paralyzed above the knees, Dominiq lurched downstairs, where he swayed back and forth and said, "It's tonight, isn't it? It's tonight." His eyes darted back and forth like trapped insects.

"Yes," Allan snapped, "it certainly is. Come on, Gloria, we're not waiting till tomorrow. We're going to that drug clinic right now."

Soon the station wagon was darting nervously through the housing development, Dominiq's sweatless body held upright between his mother and father. "Perhaps I should look at his eyes," Gloria ventured and took out the notebook in which they recorded Dominiq's symptoms. But when she peered into the large black pupils—now they just stared at the moon, heavy in the sky like a pregnant woman—she saw, instead of her own worried reflection, a strange illusion, like a photographic negative: a stony desert, cold and gray, empty and flat, with hills like chipped teeth in the distance. Slowly a face appeared within the rock, human yet not human, like a child's sculpture. As her thighs moved apart in imminent sexual arousal Gloria whined, "Could you stop the car? I think I'm going to be sick."

"What the hell," Allan said, but pulled over near the rock field.

Dominiq's head poked forward to watch his mother walk stiffly toward the tree trunks. "It's tonight," he called after her.

Allan shouted, "Gloria, our boy's in trouble. Will you come back here?"

The petrified circle, however, soundproofed Gloria, who only stared at the bitter face that floated out of the moon, larger and closer, like a sex criminal attacking at night. Suddenly the ground heaved and shook. On her hands and knees, Gloria saw the earth crack, deep fissures, narrow eyes, a thin nose, and a long straight mouth. The tree trunks stuck out from the edges of the face like stiff locks of hair. Her hands reached down to caress the dirt.

Right then something gripped her shoulder and she heard an alien voice jabber at her. Before she could squirm away Allan had lifted her up. "Will you come on?" his high voice said. "Our son needs help."

Back in the car, Dominiq turned his tearless face toward his mother. "I'm sorry," he said. "I couldn't help it." Allan gunned the motor.

But before the car had gone fifty yards he slammed the brakes. Something was happening to the road; huge cracks split the macadam, two eyes, a mouth . . . Allan spun the car around.

Back through the development, past the houses, everywhere, lawns, schoolyards, driveways, bitter faces cracked the earth. Heaving and shaking, the car doubled back, cut around, turn after turn, searching for a hole. "I'm sorry. I'm sorry," Dominiq repeated.

And Allan, as he finally found an open road, shouted, "It's all right. We'll find a doctor. It's okay. The doctor will help you."

Gloria watched the cold, cold faces form an aisle for the speeding car.

The formidable FELIX ("JAKE") GOTSCHALK, *a psychologist who lives in North Carolina, has been appearing regularly in* New Dimensions *for several issues now, a situation that is likely to continue—for his quirky, idiosyncratic style and irrepressible technological inventiveness both have such robust originality that this editor finds them irresistible. Here he is again, writing in characteristic headlong fashion.*

■

Felix C. Gotschalk

■

CHARISMA LEAK

Here comes Doctor Elkins. Yeah, his Santa Claus face *is* beginning to light up, just the way it always does when he sees me. I don't give a good old shit if he is the president of this jerkwater college reprod—I wish he would stop asking me to play golf with him. I mean, for God's sake, shouldn't a man who's been playing electromag golf for three calendrical tiers be able to break par? And he always insists that I use his teleporter to get over to the course. That is really pretty overdeferrent of him.

"Good morning, Doctor Elkins. . . . Yes, I'll be glad to have coffee with you." God, he's going to hold me by the arm again. He always does this when we enter the cafeteria nostalg. And, yes, the students are raising their heads and nudging each other with softly insistent elbows—and, yes, I can see, far at the end of the greasy-aired room, some key faculty members ready for us. Maybe three or four of them have already finished their demitasses of syrupy, bayou-mud coffee. But they won't leave the table. Not with us on the way. Never in God's world. Now even the server-clones are beaming. They beam at Elkins and they beam at me. What a coattails effect! Bayoushit—I bet these people would do anything Elkins told them to do and maybe what I told them to do. Power by association. He's going to pay for the coffee again, too. "Here, let me, Doctor El—next time? Okay." Now we have the steaming cups in our hands and are steering for the faculty table, like the captain's launch edging up to the flagship. Everybody knows we're coming—there's a quick eye-contact vector (not too furtive, not too paranoid, not too casual) and some shuffling of feet. The sociometry matrix is

69

going to change now, sure as hell; they're ready to install us as
stars and crowd around us. Miss Royal is adjusting her eyelashes
and elevating her pneumobreasts. Now the moment is upon
them and upon us. Hey, now I'm smiling my great symmetric
smile, and my wholesome brown eyes are disappearing in boy-
ishly charming dimples, and my perfect teeth are flashing their
spittlefree gloss. Don't tell me Hyman wants to shake hands
with me again. He's not kidding—well, I sure can't refuse—
"Caught a six-pounder at Lake Boeuf? Great!" Anybody'd think
I'd been fishing all my life. I don't know why I caught thirty-two
fish in two hours and Dean Stanhope didn't even get a nibble.
Maybe my charisma leak works on the fish too. I know it works
on pets, children, colleagues, clones, holobots, and sometimes,
I'd swear, even on mechobots. Now, all the faces are turned on
us, and Elkins is tailoring his comments so as to make me the
center of the sociovectors. There's that sour old Miss Seagram,
nodding at me and smiling. She'd let me fuck her, I bet, but she
probably spurts creosote from her Bartholin apertures. And I
bet she lets dry farts. Oops, Calvert is clapping me on the shoulder and blatting pizza breath at me. Why is it that everybody
wants to put their goddam hands on me? Why does everybody
seem to want a little piece of me? There's no need for me to ask.
I know. I've known for a few tiers, but I find myself testing the
limits—making sure. You see, I am a compsite personatype. *But,*
and it is a very damn huge *but,* I am an Eisenhower–Glenn–
Kennedy composite. And that is like being Elizabeth Taylor in
a world filled with eczemic sows.

The talk is flowing at us like proffered wine. They are pressing
gifts into our personality matrices, reinforcing our autoworth
parameters, elevating our sociostature, standing aside—yay,
even diving off—as we mount the pecking-order ladder. And
the funny thing is—I feel contempt for most of these people.
But I AM UNABLE TO PROJECT IT! True, I almost never get
slighted, or put on, or insulted. But I cannot seem to be other
than a guy that everybody loves. WHY THE FUCK DOES
EVERYBODY WANT A PIECE OF ME? BECAUSE I HAVE A
BLOODY CHARISMA LEAK!

Now Elkins hugs me (with reasonable unobtrusiveness) as he

enters his office, and his bird-faced secretary gives me a coy
little wave. I'm walking toward the egress-port now and I don't
see anybody. Outside, the sky is a metallic teal, and rose-petal
clouds are scudding by. The Augustine grass is so thick and
fleshy and green you want to eat it like lettuce. The air smells
of subtropical foliage, and there is a kind of ripe atmospheric
closeness: wetly pregnant molecules everywhere. Spores and
epiphytes, molds and dews, puffballs, and mushrooms with soft
erections. Far off in the northeast quad the Orleans geodome
glitters like a minifractured glass bowl. The oil and natural-gas
domes fill the south-quad horizon like blisters on algae.

Maybe I can make it back to the office unseen if I sprint
behind the Student Union building. What a shack! It looks like
a hangar for Spads and Jennys. Here goes—damn, there's Durkee. But with his 20/400 vision maybe I can duck him. Here,
I just flick behind these plantain stalks and see what he does.
He's headed this way and I won't be able to duck him but he
hasn't seen me yet. So I'll come out into the open and walk
down the steps. My corfams shine well in the sun and my decto-
lene shirt undulates airily on my compact torso. I have a splen-
did full Windsor in my cravat. Even the sun seems to love me.
It bathes me like hundreds of cupped hands: shielding, stroking,
firming up, caressing me. Some days I am convinced I shit
prettier turds than anybody I know. Mr. Durkee is getting
closer—like, twenty-five yards, and there! Those faintly ptotic
eyes behind the greasy quartz glasses light up. "Come on, man,
let's get a drink. Just had one? Well, have another." There's
nothing I can do. After all, he's my boss, my director, my bene-
factor, patron saint, protector—hell yes, he'd fight for me! And
he made me acting director when he went on sabbatical leave.
Sabbatical, my Mississippi ass! He tried to put the blast on that
geriatric Doctor Beulah Jones, and she bitched to the Synod
Board. Rather than have a big hassle, they shipped Durkee off
to finish his doctorate. Now he's asking me to go to Rene's Bar
with him after classes. He drinks vodka like it was water. Says
his wife can't smell it on him. Well, at least there is a new set
of people in the cafeteria. Just so nobody kisses me. Folger is
telling me how he likes my new car. It is a compact Olds painted

the color of pediatric feces. But you like it anyway? Thanks. At
least the flitters and the transport implants all look alike. There
is nothing personatyped about mine; but, even then, I bet my
flitter and my implants are drenched with DNA webbings that
give off a great scent.

Here I am back at the office at last. Dugan, the golf coach, just
stuck his head in the door and called me "coach." Here's a note
from Kinchen about tonight's meeting of the Charter Kiwanis,
and here's a congratulatory note from The Men of the First
Presbyterian Church: I have been elected president of that
group! Have I ever been to that church? And the phone is
ringing as usual: Gee Mitchell wants me to play poker tonight,
Ogburn wants me to go to the Coonie Club dance, and Dela-
haye wants to do another personality piece on me for the local
newspaper. Scott is looking at me, and the secretary is asking
me if she can do anything for me. You know, women really
don't seem to dig me especially. Maybe that means something
and maybe not, but it doesn't bother me at all. I mean, I'm not
queer, and I have done the stud bit for procreative quotas, and
I dig the orgasm implant and the prostate kickers and all the
hedonic gimcracks, but I guess I never was a cunt hound.

I think I am going to have to go to the john to get some
privacy. I want to get up and get out, casual-like, but I can't.
Lippincott is looking at me worshipfully as I cross the room. I'll
just flash him a good smile and cluck my tongue at him. There,
he'll be fine for maybe two hours. God, this is like running a belt
line or a gauntlet of voyeurs. Old Roger Bill is waving at me
from his truck. I wonder if it's true that he hanged a black man.
I bet he'd tell me if I asked him. Boy, it feels good to sit down.
There is nothing so underrated as a good, somasthetic, fecal
dumping. And I can press my palms against my face, rub my
eyes with my fingers, exhale, slump my shoulders, relax my
facial muscles, and close my eyes. "Is that you, Hal?" A voice
from the next stall! There is no escape. It is Ayon, the ag prof.
He wants me to be parade marshal for FFA day! The Future
Farmers of America! Futile Fuckers of Assholes! Frenetic Fruc-
tifiers! Fouled Frenchfries! Fallow Fallopians! Fellow Fellators!
Man, I am damn well going home and take a blink-out pill. But

first, I'll have to wipe my asseroonie and emerge, just when Ayon does, wash hands together, do the camaraderie bit, and then probably walk back across the concourse with him. And there goes the bell for class changing. I may have to pretend to be sick.

It's a little shaky standing here on the toilet seat, craning up to look through the elephant ears and plantains and jalousied window slats, but there! The foliage seems to part, as if it wishes also to please me, and I can see my brown Oldsmobile out on the soft asphalt parking lot. I'm going to wait until the coast is perfectly clear before I make a run for the car. You'd think that even a good charisma cat like me could navigate 100 yards without being waylaid by normos who want their autoworth parameters fattened, but it is in fact not so.

Hey, that was easy enough: a quick blat through the courtyard, a brisk striding across the white shell path, and on across the asphalt into the lego-maze of nostalgiabank autos and filmy flitters and prosthetic-looking teleporters and transporters. Now I am actually seated in the car and push the key into the ignition slot. The key feels like it should be in a sardine can. The noisy little V-6 crashes into life and I lurch the car off onto the access trench. Are all eyes on me? Have the students ceased their stupid calligraphy and turned their Cajun-brown faces toward my baby-shit-brown car? Well they might, and I strongly suspect they have. Anyway, I get on the feeder trench and ride atop the levee toward town. People are waving at me from cars. They do that a lot down here. Thank God I don't need any gas. Every time I pull into a service station, three or four attendants come streaming out. They clean the windshield, headlamps, parking lights, sonar scanners, trivid antenna, and there's this one guy who always wants to clean the white-walls. They check the oil, water, transmission fluid, brake fluid, the battery, and the central lube cannister. They prod the belts for optimum tension, press on the sparking plugs, and then they check the tires all around for exactly 28.5 psi. They usually want to clean the inside glass and vacuum the floors. Another young guy always shines the exhaust extension like it was a favorite boot.

Who's that behind me? It's Bidot Lacache and he's flagging me down. Old dumb-ass Lacache. So I'll ease over onto the shoulder by Doc Markham's allergy clinic. Doc is a crusty old M.D. bastard, but he is cordial and subordinate around me.

Now Bidot is striding self-consciously toward me and his face is one big trusting smile. I wonder what would happen if I would clench my fist and slug him right in the mouth? Hey, I'm tempted, but I know I couldn't do anything like that. Something very deep in me disallows that response. Shit, that would be like Santa Claus slapping a kindergartner. The effect would be eradicable—or whatever that word is. Can you guess what Bidot wants to give me? Garfish filets and nutria pelts. He happens to have some extras. Well, fuck a duck, I can't refuse. It's free food and I'll be making Bidot happy.

I finally make it home. The ingress port rolls up nicely, obediently, and the air-conditioning feels nice in the tunnel. The hoops of the rug writhe deliciously under my feet, and the banister feels cool and smooth as I mount the escalator. Speaking of mounting, and cognizant of the imagery the term evokes, I see my adoring Schnauzer reprod has mounted the cat again. The cat is about twenty years old now and likes to please me by allowing the dog to mount her. What the hell could get into a dog to get him to hop a cat? What estrus tropism this? Why would a salt + pepper-colored dawg climb on a geriatric tabby-matron? Now their little show is over and they come bounding to me.

"Did you bring any ale, dummy?" Susan's rasp sears the cool air. (What all but blatant sacrilege this? Who hath not got the word on me? Who purporteth to address me thusly? Who, prithee, pray tell?) All you hairy-ass studs know who. All you thick-necked bulls, with variegated flaccid pricks and taco breath—no need to guess.

"No, darling," I offer.

"You got ears, haven't you? You know, audio receptoports?"

"Well, certainly, darling—"

"And you comprehend simple chains of linguistic input, don't you—things like BRING HOME SOME ALE? EMPTY THE SMELLY GARBAGE? STAY ON YOUR SIDE OF THE BED?"

"Really, Susan, I don't want to argue—"

"Well, I *do,* you dumpy little fart."

"You are being insulting."

"Your perceptual acuity is startling, Dick Tracy. How long did it take you to nose down on your first clue?"

I walk away from this consort-surrogate, wondering why my charisma doesn't seem to work on her. I flash my best visage at her and she looks at me as if I am a funny little ball of nit. In any case, I almost like her bitching, especially compared to all the autoworth fattening I get everywhere else. So I autovector medial sheepishness and plod off toward the sleepdeck.

"Where do you think you're going?" she asks, her voice flaring out at me like a chameleon's long sticky tongue.

I tell lies fairly well: "I am ill, madam, and I am going to bed for a few hours."

"Well, I want some goddam ale."

"Dial the aeromart or the pneumopak delivery service."

"They cost extra."

"Live it up, lover."

"Oh, disappear."

Thank God I am actually and finally alone herein one of the somno cubicles. Well, not exactly—the provost trivid camera is in the bulkhead, but there's no getting away from them. I usually taunt the camera with noncomputable jazz like "Come off that wall, you myopic-looking four-eyed hive of circuitry!" The camera's interpretive matrices can't handle anthropomorphic statements. Anyway, I peel off my velour jacket and empty the pockets: two stylus pens, a mustache comb, two blatters of amphet, a peristalsic wriggler, and a jumble of notes on 3 × 5 cards. As I look at the little pile of things, I feel a swelling private delight. These small objects are my very very own: extensions of my digital apparatus, a personal grooming item, chemical pellets to brighten my mood, an hedonically toned sensuo-implant, and my very own scribbles. I can draw them unto me, untouched by the swarming normos with their empty cups and nadired autoworth histograms. A gentle Mozart figure pulses in the transducer as I hang my life-support girdle on a favorite antique hook. I can feel the graviton field easing up on the g-loading. I close my eyes and slowly deflux the couplers on my ruffled dickey shirt. The sheer satin privacy of the moment floats me off in space, encapsulated in a warm fetal amnio. I sit on the edge of the bed and sigh aloud. I am a rough burlap sack, stuffed with fine russet potatoes, and I am reaching in to remove each one, slowly, carefully, ritualistically, until I am emptied, collapsed, deflated, reamed, steamed, and dry-cleaned. I pull off my star boots and the fuzzy socks, warm isomorphs of my thick calves. My toes wriggle like grubworms on a hook. I stand, like a sodden anthropoid, and deflux the leotard-sheathing. It drops to the deck and I stand there unveiled and vulnerable in my genital pod and Buster Brown tee shirt. The ritual is almost complete: my pockets yield keys and thumbprint plates, identocubes in shiny flat interstitial mazes, and a wonderfully mundane handkerchief. Even an Eisen-Ken-Glenn composite has to wipe his nasal apertures. And I even pick fresh green snot if I have any.

And now I am blowing out my breath, like a weightlifter psyching up for a key press, and easing onto the inflated gelatin bed. I set the thermal controls, impatient for somnolence, and palm the blink-out cubule open, extracting one of the pellets. I lie back and pop the blatter into my arm and feel a delicious coolness, as if iced cognac were replacing my hot sticky blood. I sink deeper in the bed, supine and spread-eagled, like a sodden colossus in jellied quicksand. My lids close like membranes stretching languidly over agates. A soft roaring begins, far off in my personal galactic life-space. I soar lightly over lava beds and eucalyptus groves, skim icy-blue crags, spear rearing black thunderheads. I sift porously through space, the acceleration flattening my face. At last I am nobody. I am a flat gray monolith, a diffuse zephyr, a sheet of rain, a sizzle of fire, a Moldau, a Nile. The sweetest gift to me is the extirpation of my identity. Ah, the joy of having no concept of self. I sleep.

I was zipping into diaphanous white trouser-pipes when the consort irised the somno port open. She stands there, like a whore in a door, and gives me a once-over. Anybody would think she used her cunt as a repository for nails, bobby pins, dental floss, or Sen-Sen; she sure as hell doesn't use it as a

constrictive sheath around my stalk. "Hey—Mister Wunner-
ful," she says, in a skillfully modulated taunt, "your visophone
has been flashing all afternoon, and the message center is clog-
ging up with cubes." "Thenk kew, dolling," I say, snapping to
attention and bowing ever so slightly. Maybe I can charm the
old sow into the sack for a quick lay before dinner. She seems
to mellow a bit, but then she turns and plods off down the hall,
like a tired charwoman. When I enter the solarium sectant I see
what she means: I have had eleven visocalls and eight com-
muniques in five hours. The dog is nuzzling my leg and the cat
has made a truly magnificent leap all the way to my shoulder
epaulets. It is purring and trying to suck my ear lobe. The
atmospheric molecules crowd around me like happy bees, and
the cologne seems to say, "You picked *me!* You picked *me!*

I riffle through the message plates, and it's the same old jazz:
Some engineers want me to speak at their colloquium, the
provost cadets want me as a consultant, a chemist is begging me
to co-author a book with him; Dean Gugliemo is calling from
the club, Jack Stans wants me on his deer-hunt stand (I missed
a clean shot recently), and a contractor wants to build me a new
geodeck. I don't have any surplus of credit lines, but he wants
to advance all the vouchers himself—keeps telling his friends I
am "his boy." Well, at least here's a switch: I am five months late
with a fuel blastula account, and the Credit Synod is giving me
a final chance to pay up. The Harvard Club wants me to join
their bicycle gymkhana, Calvert is inviting me to a bridge tour-
ney, and here's someone I don't know, asking if I will come and
talk to his teenage son about Jesus!

I think I would like to hear some more pure Mozart, but the
transducer is blaring some brand of martial dissonance. Now
the dog is barking to go out, I have a stack of paperwork back
at the office, my prostate is acting up again, and I think Bob
Hague is making the copulation scene with Susan. A strange
resolve is nudging at me—where did it come from? I feel some
glimmers of tranquility in the distance, like soft silent lighten-
ing blooming in wet clouds. I am beginning to know what I
must do: I must disconnect myself. I am burgeoning with the
input needs of too many goddam normos. I must disconnect. I'll

need a private place to do it, but that won't be any problem. Of course, it will be illegal, painful, maladaptive—but then, maybe the Synod adaptability indices are wrong. After all, who says I always have to please other people? So many of them draw strength regularly from me that I feel like a glucose bottle over their failing white torsos—an organismic donor of generalized life-energy. Why do I have to wave at the neighbors and friends, listen to the same old jokes at the bars and clubs, and make believe it's funny when Durkee gets drunk at Kiwanis and passes out with his face in his spaghetti? And then to watch him wake up in the middle of the speaker's presentation, look around like a dinosaur in a lake, and blurt out, "Hey, where's old Charley Smith?" And with the spaghetti strands clinging to his widow's peak like some absurd parody of Medusa. So the action comes: I make a fast, azimuth-true stride down the hall to the drop-shaft and out into the autoport. I slide into the Olds and back out of the drive faster than usual. I guess Susan is wondering why I grabbed up the box of X-acto knives from the workbench. She thinks I don't have the guts to disconnect—to cut out my persona-implants. But I do in fact have the requisite guts.

I zip through town and up the bayou to Woodmead, a very large-scaled plantation home done in Greek Revival. It is abandoned but not vandalized and visited by all the area nostalgia buffs. I park the car in the soft impacted loam of the drive and get out. The sun is setting like a humid blister behind the gnarled and moss-skinned branches of the live oaks. A blue heron flies past on fragile butterfly wings, its eyes disproportionately bright and somehow cruel. The untended grass is high, mysterious, undulating, and the trailing gossamers of Spanish moss are like funereal tinsel. The silence tranquilizes me nicely, like camphor breezes flowing into my auditory sensors. I listen closely and hear the sawing of insects in the fields, the rustle of the grasses and the yucca blooms, and the dull swish of a flitter skimming the bayou. I approach the house like a tentative prodigal son. Soft detritus litters the shallow stylobate, and wasp nests cling stickily to the walls. The door yields readily and I step into a dark, high-ceilinged foyer. A few quiet steps away and I see the staircase against the wall, ascending, massive, and somehow ceremonial. To either side of the central hall are large rooms with walls eighteen inches thick. The attic beams are said to be fourteen-inch-square heart cypress. There is a melancholy here that seeps into me like welcome elixir, embalming, diffusing, filling up. I begin to climb the stairs. Is that a human form on the landing? Skull-like face, whiter than ash, ebony physiognomy? No. It is a delicious fantasy, mired in the memory blanket of the past. The air is both musty and fecund on the second floor. Corinthian columns stand at both ends of the hall, and the ceilings float up to their twenty-foot asymptotes. The light is fading and the darkness is like warm velvet. My footfalls are soft, slow, and I breathe contentedly, pouring out slow full spumes of frost and warmth. There is nothing so full as an empty house. Surely ghosts cling to the high corners of the walls, like convex webs, little matrices of ancient dust and metal flecks, bone and parted flesh, rotted, dried, stratified, exfoliated. What has brought me here? Privacy, of course, but I could have locked myself in any room at home. I have violated expectancy parameters. I am supposed to be predictable. I don't threaten anyone and I am loved, but I am not happy. The sweet silence of this place seems to make me happier. Perhaps it is because I am absorbing memory-trace engrams from the environment, rather than having people pawing and extracting and reeling mtv's out of me. The cantilever steps to the attic cling to the circular tower shaft. I climb in reverent excitement. The door to the huge attic is like a portal to heaven and/or hell. I grasp the knob gently, as if it were an egg, and turn. The door opens silently and I can see the huge beams creeping upward into the ultimate chiaroscuro under the roof, like bridge trusses. The heat is dry here, an urgent compromise of steaming humidity outside and inside shieldings of cypresses which stood for decades in the black waters of the swamp. I move under the beams and sit on the floor. Surely this is the womb and I should tuck myself into a tight little fetal ball, but my psychodynamics just don't work that way. I simply want people to stop sucking on me like I am some general comfort-tit-of-the-world.

I dial an energy-chaise at a nice height and sit on it. It's a little hard (but itchy, erotic fun) to autovector flare energy through the vitreous humor, but I do it anyway, and my eye-beams are like twin laser cones or tensor focals. I open the X-acto box and examine the blades: hawkbills, straights, scimitars, serrates, crosscuts, scapellas, multiples. I clip the hawkbill in and hold it like a pencil over the smooth ventral white of my forearm. About half an inch below the rosy surface is the John Glenn personaplant. I barely touch the point of the knife to my arm, and a crystal-clear pinch of pain rankles through my neural filigrees. I dab at the area, like a painter with a sharp brush, but it still hurts like holy hell. I am breathing unevenly and I feel fretty and immature. But no one can deal with true pain—pain in the searing yellow sense of tissue damage. Drawing a blade over the resilient mound of my forearm is like splitting a gelatinous melon and I cannot take the pain; so I use one of my rare implants: morphine distillate sprayed from my mouth. I cut quickly and deep, and the implant gives off high-frequency vibes. The mechovoice from the leasing co-op begins: YOUR ORGANISMIC INTEGRITY IS ATYPICAL. SEEK ASSISTANCE OR CODE IN YOUR LOCATION. I always wonder how the leasing people can keep such close tabs on their implants. The blood is flowing down my arm like Ferrari paint on a white sheet, and I do a quick and ragged cut inboard, toward the crook of my arm. I start to sponge away the blood, but suck it instead. It tastes nourishing, like thick pure soup with iron garnishments. A few beads of oily sweat ooze through the skin at my temples and I think of osmosis and selectively permeable membranes. IMPLANT SPACE VIOLATED IN TWO PLANES, the voice continues. TAMPERING WITH SYNOD PROPERTY PORTENDS WAIVER OF CIVIL PROTECTION. CODE IN THE NATURE OF YOUR TRAUMA. Oh, fuck you, Jack, I say, softly urgent, and I make a deft abscissal cut. I get memory traces of plugging watermelons. TISSUE DAMAGE IN THREE PLANES. AZIMUTH READINGS SUGGEST SPECIFIC EXTIRPATION OF IMPLANT. THIS IS NOT ADVISED. REPEAT. THIS IS NOT ADVISED. IT IS ILL ADVISED. YOUR ORGANISMIC SAFETY IS THREATENED. CODE IN YOUR LOCATION AND/OR FILE VOUCHER

FOR CRISIS INTERVENTION. You hive of Hong Kong circuitry, I spit at the voice, I'm going to dig you out of there in
about one minute. The square-shaped incision is finished and
one of the sides is spurting slow blood. I use the fusion torch to
seal off what looks like an artery or a vein, but now the soft plug
of meat won't pull out. It is as if the flesh has sent tap roots into
the microstice lattice of the implant itself. The morphine is
starting to wear off and I feel queasy. I redo all four cuts, deep
down, past the bottom edges of the pak, and the blood flows
freer. Now I get a pair of needle-nosed pliers positioned over
the patch of discoloring flesh, the jaws like a pterodactyl beak,
and my index finger and middle finger inside the caliperlike
handles. My thumb, fourth, and fifth finger close the jaws in a
careful exploratory scissors movement. The vibes of the pak
increase as the pliers notch on to the pak edges, like grabbing
a domino. I spume on some more morphine and begin to
wrench the pak loose from its warm fleshy nest. WARNING.
WARNING. SYNOD PROPERTY IS BEING DISTURBED.
YOU ARE IN SOME DANGER. REPORT IN TO CENTRAL
CRISIS BANK. PROVOST ROBOTS ALERTED. SIGNIFY
YOUR RECEPTION OF THIS MESSAGE. Jam it up your ass,
I say to the mechovoice. As if there weren't enough normos
feeding me verbal jazz all the time, now this mechovoice comes
in like a new bell. I shut my eyes and rock the pliers. The pak
grates across the bone and my emosensors flare up almost to
limits. I bite on a sponge and give an earnest pull, breaking the
implant loose. It comes out, bleeping loudly, and trailing tiny
sinews and stitch-meldings and blood. Hey, I feel different, but
then I'm supposed to, minus one personapak. I'm glad that my
intellective parameters are programmed to be independent of
my emotional constellation. I'll be able to keep a cognitive rein
on the changes and not get really shook by the emosensor inputs. I mean, suppose you feel quiescent, and all of a sudden
panicky feelings flush through you. If you even halfway ready
up for the change, it can be handled, like bracing up for a
six-inch jab in the gut. The pak's little noises are softer now.
Now for the Eisenhower pak: It is in my inner thigh, close to the
surface. I position myself to look at the area and it is like trying

to see past the lint into the secret twists of the umbicular socket. The Eisenpak has always felt good—a little itchy at times, but substantial, predictable, wholesome, reliable, perhaps even valid. It is fun to stroke; it feels like a pillbox with a crusted lid, all covered by a thin rubberized sheath. I think the inner thigh used to be called an erogenous zone.

It's dark outside and the insects are singing like tiny raucous choirs. I bet that Susan is fuming around, bitching hypochondriasis at whoever she can collar—but wait, she may be getting laid by that big stud next door. But, *but,* more important perhaps than either is the fact that everybody will be wondering about me. Well, let them stew in their wonder. I'll just draw a simple scapular edge along here—Christ, that's tender! A little freon from the torch will help. There, the skin separates easily and the epithelial strata bare themselves. The abscence of pain inspires spurious confidence in my autosurgical techniques. The displacement of tissue by a blade is really pretty crude, though —I can use the torch like a tool, or like a knife on soft butter. I anneal the edges of this simple slit, like serging carpet, and ease the pak out. The voice beams in again, weak but still insistent, telling me that my organismic integrity is deteriorating, adaptibility parameters skewing, and that the provobots are looking for me. But I don't care. I feel Godlike now, all Messianic, what with just the Kennedy pak left in me. It is the pectoral area and is gold-plated. Hey, this will be easy enough: like squeezing a blackhead with one hand, then a moderate prehensile calipering of the fleshy tit, a tiny cut with scissors, and the little cylinder appears, its cobalt head patterned with microcircuits. This is a little like taking out a fat acupuncture needle—there! What the hell—I seem to have slumped down, shrunk, been diminuitivized. But I know this is just an emo-feeling. *Just* an emo-feeling! I know what's in store, now that I have done the deed. My cognition will remain at centile ninety-two, but my personality constellation may do almost anything. The prediction is that I will be anonymous, but who really knows? I should be able to blend into any milieu, colorlessly, innocuous. Maybe now I can get some rest.

It's dark as pitch and my visual flares are losing power. I

gather up the three little men of my former personality and drop them in a bag, much like pieces of old vegetables. Two little squares of tile and a fat pencil—that was good old me! I stand up and I feel short. The darkness is more ominous now. Darkness is the absence of light. Who said that? Arch Oboler, on the old "Lights Out" radio show. See? My intellective parameters can still flick out for informational esoterica. I walk across the cypress platings, my gait ambling and shuffly. I reach for the door handle and bend my finger. I turn it counterclock and pull. Nothing happens. Push. Nothing. Clockwise and pull—what the hell is wrong? Oh yeah, clockwise and push, and the door springs open, banging against the wall. God, it's black out here, the stairs are too narrow and steep, and my life belt feels like a sodden inner tube. I reach out for the banister and a splinter darts into my palm. I snatch it away and feel swayings in my semicircular canals. I am going to have to take extra care—I feel locomotor ataxic—hey! I was drunk the other night and was trying to make it home from the blatter parlor. I was doing fine, until I rounded a corner and some guy stepped on my hands! ha ha? ho ho? hee hee? Man, if I had told that one at the faculty table this morning, the laughter would have been loud and nothing short of approbatory—well, smell me, fellows.

I made it off the circular stairwell and here I am shuffling along the upper hall. A shiver cups little radiates down my back and I have the feeling that a cobweblike gossamer figure is close behind, walking on dusty pseudopods, its willowy breast just an inch from my back. My dimming visuoflares pick up a form on the floor ahead. It is a rat, scudding right at me (I thought rats were negative-phototrophic). Shit, the little thing means business—hey! It's squealing and jumping up at me! I raise my arm and feel the soft underbelly hit me and the tiny scrambling claws. In my mind's eye I see the sharp yellow teeth, ragged, clicking, gnashing. I wrench my umbicular bezel for a protective isomorph and the rat keeps bounding up at me. I kick it and it slides against the wall, like a beanbag. I bend over to look at it, and so help me, the little eyes look at me as if to say, you zero, you cipher, you big nothing!

I try to get down the main stairs quickly and almost fall. I see dozens of specters following me, gesturing and urging each other on, pointing, beating their waving breasts, heads lolling, mouths agape. I lumber across the foyer and wrestle the door open. A snake is on the porch, all wreathed in warm scaly coils. I crash through the yucca plants to avoid it. What's wrong—why am I fleeing? Surely I can autovector some composure. I can still be cool, I hope. Sure, I stop and look around, but my chest is heaving and my emosensors flaring. I try the exhalatory blowings, but I am like a winded trumpeter. The live oaks loom strangely in the fetid gloom. I get into the car and bang my knee —goddam, that smarts! I can't get the keys out of my pocket, so I open the door and get halfway out again, standing crazily on one leg and digging in my pocket, while my foot begins to slide on the soft spongy soil. I try to force the key in and it is upside down. I get it right and then find that the key won't turn because the steering wheel lock is engaged. This has happened before, but now it feels more than usually baffling to me. By moving the wheel slightly and fitting the key in and out, I get it free, and the key turned. I notch it to start but nothing happens. Then I see the gear selector at 4, nudge it into N, and the starter spins noisily. The engine finally catches after four trials, then dies, as I try to drive off with the handbrake engaged. Christ, look at all the minutiae going wrong since I got the implants out—hey wait! Could it be that I will now be flooded with negative stimuli? God, I hope not. I don't mind being the kind of guy who blends in with the wallpaper, but I don't want to be a focal scapegoat or a communal whipping boy.

The car slews out on to the road, and I think I feel adequate. I reel out the umbilicus and plug it in the console. The panel lights spink on, and the homeostasis readouts rank me at minus 2.2 standard deviations. That's pretty far into the tail of the curve—almost a reciprocal of the two plus which I usually read. Maybe I should feel a lot worse, I don't know. I think it is the intellective consistency making the whole bit bearable enough. The car engine is overheating, and some smart-ass in a Corsair reprod flitter keeps buzzing me. The propeller is strictly holographic, but it still can scare the piss out of me. The road is full of old chuckholes and sugar-cane stalks. I get to the bridge, but it is opening for a string of barges to come through. My back is hurting and I have to take a shit. My tongue feels like a snail in a cold grease bucket. I try to pick my nose but it is dry and empty. I doze and wake up slobbering on my tie. The car won't start for several minutes, a mosquito got in and is whining around my ear lobe, and the air smells like a fish market. Everything is going wrong.

I make it home and into bed before Susan barges in, arms akimbo, in full stride yet.

"Where have you been, dumbshit?" she rasps, her tone combining casualness and taunting in optimum amounts. I give her a casual look and a long pause.

"I am not in a court of law, madam, nor are you an examining barrister."

"You don't look right, and you're giving off strange auras—what's wrong?" Before I can firm up the blanket flux, she snatches it off.

"What the hell, you pea-brain, you've taken out your implants!"

"Have I? I hadn't noticed."

"You can't do this to me, you ant—"

"What, my dove?"

"You know very damn well what I mean. You're not marketable without implants, and you'll probably get shipped off to a reconstituting farm." Susan's surliness sags and I can see that she is going to cry.

"Allifuckingator tears!" I grate, trying to hiss some alimentary bad breath at her. Her hair is full of plastic curlers. She looks like a goddam turbo-jet copter.

"We'll have to sell the dome and move to God knows where."

"Good," I mumble, "I'm fed up with conspicuous consumption."

She sits on the chaise and looks sadly at me. "Why did you do it?"

"Because I am sick and damn tired of being the great white personality of the world. I'm everybody's favorite son, all grown up and successful. I have been an optimum interactional ploy and buttress for about ninety percent of everybody I've met since I applied for the implants. I'm tired of everybody pawing at me."

"Surely you could live with it."

"Easy for you to say, Miss Nondescript."

"That's unkind, and besides you are going to piss me off again."

"Then you better teleport home to your mother." Before she can make a move, I snatch up a blink-out pellet and snap it into my wrist. Delicious waves of tranquility pound me silently into surf, sand, palms, dunes, filigrees. I lapse into sleep.

I dream I am fencing with a smiling young man. He has a Bowie knife and I have nothing. He steps in repeatedly, piercing my deltoids, pecs, triceps and stomach with teasing snaps of his long arms. He binds me in a chair, forces my mouth open, and cuts the corners of my mouth with a shiny razor blade, saying all he wants to do is widen my lip line. A jangling alarm clock awakens me and I feel exhumed, like death warmed over. I swing slowly onto the deck and look at myself in the mirror. The three wounds are blue-black on my flaccid alabaster body. I try some side-straddle hops without too much discomfort, have a quick sonic bath, and dial a protein blastula breakfast. I don't hear Susan—maybe she went to her mother's dome. I'm going to get canned at the office, I'm sure of that, and I don't think I really care. Well, here's some tight boxer shorts from Neiman-Marcus and a dandy mesh tank shirt. I pull on some eggshell-colored Bermudas and a toga-sheath. I wonder where the dog and cat are?

I amble down the slick hall and out the egress port. It is about eight in the morning, but already the temperature and the humidity must be coincident at about seventy-eight. The auto-port smells like gasoline and tomcat piss, and the car smells like pizza. Nobody waves at me during the drive to the campus; in fact, a student in a Vette cuts me off at the gate. Damn, she sneered at me, too. Some geriatric in a Peugeot is tailgating me, and I am starting to sweat. I park the car and shoulder through a small group of students. They take no note of me and yield no ground. They seem to fall silent as I pass and then they snicker.

Is that paranoia I feel? I feel conscious of my posture, my gait pattern, the swing of my arms. They don't swing in easy cadence—aren't they supposed to move in some definite relationship to stride? I feel vaguely asymmetric, as if leaning slightly to one side, like a listing ship. My facial muscles are a bit tight and faintly quivering. God, was that a tic I felt? Coming through the mews, Lindsley looked at me, smiled knowingly, and snapped his eyes away, as if he were watching a tennis match. I enter the office, feeling furtive, and no one raises his eyes.

"Doctor Elkins wants to see you right away," says the secretary, not taking her hands from the typewriter nor her eyes from the trivid cube. So this is how it feels—almost two full hours of environmental exposure, and no inputs to reinforce my autoworth parameters. "Any messages?" I ask her, and she nods at my empty mailbox. "Where's Durkee?" I lean in, and she seems to be offended. "*Doctor* Durkee is in administrative staff conference until ten." I walk for the door and it seems far off, and I feel like I'm walking on a stage. Elkins is cold to me, says some faculty members are angry at me because I told a school official about how drunk some of them got at the last party. I act lame, and my incredulity never quite surfaces. It is as if I am a stranger. I approach the faculty coffee table later, and the four men there get up and leave. I sit there for several minutes and drift back to the office. My appointments have been canceled and I have a message to report to the infirmary. This is it, I say to myself and out loud, once out into the hall.

All dispensaries, clinics, and infirmaries smell alike—something like merthiolate and floor wax. When I enter the room, two hulking provobots grab me. I couldn't fight them if I wanted to, so I do the waxy flexibility bit and hope they don't rough me up too badly. They get me supine on a table and flick on tractor beams. Then, Doctor Morvant, Doctor Ellis, and Provost St. Marie come in, as if right on cue. They examine my wounds and ask if I willfully extirpated the implants. I try to say yes, but my face feels novocained. They seem to accept my silence as admission and they leave. What bedside manners! I might as well have been a wart or a turd. I can hear them talking. I have to go to the funny farm for some new DNA chaining and some new persona implants. Who's that they're mentioning? Dixon? No, somebody named Nixon. And somebody named William Rogers. Hyman Rickover? Oscar Levant? Hooray! Huzzah! I am to be a new man.

MARTA RANDALL *lives in northern California, contributed "A Scarab in the City of Time" to the fifth* New Dimensions, *and is the author of a novel,* Islands *(Pyramid Books). She reports herself at work on a second novel— punctuated, however, by bursts of short-story writing, one of which produced this ingenious variant on a classic time-travel theme.*

■

SECRET RIDER

> "Foundering between eternity and time,
> we are amphibians and must accept the fact."
> —ALDOUS HUXLEY,
> from *Theme and Variations*

I

She had followed him across the galaxy.

Twice.

Always arriving the barest moment too late, always just behind the jet that left, the ship that sailed, the tauship that taued
the day before, carrying him with it. On Gardenia they told her
he had gone to witness the Rites of the Resurrected; she flew
over the face of the globe, pushing the sled to its limits above
the checkerboard jungle, arriving in time to see the thin con-
trails of his jets leaving the Awakening Place toward the Port.
Followed him to Asperity, to Quintesme, to Jakob's World, to
New Aqaba, where she thought she saw him entering a sky-blue
mosque. But, again, she was wrong. To Nineveh Down. To
Poltergeist. To Jason's Lift. Past stars as yet unnamed, booking
passage on the quickest, the fleetest, second-guessing his guess-
ing mind.

She had something of his, sewn under the skin of her thigh.
Kept warm and secret, although it demanded neither. Perhaps
he no longer needed it, certainly had forgotten it might have
existed, but she had it and wanted to give it to him. Besides, she
loved him.

On Murphy's Landing she shared a hotel with him, unbe-

knownst to either of them. Had arrived, body-time at sleepless
dawn in the bright morning light; had registered, slept, woke
at planet-noon to ask the questions she had been too tired to ask
before, discovered he had just, barely, left. And no room on the
ship for her. Didn't weep, but wanted to. What use?

Back home, her children grew older and younger, cities failed
and flourished, she herself died many times. On Asperity at
1852 Earth Time, on Jason's Lift at 3042 E.T., on Soft Conception at 1153 E.T.; Constantinople toppled while she argued
with border guards, New Jerusalem rose to the stars as she slept
exhausted in the arms of a stranger on Endgame II.

I I

Tau travel does not necessarily do odd things to time, nor is it
true to say that time does odd things during tau travel. Were
tau a linear projection, a straight line running alongside the
other straight and infinite lines of the universe, it would be
possible to say that there is some correlation between the Y of
tau and the Z of time, would be possible to perceive a corre-
spondence and arrive at a formula for controlling tau-shift. But
tau doesn't work that way. Leave Parnell for Ararat and when
you arrive Parnell may not have been discovered, might have
centuried to dust in the wake of your passing. Ararat, clear in
the telescopes of Parnell, might be still a formless cloud shivering in the pull of gravity's shaping. Tau takes you to a place, but
the time is of its own choosing, and random. And so the terminals, the gaping jaws that connect real space and tau space;
time-machines, capable of plucking a ship from tau and sending
it into reality precisely at the time demanded. Which may or
may not be seven months' time from the beginning of a seven
months' journey. Why dismiss the possibilities of a burnt planet
that once was green, simply because it met its death four thousand years before the Terran seas were formed? Or because it
had not yet been born, not in real-space? Humanity, not content with having the universe for a playground, delved into past
and future, and lost itself amid the ages of the stars.

III

She lost the trail on Nueva Azteca, spent hours and days tracking those who had served him or seen him during his brief stay on the pyramid planet. A porter at the hotel had overheard his plans to book for Leman, but the port records did not carry his name for that destination; the Colonial Administrator's office offered the information that he had requested a visa-stamp for Hell's Outpost but, again, there was no record of his departure.

She got drunk on heavy beer and sobered in steam showers, accepted an invitation to ColAd's yearly celebration and spent the evening curled in a corner, hopelessly scanning the tri-dims of Galactic Central that floated through the noise and scents of the transparent room. Queried every shipping company serving the planet and sat back to await the answers to her questions. They came in over the next planet-months; no, and no, and not since five years back and then in a completely different sector. She swam in the dark red waters of the inland sea and safaried across the endless plains that girdled the planet at the equator. Cupped her hand over her thigh in the night and never considered going home.

IV

He had been with her during the birth of her daughter, floating weightless with her in the labor sphere while her body paced through the rhythms of childbirth. Had kept her mind on the hypnotic convolutions when she tended to wander, helping her pulse love and warmth toward the tiny soul working its way from her body and, finally, had taken the wrinkled, squawling infant from the doctors and placed it in her arms, sharing her joy.

She had feared, during those last weeks before delivery, that the coming changes would also change their love, that in some manner the intensity would dissipate the fires of their first loving, three months back. Yet he had accepted this doubling of herself, as he had accepted her rounded belly, with a fierce tenderness that in its own fashion equaled the depthlessness of her own love.

He left Interplanetary and took assignments closer to Terra; she refused an engineering assignment that would have taken her halfway across the sector and contented herself with minor jumps through Terra End. They calculated their comings together carefully, always reappearing on Terra a week planet-time after they had left. It didn't matter that their bio-ages shifted, that each one was, alternately, older and then younger than the other. Accept off-planet jobs and one had to accept the mismatch of planet-time and bio-age. They loved, and bio-time had little to do with that.

But the time-shifts made it harder to note other differences, harder to decide which were the natural changes of age and which were the unnatural transmutations of illness.

Until the changes became very clear, and now it was her turn to sit nervous in waiting areas, to help him through the tests, to await not the delivery of a child but the delivery of a verdict, an opinion, an identification. First with hope, then with faith, through his growing desperation. Waiting.

Two years had passed for her daughter, seven for herself, six for him, when they told her that he would have to die.

V

The night the last negative answer arrived, she pulled a dark clingsuit over her slim body and ventured into the Aztecan evening to drink, smoke, ingest, sniff, swirl, unsync—all, if possible, simultaneously. Started high and moved lower during the course of the night, from the elegant dignity of a crystalline cube that floated over the apex of the largest pyramid to an expensive tourist club clinging to the sides of a seacliff to a raucous gathering at the home of the Attache for Sensory Importation to a neighborhood saloon where they threw her out after five Bitter Centauris. Found herself, at dawn, half draped over a table at SeaCave, a spacer's bar at the bottom of the bay where she had been once before during her quest, but not in her present condition. Peered at the double-imaged, blasted face across from her and asked her usual question.

"Yeah, I know the knocker," the harsh voice replied. She extracted the words from the stoneapple haze, pulled herself nearly upright and forced the double images to resolve into one.

"When?"

" 'Bout three runs ago. Booked passage from here to Augustine. Funny knocker, came on board something unusual." The voice paused.

"Want another drink?" she asked.

"Naw, I'm up enough."

"Food?"

"Cash," he suggested.

"Cash. Okay. How much?"

"How much do you want to know?"

She considered, then excused herself, found the dispos and cleaned her stomach, bought a sobor from the vending machine and pressed the vial to her arm, felt the coolness of rationality return. Made her way back to the bar and sat beside her informant.

The blasted face turned toward her and now, without the deceptive veils of high, she could see the spaceburns and fightburns, the scars where an eye had been replaced with a maximum of haste and a minimum of skill. The hand wrapped around the vibraglass had thick, splayed fingers, some one joint long, some two, none of them whole. Rivers and streams of scars flowed down his neck and under the top of his battered tunic, emerged again to run down his forearms and fingers.

"Pretty, ain't I?" the spacer asked, grinning. There was no telling where the scars ended and his lips began.

"Why don't you . . ."

"Get fixed? Why bother? Not bad enough yet, give me another run or so and it'll be due for a clean-up, then I'll just bash it up again." The spacer shrugged.

"Want another drink?" she asked.

"And cash?"

"Sure. How much do you know?"

"How much've you got?"

"I want to know what you meant by boarding unusually."

"Ten skims."

"Skims?"

"Units, graffs, get me?"

She pulled ten from her hip pouch and put it on the table, covering it with her hand.

"Talk."

"Well, it was about five to lift-off . . ."

"To Augustine?"

"Yeah."

"Augustine when?"

"Five skims."

"Later."

"Your chips, lady. So everything was pretty much battened down, we had the hoppers in gear and were just about to cut cords when this knocker comes sprinting over from Main and through the cord. Seems there was a cancelout about half hour before lift-off and this knocker came in on stand-by, just made it to the port on time."

"Go on."

"That's ten skim's worth."

"The hell it is. There's nothing unusual about someone boarding late, there's always one."

The spacer shrugged. She lifted her free hand and ordered a DoubleTaker for him, a glass of innocuous JelWatr for herself. The drinks arrived and the floating tray hovered for a moment while she pressed her thumb to the plate. The empty glasses winked out, the transparent cover of the tray snicked down and the tray floated away.

"You gonna give me the ten?"

"If you finish giving me ten's worth."

Their eyes met over the radiant blackness of the table, then he dropped his glance and poured the 'Taker down his throat.

"Okay, lady. What was funny was he wore the wrong name."

She pushed the ten to him and replaced it with a five.

"Augustine when?"

"Twenty-five odd, seven down."

"Name?"

He watched her add another five to the one already under her palm.

"Called himself Johan Ab'naua, but before we reached the grab he, uh, asked me to get rid of some old tags for him. They said 'John Albion.' "

She pushed the money to him, sat back, finished her drink.

The next day she booked passage for Augustine, twenty-five odd, seven down.

When she got there, he was dead.

VI

Or, at any rate, Johan Ab'naua was dead. The body was prepared for burial, but she bribed one of the morgue attendants to let her see. Tension twisted within her as the tall woman led her down to the cold vaults, swung open the heavy door and ushered her into a room with numbered doors lining the sides. Her hand drifted down to rest lightly on her thigh as the attendant selected the appropriate door, opened it, and the transparent rectangle floated into the room.

The coroner's report, 'hezed to the end of the rectangle, was quite thorough. It talked about traces of radiation damage and talked about traces of chemicals found in the body, mentioned half a dozen, each one fatal in the proper amount. Talked about an excess of water in the tissues and speculated on immersion before the deceased deceased. Considered the fusion burns, speculated on the possibility that weapons were used to put the deceased out of the misery undoubtedly caused by the above-stated factors, or, perhaps, to disfigure the departed beyond recognition. Or to cover the radiation, and the poison, and the water. Mentioned the difficulty of effecting a true recognition from the remains and boasted of positive identification achieved through thorough and painstaking work. The amorphous mass in the glass coffin, the coroner's report insisted, was all that remained of Johan Ab'naua.

She glanced inside the rectangle quickly, then thanked the attendant, passed over the balance of the bribe and returned to her hotel.

VII

Was he dead because she hadn't reached him, or dead because she had?

Their times, she knew, had crossed before. Even before he had journeyed out so far, even before she had tucked a secret in her thigh and followed him, their various whens had crossed and recrossed—he older and she younger, or she older and he younger, backward, forward. It was possible that at some future biological date she would meet him before his death, would give him the ampule stitched beneath the skin of her leg. His death was no reason to end the quest. It was, simply, a matter of timing.

Somewhen, curling through the intricacies of tau, John/Johan still lived. Somewhen on this very planet he lived, but that past was closed to her as completely as it would have been without tau. There are laws that maintain the continuity of planet-time, strictly enforced regulations proscribing visits to a planet at any time previous to one's first planet-time visit, that forbid jumping on-planet itself. How else to cope with the ensuing chaos, how maintain a measured sanity in the face of life when tomorrow is last week and yesterday happens next year, when your great-great-great grandfather drops in for a drink ten minutes before the arrival of your current lover, who hasn't been born yet? They try to enforce planet-time laws as strictly as the universe enforces the laws of gravity, as rigorously as light follows the dictates of real-space. Or she would have leaped backward after that first near miss, countless planetfalls ago; would leap back now, into John's Augustine life.

Yet, had one the time, the resources, the contacts, the courage, there was a way to circumvent the laws. Name changes, print changes, the subtle individualities of the body rearranged, and one could slip by the guardians of time, revisit the past of one's present. John must have done it. Otherwise, why the change of name? Why the end of the trail on Nueva Azteca, why the misnamed body lying frozen in the morgue?

She could not duplicate his feat. She lacked the resources, the contacts, perhaps even the courage to have her life changed. And so, again, it came to this: a matter of timing.

She rose from her bed, wrapped herself in warmth and went to trace his death through the glittering austerity of the city.

VIII

Augustine is a sovereign nation, a chartered member of the Union of All Worlds, and consequently information was harder to obtain than it had been from the various ColAd agencies on Nueva Azteca. His effects? In storage, where they would remain for seven years unless claimed by a relative. Could she, perhaps, prove relationship with Johan Ab'naua? No, not with Johan. Sorry. After seven years the effects will be destroyed. She looked at the pinched, bureaucratic face before her and dismissed the idea of bribery.

She had no better luck at the port. The passenger lists were closed, confidential. But the clerk was sympathetic and suggested the files of the local newsfax, the public lists of entry and exit taken not from the port but from customs. So she booked time on the public computer and keyed in her request.

Johan Ab'naua had arrived on Augustine ten weeks before. Had been discovered dead in a back alley in Port Sector four days ago—a small story, that. Violent deaths in any port sector are far from a rarity. A holo from his passport accompanied the story, a chip taken from the main crystal, for the resolution was fuzzy, the colors off. But she recognized John Albion's face behind the subtle changes. So.

She thumbed the connection closed and went out to wander the city.

IX

They had tried to build Augustine austere, straight, square, grim, but the planet itself defeated them. The world's basic stone was a refractive crystal, hard and shimmering, and only it would stand up to use as a building material. The architecture of the city was all cubes and rectangles—small, severe windows and disapproving right angles, built of glimmering, color-changing crystals that reflected the flowing of wind and temperature, turned the monastic blocks into the unexpected wonders of a drug dream. The citizens strode purposefully amid these hulking fantasies, dressed close and severely, grim of eye and lip. She hurried past them, knowing that their sour glances were not for her alone but for the entire universe that, in creating their planet, had played them such a dirty trick.

As she wandered away from the city proper and more deeply into Port Sector, the texture of the city changed. The buildings were now covered with layers of grime, the filth bringing them closer to the ideal of the founding fathers than the more respectable, and clean, parts of the city. Yet the people were less grim here, the spacers decked in the usual collection of charms and artifacts, no two alike and not a one drab. She moved among spacers and whores and drug pushers, asking questions, and at last stood in a small alley that ran between a block of tenements.

Nothing there, of course. Nothing to tell her how or when or even where he had met his death on the oil-streaked pavement. She walked the alley twice, staring so intently that she felt intimate with each small crevice and corner, each pile and heap, each crack and discoloration. She found no answers to her silent questions; the walls kept their counsel, and after a while she left.

X

Evening of the thirty-hour day was beginning and numerous establishments in Port Sector had their glaring come-ons already lit. She wandered past, unseeing, her dark hair tumbling over the neck of her suit, reflecting back the lights spilled from open doors.

"Hey, spacer, wanna night?"

"Gimme some, will you?"

"Fucking knocker!"

"Lady!"

"It'll cost you, junk."

"Hey, lady!"

"Jump it, jump it, jump it!"

"Lady, wait up!"

She felt a heavy hand on her arm and raised her eyes. The spacer beside her was unfamiliar.

"Yes?"

"Hey, don't you remember me?"

She looked more carefully. The man had never been good-looking, but his face was smooth, eyes clear and as yet unreddened by the night. Coils of orange hair, thick eyebrows, ears decked with small, mismatched cascades of jewels, body draped in iridescent shamskin. She shook her head.

"Oh, yeah, I got cleaned up. You asked me about some knocker, back on Nueva Azteca, remember?"

"Oh. Yes."

"Find him?"

"Sort of. He's dead."

"Care." The spacer raised an eyebrow. "Matter?"

"Yes, it matters."

"Care. Here, I'll stick you a drink. I need one."

She shrugged and he guided her into a dim bar, snapped his fingers for a tray as they sat behind a grid.

"You wanna JelWatr?"

She shook her head. "Whatever."

"Okay. Two Tri-levels," he told the tray, and they sat in silence until the drinks arrived. The spacer thrust his thumb at the printbox, grinned as the green panel flashed, and turned to her.

"Got paid," he explained. "You bruised?"

"I suppose."

"So goes."

She shook herself from her lethargy and glanced up at him. "How'd you get cleaned up so fast?"

"Went up to Sal, got it done in time for my next run out."

"Sal?"

"Salsipuedes. Oh, you're a knocker. You know about time regs and all that? Right. Well, you can't always get enough spacers for a run in the start port, 'cause some of em's been to the stop port up the line, see? So most ships stop at a Salsipuedes just off orbit and pick up crew, then drop them off at another Sal before the stop port. Lots of spacers get stuck that way, 'specially old ones that work just one sector and have their times so screwed up that there's no when they haven't been up the line anywhere."

"So how long did the clean-up take?"

" 'Bout a standard year. I, uh, jumped."

"Jumped?"

"Yeah, there's no time regs on a Sal. You just gotta watch out you don't meet yourself, if you're the superstitious type. Lots of spacers don't care, though. Last time up there was one old junker sitting in the lounge talking with five others of himself. Me, I don't want to know what's going to happen. Can't change it, anyway."

She felt the first level of the drink tickling at her mind and pushed the low, sweet euphoria aside.

"Look, can a . . . a knocker spend time on a Sal?"

"Yeah, sometimes. Hey, drink, you're not down to second level yet."

She raised the vibraglass to her lips and drained off the second level. It flowed down her throat like liquid stars and she felt dizzy as it hit her stomach.

"Can a knocker jump around at a Sal?"

"Maybe." His eyes narrowed and he tugged at one earring.

She considered the remaining liquid in her drink, slowly swirling it against the invisible sides of the glass.

"Look, I want to know how to get on a Sal and how to jump around once I get there."

The spacer grunted noncommittally, keeping his eyes on her.

"How much'll it cost me?"

"You alone tonight?"

She met his eyes, paused, finished her drink. And nodded.

XI

"This all of it, knocker?"

"It's all I know. From Terra to Neuhafen, to Gardenia, to Asperity, to Quintesme and the radiation labs. To Jakob's World, to New Aqaba, to Nineveh Down for the baths. To Poltergeist, to Jason's Lift, to Endgame II, to Murphy's Landing. To Nueva Azteca, to Augustine. These flights, here, these times, these ships."

"Okay, gimme another cup of that stuff. Now look, here's your sticker. All these jumps, here, they're long hops, five lights or more, see? You book for one of those, you've got to be cleared before you leave the start port. Too much trouble with knockers who make it to stop port, and then the company discovers that they've been there before, up the line, and can't afford the passage back, see? So they check you out before lift-off and save themselves the trouble. And since you *followed* him along the line, you might as well count these hops out."

"Couldn't I get on board as a spacer? They're dropped off on Sals after long hops, aren't they?"

"Yeah, sure, but look, knocker. See the band, here? It's my registry, my license. Implanted when I finished training. No way to forge one of those. Seems like you'll have to try it here, between Azteca and Augustine."

"But that's so close . . ."

"It's the only way, knocker. Sorry."

XII

The sack vibrated gently against her shoulder as she stood by the port at the jump station, watching the tau-ship move ponderously into the coil. The huge bulk slid between the heavy, curving bars, jockeyed the final humps of its tail section into place, and paused. Then it began to shimmer, so softly at first that she was not sure whether the shivering was within her mind, her eyes, rather than in the resting ship. The shimmering

coalesced, expanded, sent tendrils of change over the innumer-
able curves and bumps of the ship. Light spilled through the
bends of the coil at odd angles and odder wavelengths, a flow
of molten crystals, an agglomeration of colors, a sudden transparency that wavered, disappeared, re-emerged larger than
before, grew to cover the magical creation within the coils, and
the ship vanished, the gaudy display cut off as abruptly as if
someone had thrown a master switch and plunged the show in
darkness. She shut her eyes, opened them, stared at the inert
and empty coil, where not the least iridescence remained to
mark the passing of the ship from one time to another. From
on board ship, she remembered, it was the coil that shimmered
and restabilized as the translation through time took place, the
universe that shook and was again steady. But nothing matched
the display as seen from the jump station.

She stood alone at the receiving lock, the only one to disem-
bark at Azteca Sal. The bursar had been furious because of her,
aggrieved that her previous presence on Nueva Azteca had
marred an otherwise smooth flight; had raged and stormed into
her cabin, waving the GalCentral faxsheets and cursing. She
had shrugged, forfeited the remainder of her passage as a result
of her "carelessness" and stepped into the shuttle to the Sal
without a backward glance.

The corridor stretching from the lock area toward the heart
of Salsipuedes was bleak and unmarked, made no echo in response to her footsteps as she walked its length. It angled to the
right and opened into an empty, ovoid room. She walked to a
semiopaque shutter set into a curving wall and rapped impatiently.

"Oh, yeah, hang it," said a voice and the window sphinctered
open. "Right, you're off the *Hellion*, bursar called. Want a
bunk?"

"I want to jump, fourteen even, two down."

"Can't, not for another week. We've got too much coming
through, can't take energy to hop a knocker around. Bunk in
G'll cost you ten, private sixteen. Private? Right, level H, section four, back two. One week, okay."

She pressed her thumb against the plate and turned to go,
code key in her hand.

"Hey, knocker!"

"Yes?"

"Thumb's okay here, but it won't buy you anything else on Sal."

"I know."

Her room was a bleak cube with a bunk, a clean-unit and one chair. She stowed her gear and, following the remembered words of the spacer, found her way to one of the many mess-chambers.

XIII

John Albion was/is/will be living/dying/dead; sucked into the dead/dying void. John Albion had been/is/will be sitting in the warmth of her home and talking of something very small, something very alien, something very much in his bones which has/is/will be killed/killing him. Conjugate the tenses of time travel. Verbs are illusory.

A disease. An organism. The marrow. The blood. An explosion of time, but biological time; inescapable, certain. A searching. A sampling. A yearning, a leave-taking, a sudden aching absence. A movement of machines. A discovery. A synthesis. An ampule of clear fluid. A quest. A death.

Despite or because of? Too soon or too late? An idiot's question, a useless knowledge. What is/was/will be/is/was/will be. Immutable mutability; the ultimate paradox.

A discovery, a quest, an ampule in the thigh. A walk down the corridor of Azteca Sal, a seat in the midst of confusion. Because they always were/are/will be.

XIV

Noise. Fumes. Dim swirls of ersatz smoke. Raucousness. Belligerence in the corners. Shapes hulking and moving through labyrinths of sound and scent.

She sat, ignored except by the trays that brought her food and drink, accepted the flat notes she pressed upon their surfaces. She felt the small curious tensions her presence produced as though, without a halt in the uproar, she was being watched, evaluated, measured and metered on scales she only dimly comprehended. She, in turn, watched and measured.

A spacer moved by her for the fourth time. There were three others of him in the room, and each apparition ignored the other three. Another spacer, gray hair cut ragged about her gray face, leaned over a nearby table.

"When is it?" she pleaded. "When is it?" And received four conflicting answers in reply.

Music from somewhere, as disjointed as the echos of the room. Dancing of a sort, on tables at the far side. Trays floating and bobbing among the shapes, never spilling, never knocking, ever present. And, once, a familiar face.

Seamed and gnarled, a river of scar tissue and a misplaced eye. No mistaking that, but though she raised her face to his passing and called, he did not look back. She wavered, uncertain, then pushed away from the table and crossed the room.

"Hey . . ." she began.

The hideous face turned, the eye winked.

"Yeah, sure, knocker. But I keep my nose out of my own business, see?"

She nodded, found her table again. Soon afterward she returned to her own cabin, curled on the bunk with one hand over her thigh, slept fitfully.

She spent the second day sprawled on a chair in the messchamber. Watching the eddies of the crowd, the changing sounds and moving faces, drinking sparingly. In the evening someone offered her a vial of stoneapples; she took a small sniff, returned the vial with thanks and it disappeared back into the crowd.

The third evening someone finally approached her. A slim spacer, a woman in middle years with quick, nervous eyes and a thin mouth, two or three scars meandering down the curves of her neck.

"Share your table, knocker," the spacer said and swung her legs over a stool, dropped her drink on the table, slouched down and peered over.

"Sure. Want another?"

"Alla time. Name's Kalya."

"Name's unimportant."

"Up to you, knocker." Kalya captured a passing tray and ordered the offered drink. "You waiting for something special?"

"Jump time."

The spacer smiled. "On which side of regs?"

"Whichever side I can find it."

"Cash?"

"Sure."

The drink arrived and was paid for, then the spacer stood from the table. "Follow me, knocker. There's always a spare coil somewhere."

XV

They followed the mazes of the station, branchings and turnings, and Kalya always ahead or beside her, words tumbling forth as she waved her drink to punctuate her sentences. Spacers called it "coiling," only knockers called it "jumping." This was one of the better Sals, always something going on. Sure, there were always illicit coils on a Sal. GalSec made sweeps for them, but all you had to do was coil forward to see when the sweep was, then move the coils to different whens; it wasn't hard, you dismantled them and put them through the coil that remained behind. Yeah, sometimes you saw a bust, no help for it, if you made it, you made it; if you didn't, you didn't. A game. No care. Small, one-person coils, some larger, some as big as an entire mess-chamber, but those were difficult to maintain; the power drain had to be managed and camouflaged from Gal Sec. There was one here at Azteca Sal, a party, maybe she'd like to try it, sure, it'll get you there, we'll drop you off on our way, nothing like it. You're loose, knocker, know that? And tense, like a spacer on job. You're not GalSec 'cause I'd have seen you, or you wouldn't be here, would you? Jarl tipped me, you're quick. Here, knocker. Here.

A door like any other on Sal, a gleaming metal circle with palm receiver on the right side, protruding slightly from the brushed silver gleam. Kalya pushed her palm to the plate, the door sphinctered open and they stepped forward.

Into nothingness.

She spun, seeking the door, but Kalya grasped her arm, laughing.

"Easy, knocker, easy."

She glanced down to where her feet floated, toes pointing down, nothing underfoot; a darkness from which her companion stood as the only illuminated figure on a blackened stage. "Easy, easy, easy." Her hand spread urgently along her thigh, her throat constricted, knees flexed instinctively to absorb the impact of a fall. But there were no swift rushings of air past her frightened cheeks. Kalya laughed. Shudder. Strain.

"Easy, easy. This is only the entrance, we're not into it yet. Calm, knocker. Quiet."

She straightened, touched her hip-pouch, chin, hair. Wriggled her toes experimentally against the resilient emptiness. Calmed.

"When are you headed?" Kalya asked.

"Fourteen even, two down."

"Cash?"

She fumbled at her pouch, produced a fistful of notes, handed them over.

"Good. I'll toss it into coil, we'll get you there. Ready?" The spacer hooked an arm over an invisible something and, reaching out her other arm, offered it for support.

Floating, unable to imagine the next stage, she drifted passively on Kalya's proferred arm. Felt the roundness of a door circling her. Kalya pushed them through and the invisible door snicked shut.

XVI

For we exist in time. Time is what binds molecules to make your brown eyes, your yellow hair, your thick fingers. Time changes the structures, alters hair or fingers, dims the eyes, immutably mutating reality. Time, itself unchanging, is the cosmic glue, the universal antisolvent that holds our worlds together.

Passage through a coil releases time, and the body dies. Energy remains, the components, the atoms remain but their structure is random, for the glue has been stripped away and the time-bound base no longer exists. When coiling ceases, time rebuilds the molecules to its own specifications, the glue snaps back and the self in time is recreated.

But the soul, the mind, the essence has no time, dwells in an eternity and is bound to the "now" only as it is bound within the molecules of the moment, only as it is caught in the cosmic glue. Matter, here, is transcended, the sum of the parts is more than the whole, and is capable of existence apart from the base. An analogy: mind as gas, time as the sphere in which the gas is enclosed. Break the sphere, divorce mind from time, and the essence is free to roam eternity, consistent only unto itself. Drugs release the mind from a realization of time, temporarily. Pain, starvation, flagellation, intense mysticism release the mind but, again, temporarily. By defrauding the brain, by convincing it for the hour or the day that there is no true physical base, the mind reaches toward infinite ecstasy, encompasses a portion of the god-head before it is snapped back to the temporal.

And coiling releases the mind. By destroying time, by revoking the bindings. Coiling is the possibility of endless transcendence, broken only by an act of will.

XVII

As though signaled by the shutting of the portal, bright colors, sounds, smells leaped from the room before her, random coalitions of color and shape danced by too swiftly for her mind to give them meaning, and the deafening noise battered at her ears. Chaos. Bewilderment. Fear.

Kalya laughed and stepped into the maelstrom, crying, "Come, join the party, the party, the party," and was lost to sight.

"Kalya! Wait! How?" Nothing. She strained her eyes, searching the moving seas before her for a glimpse of a familiar face, arm, anything, but the rushing refused to yield coherence. Complicated abstractions presented themselves, vanished, re-formed, exploded into a million further abstractions; rationality exiled from the universe; the senses reeled.

It is a hoax, she thought bitterly. *A paltry joke played on a stupid knocker. A fraud.* And she flung herself forward.

A brief wrenching as she passed the barrier, a metaphysical twist and she was within. She glanced down, once, and screamed, closed her eyes, refused to glance at what she had become/was becoming again. Sound and color sliced through, quick hard lines that melted, honey-like, at her ears and be-came only slow thunders. Infinitesimal tastes hovering through the air, past and presences, a million brushings and her brain lost in sensations for which there were no names, the ordering of the universe exploded in a spacer's game.

"When are we?" she demanded of a flickering form. "Where are we? What? How?"

"It is the end of the universe," the void said seriously. "Very popular. Quite pretty. Look."

She looked and would not look again, turned and fled through the fabric of the room.

"Stay," she commands a passing face. "Help, stay!"

The face dissolves before her, and a voice says, "Why here? When did you come? How?"

"Kalya brought me, I'm lost."

"Bitch! I told her to clear, but she meddles." The sense of glare, an amorphous swirling, a purposeful stride.

"No, don't leave me!"

An impatient hand, a jerk that sends her stumbling after the form. Which changes even as she watches it, shifts through the spectrum, becomes, briefly, a quick warm scent on the air, spills outward, condenses. And still the image of a hand on the image of her arm, dragging her through chaos.

"Kalya! Bitch!"

"No," she pleads. "Just let me out, please."

"When?" the jellyfish demands.

"Fourteen even, two down. Please."

The dragging changes direction. She abandons herself to it, cuts off visual impressions, feels the insidious tickling of change. Then the sensations lessen, disappear, and she opened her eyes to find herself back in the room of nothingness, still grasped by her rescuer.

The face stabilized, somewhere between the scarred monstrosity of Nueva Azteca and the smooth youthfulness of Augustine.

"When are you?" she asked.

"Two years after Augustine. Just passing through. Stopped at the party. Didn't know."

"What happened?"

He shrugged, a quick motion of the shoulders beneath the soft scales of his robe. "Spacers get used to it, get their kicks that way. Frame of mind."

"But a ship, it's not like when . . ."

"Different. Ship coil's phased, quick. That one's not, completely random, not linked to a durator."

"So when are we now? How do I get back?"

The spacer grinned, stretching one scar wide, and reached a hand through blackness. A twisting, a writhing and she cried in fear, believing that the insane influence of the room had entered even here. But the twisting settled, the darkness remained intact. The spacer palmed open a door and ushered her into a corridor.

"Fourteen even, two down. Ship well, knocker." The spacer popped back through the door, and the snick of its closing echoed in the empty hall.

XVIII

She gazed down the pitted and pock-marked corridor, noting the stains on the stainless walls, the crackings in the floor underfoot. Wondered briefly if another trick had been played on her, if she had been deposited far in the future rather than three months in the past. Decided that she was not going to re-enter the insane party to find out and began walking down the hall, looking for a known place from which she could chart her course back to the intake port.

She peered surreptitiously at the spacers she passed but found no one familiar, even considering the time-jumping fluidity of a spacer's face. Yet, after a time, she spotted a face that looked, if not familiar, at least friendly, and she approached.

"Spacer?"

"Yeah?"

"When is it?"

The spacer stared at her, taking in all the small differences that branded her as a knocker, and smiled.

"Fourteen even, two down. Last I checked."

"Thanks. Where's the intake port?"

"Same place it always is. Follow that corridor, take a right at the second intersect and you'll find it."

She found it. The agent irised open the window and peered out.

"Yeah?"

"I want passage on the *Claudia Frankl*, it ought to be through here tomorrow."

A swift hum of machinery. "Right, there's space. First class, second class, nothing in stasis."

"Give me first class, I don't care where."

She pressed her thumb to the plate and a bright vermilion flashed across the face of it.

"Here, knocker, gimme your thumb a minute."

She pressed her thumb against the new plate and the agent palmed it, disappeared, came back a moment later carrying her credit plate and the sack of belongings with which she had entered Azteca Sal, three months in the future.

"Arrived yesterday morning through the cargo coil. Here, look, here's the notation on the log. So I'll enter it in the PDL for, um, seventeen odd, four down, and when the agent up the line opens the PDL, there it'll be, bright and clear. And the agent'll shoot the stuff down the line, and I'll receive it yesterday and give it to you today. Enter time-change in your credit tape, right. And next time, knocker, take your gear with you, it's simpler that way. Try your thumb again."

This time bright green glowed from the panel, and she took her sack.

"Can I have a bunk for the night?"

"Sure, one in Temp'll cost you ten, plus six for cargo-jump, press again. Level A, section nine, bunk fourteen. Down the corridor, first to the right, one up. Be at Intake at fourteen two tomorrow, sharp. The shuttle doesn't wait."

"Thanks."

"Sure, knocker."

She stowed her gear in the locker at the foot of bunk 14, checked the time, then piled her clothes over the locker and swung in. Spent no time thinking of the room in which she had traveled time; her mind settled on the future, on tomorrow, and for the first time in her quest she did not sleep at all.

XIX

We'll get off at Augustine Sal, yes, and jump to somewhen where neither of us has been before. And he'll have taken the medicine, of course. A small home somewhere, a place that needs engineers so we'll be able to work. In the quiet, like the beginning, me and John, John and me, until it's time for Augustine. Since it has to happen.

He'll be changed, of course, but he'll remember me. His hands are swift and gentle, his hips are sweet. Brown and golden, brown and golden under my hands, between my thighs, laughing softly at midnight from a soft bed. When he looks toward the sky his eyes narrow against the glare, with small crinkles at the corners. Brown. His mouth is honey.

Some new star, perhaps, some just-discovered world, to build a city, a seatown, a spiraling cluster of lights and sounds. Such solid geometry we make together, me and John, John and me. New animals, new plants, we'll have a garden and he'll take a small greenery in his palms and urge it easily to the soil, things leap to life at our touch, cities and subways, fruits and flowers, tiny birds rest on his shoulders.

And to wake to find him sleeping, thighs under my knees,

arm across my stomach, head on my breast, his breath is easy
as he sleeps, and his hair spills over my shoulders, brown and
golden, brown and golden. As it was before, and for almost
forever. Until Augustine. Of course.

He'll open the door, smile, open the door, irising to his face
and hands, to his legs and smile, to his chest and arms.

When he sings his voice cracks, leaves him stranded in laughter on a high, subversive note. He'll build vaulting arches across
the seas, from my city to my city, and together we'll shape
worlds.

Until Augustine.
Until Augustine.

XX

She stood before the closed shutter of his cabin, feeling tension
twist knots upon knots within her. Pressed the call button on
the wall. Pause. Pause. He's not here. He's asleep. He's not
answering. He's . . .

"Yes? What is it?" Suspicious.

"Mr. Ab'naua? I have something for you."

"Who are you?"

"It's a medicine."

"A medicine? Who *are* you?"

"Please, Mr. Ab'naua. John, please let me in."

The door sphinctered open suddenly and he stared at her.

It was as though he carried a fire within him, an inward light
that bathed his skin with a deep bronze glow. That ate him from
within, for his cheeks were deep and hollow, his eyes impossibly
large in his narrow face, his wrists and ankles much too heavy
for the thinness of his limbs. A medicinal smell reeked from the
room behind him, crept out into the corridor as he frowned at
her.

"May I come in, John?"

His eyes hardened, hand moved toward the door's controls.

"You must be mistaken. My name is Johan."

She glanced at the back of his neck, where her fingers had

often massaged the tension from him. Glanced at his hand resting at his side, at the slant of his shoulders, the curve of his hips.
She could have sculpted each slight plane and angle of him in
plasteen, with her eyes closed, despite the ravages of the disease.

"John," she repeated positively.

"Sorry, lady, the name's Johan." His hand touched the controls, but she caught his shoulder with one hand and with the
other forced his face toward her. A deliberate, furtive blankness
echoed in his eyes.

No, she thought furiously. I shall not be robbed of an ending
to this, I shall not be stripped of seven year's wandering. She
snatched her vibraknife from the pouch at her hip and, before
he could respond, she sliced through the skin of her leg, reached
within and withdrew the ampule, held it red and dripping
before him. He stared from it to her face, to her bleeding thigh,
to the vial once again.

"It's for your marrow disease," she snapped. "It's the cure.
I've been following you for seven years to give it to you and
now, by damn, you're going to take it."

His hand rose, then grabbed the vial. He snatched at her arm
and pulled her into the cabin.

XXI

His eyes were the wrong color. Teeth smaller and more even
than she remembered them to be, lips thinner. But his broad
fingers were unchanged, and she watched them expertly stitch
the incision, spray a healer over the area. The deep tingling of
healing tissue warmed her thigh, drove out the coolness of
seven years' constant anasthesia.

Shimmering bottles lined the walls of the room. The table was
littered with tubes and cans, the foot of the bunk held tiny reels
of books scattered among the jars. She looked at them as she
told him of the research, the synthesis, the quest. Inspected
them, rather than inspect the harsh, bright, wrong light of his
eyes.

He listened impatiently, fingers tapping against the cleaned ampule, and interrupted her before she had finished.

"Yes, naturally, you've come a great distance," he said, waving away her travels with a sweep of his unchanged hand. "But, of course, you didn't see those planets as I did, you couldn't know, could you? I've been so far . . ." And he told of a search for health, of one frustration after another, of failures on differing planets, of promises made and promises broken. He talked of healers and doctors and those who cure through the soul; of the resurrected natives of Gardenia and the immortal proto-organisms of Neuhafen. Expounded. Declaimed. Praised and excused. Wise men, healers, saints, gurus. Charlatans. His wrong-colored eyes glowed, his hands moved impatiently through the air as he described the promises of the healer he had changed his name to visit.

"And, of course, I was suspicious when you called me 'John,' " he explained. "If Galsec knew . . . But they won't. This man, this monk on Augustine, he's spent much time on Neuhafen, he's communed with the proto-organisms. I've been there, of course, but you simply can't make any contact with them, fleetingly, like that. This man spent *decades.* And, listen, he can cure me. He . . . he can make me immortal!"

"But *this* is the cure," she told him through her confusion, and he smiled, lofted the bottle, watched it spiral through the air and made no move to catch it. She cried out, grabbed it before it shattered on the floor. Crouched, staring at him.

"But it's no good to me," he explained. "The monk can't cure me unless I'm ill, that makes sense, doesn't it? And to be immortal, to live forever! He can really do it, I've heard from people who've known people, I have it documented, here, and here. Take this one, read it, it'll convince you."

"But, John . . ." she protested, reaching the ampule toward him. He waved the vial away without looking at it.

"No, really, he can, it's all here. I know. I didn't believe it at first either, but this will change your mind, I know it will. Here, take it to your cabin with you, keep it, I have another copy."

"John . . ." with despair.

"Johan, please. Of course, it was quite kind of you to bring me

the stuff. You couldn't tell that it would be useless, could you?
I had no inkling, of course, but this thing of mine is actually a
blessing, you have to consider it as a catalyst, if it weren't for
that the monk wouldn't even touch me. He's a saint! A wonderful man, he'll change and cure me, they say he's immortal
himself, you know, but he claims that immortality isn't important once you've reached the higher planes. We can't all do
that, naturally, we have to settle for simple immortality and
wait for time to mature us enough so that we can attain saint-
hood too. It takes time and work, I know, but I'll have forever
to do it in!"

"John, you're going to die on Augustine!"

"What? Nonsense, of course not. Listen, this monk, this
saint . . ."

XXII

So she decided that he wasn't John any more after all. That he
was indeed Johan, someone who carried within him the essence
of her lover, but transformed, transmuted, beyond her. She
spent the remainder of the trip in her cabin, disembarked,
pursued by angry bursar, at Augustine Sal and watched the
Claudia Frankl shimmer from her life.

And, when you come to cases, John *had* died on Augustine.
Had/is/will.

Which is paltry consolation.

She could have entered the coil at Augustine Sal and burned
time away in a blaze of confusion. Could have died for love in
the bleakness of space. Wandered unconsolable among the
stars. Done any number of dramatic things. But she wasn't a
very dramatic woman, so she booked passage for Terra, arrived
three months after her departure. Returned to her work, raised
her children and, eventually, died of old age. Was puffed to
chemicals in the mortuary, with appropriate ceremony.

And that was that.

That BARRY MALZBERG *writes somber and disturbing stories of schizophrenia and moral paralysis is, of course, not news; but that he is also a wondrously comic writer is a fact that few readers seem to recognize. To be somber and funny all at once is a rare gift but one that is discernible in most comic geniuses, from Swift and Jonson to Kafka, Buster Keaton, and Joseph Heller. What? You don't think Kafka's funny? Then you probably won't chuckle much over this latest Malzberg.*

■

Barry N. Malzberg

■

ON THE AIR

i

dial slow. easy to get nervous when putting it in, easy to lose the
direction altogether and that is why it is important, it is important man to move the wheel slowly, not get fucked up between
the twos and the threes, get it right. two one two. three seven
six. five four two *one*. there. the first bleep sounds like a near
busy and you don't like that at all, that means that all five lines
are jammed up and god alone knows when you'll be able to get
through, how many times you'll have to sit here racketing the
numbers against themselves, busies are no *good* man they are
a bad scene but it goes through, that easy purring ring coming
soft out of the earpiece and you know you are set. on the dial
this frigging cunt she is talking about her problems with the
group, just going on and on but stevie is already making the
good-restless sounds that means he's about to split and leave
and maybe you'll be the next one in. once you get the ring-in
it is just lights on the dial, stevie can push one or four-oh or
seventy-three for all he cares, he has explained that and it is
random. call late and get in early; call early and never get in at
all. it is not fair but then who ever in the words of our late great
prez ever said that life is fair? ring in the earpiece. got to go,
stevie says on the *rad*-io, got to take care of business and the
lady burbles burbles in stevie's ear but her voice is already soft
and going. she knows when she is done. got to *go* my dear stevie
says and then just like that he is saying hello into your ear.
seven-second lag a truly great thing to keep the fuckers and

119

suckers and mother-fuckers off the air. while the radio is still playing stevie saying goodbye to the cunt he is saying *hello you are on the air now* into your ear but this will only come out on the radio seven seconds later so if you say fuck or twat or eat my shit stevie will hit the switch with his hand and you will be canceled off. hello, stevie says again, who is this ringing my bell? in ten seconds you will be *off* the air if you do not move.

quick then, one hand flick off the switch of the radio, first thing the experienced phone talker does, second cuddle the receiver into the chest come forward then into a confidential posture. 'hello,' you say, 'stevie?' although you know it is him of course this is just what is called an instinctive nervous reaction. going on the air is an uptight-making process; stevie knows this has warned us against it many times. let it all hang out, reel it out, stevie says, forget the jet-lag and the fuck-switch or you will not be able to wing it which is the principle of free form.

'hi,' you say, 'how are you?'

i am all right, stevie says. i am not complaining.

'the topic for this evening is drugs,' you say, 'i had a few comments on the drug situation in relation to what this previous caller said.' stevie likes you to give the calls what he calls *reference* so that they do not *hang out in the open*. 'if i may continue.'

you may continue. this is your radio.

'good,' you say. you draw yourself into it the way that you always do when you go on the air. somewhere in the hall there is the sound of movement, somewhere out on the street there is a siren which comes through the open window but these are ignored, you draw yourself into that ball of flame which is contact and going on the air. 'now i don't know about drugs,' you say, 'not really being a user but i want to say—'

if you don't use why shoot off your mouth.

that is stevie. he is often insulting but inside there is this core of real warmth which can be perceived and gotten hold of and despite the cynical exterior at almost any time can break down into tears if he is really moved. i have heard him in the early-morning hours near the end of his shift weeping and telling of his childhood. 'stay with me, stevie,' you say, 'and i will explain.'

you ain't explained anything yet. you are just calling in to hear yourself talk on the radio.

'listen here, stevie,' i say assuming an atttitude of command without which call-in live radio is nothing and you are merely at the mercy of the host who merely uses you for the purposes of his own moods and passions, 'you will let me explain what i have to say and then you will understand exactly why i have called in.'

i have heard your voice before. i think that you are one of the regulars.

'everybody is a regular, stevie,' i say, 'once you call in or even try to once you are a regular.'

that is the truth, he says, that is the truth.

ii

it may be asked why i am writing these memoirs in lower-case type without capitals that is to say and my answer is that the typewriter has a bad shift key and a poor spacer when you get into the upper-case leads. there are those who will say this is bullshit and the real reason for this very jazzy and self-conscious method of diction is because i am trying to reproduce typographically the feeling of anonymity of the caller in live-show radio and how oppressed and small they feel and deprived of that true sense of identification which would enable them to capitalize capitalization being a way of establishing names and dating but i say that this is a load of crap as i make my points as stevie has always asked us to in my words and manner of speaking and not in any tricky methods which would only get you bleeped off on the cuts anyway.

iii

others may say of live call-in radio who needs it? who needs memoirs about this horseshit much less from one of the call-in creeps themselves or himself? live-call-in-radio shows the isolation and emptiness of modern life, lost souls in their separate shells in the city desperately trying to establish communication with the host who in his invulnerability and lack of known feature can be called god and that is all you can say about a country which has so taken power out of the hands of its citizenry to say nothing of a sense of purpose that they are reduced to call-in radio to get their rocks off. this is a lot of crap because only a very small percentage of these so-called anonymous and frustrated citizens call in and they are not representative of citizenry in general being in fact very strong and individuated types who wish to change their lives by assuming control over them hence the call-in. one who calls in is already three quarters of the way to being an individual and from my analysis of the many people who will be on the air during the night because you must listen as well as talk to get into the beat of the show i would like to say that they represent a high grade of intelligence and articulacy well beyond modern politicians for instance and do not feel at all helpless at least i do not think that they feel completely helpless or otherwise why would they call in at all, eh? that is the question i would like to put.

       i v

my name is raoul the caller; raoul the call that is how i identify myself when i talk to stevie which is every so often although he does not still recognize my voice reserving recognition for real regulars of the sort who call every night whereas i only call when i have something to say and to contribute to the discussion which in my case is no more than once or twice a week. raoul the call has a ball. 'listen here,' i say, 'about these drug problems, this situation you are talking about i have had some experience with drugs and i tell you they are a downer altogether. one does not need drugs to take the ultimate trip.'
    what is the ultimate trip?
    'well there is some who say that death is the ultimate trip and others who say sex of course but to me the ultimate trip would be actual spaceflight and that is what i want to say i am doing. i am going to go on a spaceship tonight. i am going to go to

venus by way of the moon and i wish to tell that to everyone.'

that is cool, stevie says, that is real cool that you are going on a spaceship. you have a spaceship in your backyard or are we talking of one at kennedy airport which you are boarding?

'now that is ridiculous,' i say knowing how stevie can ride over you and start to abuse unless you pull him up short at the beginning also thinking of the seven-second lag and the knowledge that if i get too clever with him he will cut me off. 'no one has a spaceship in their backyard particularly on west 93rd street between amsterdam and columbus avenues which is a courtyard of about two feet square and there are no commercial spaceship flights going from kennedy as far as you or i know. i am going to will myself to venus by way of the moon, inner space is a condition of validity of travel which is a proper metaphor for any external reality and one can travel if one wills himself to do so.'

you are losing me, stevie says, inner space and external reality and validity. i do not know validity. i recognize your voice now. you are raoul the call.

'that is right,' i say. i am cheered because usually stevie does not recognize my voice but this proves that i have made an impression on him or then again that he will admit i have made an impression on me. 'i am raoul the call and inner space is the proper conjecture for external reality. i am going to board the ship of my soul and go straight out to venus with a moon stopover.'

far out stevie says, you are one far-out guy.

'i am going on a long trip.'

are you carrying any messages?

'if you wish me to,' i say, 'i will carry any messages you wish. but i have been on venus and the moon many times before and i wish to assure you that they are uninhabited with conditions not conducive to life and there is no one to leave the messages for except coliform bacteria which can make it occasionally in the methane swamps of venus.'

oh man stevie says you are far far out you are wild. how many times before have you gone?

'i have gone to venus sixteen times and the moon eighteen

and mars once. mars is so hot that there is no way you can even do any sightseeing even under glass. later on they will open the mercury shoot but this will not be for several years. there is nothing on mars or mercury either by the way,' i say.

you are flipped out, stevie says, you are freaked out, you are flippo. raoul the call why you do this to me?

'the topic was of general interest tonight,' i say, 'not limited to a special subject and i thought that the discussion of drugs and trips before led naturally to this. i have been wanting to tell you for a long time of my exploits and this seemed to be a good time to do it.'

you are too much, stevie says, you are too much. he pauses and i wonder if he is going to cut me off the way he will often do to move onto the next call if he feels the show is lagging but he does not want to leave this one go i can tell if he can. he begins to ask me what methane gas is and i tell him giggling a little because even thinking of methane make me lightheaded.

v

stevie holds me on the line after a time and takes other calls. gang-calls are a technique of the modern switchboard; he can bring in as many as ten talking to each other and on the air at once but he settles for just five this time. naturally they all want to talk to raoul the call about his trip to venus. some feel that raoul is crazy or being sarcastic about drugs and their effect on consciousness but at least two are very serious and want to ask me further questions. how long has this been going on? how long have i now been flying to venus with stops on the moon? does modern technology admit of this possibility? do we have the machines and the government is sitting on the information as it has sat on so many other things and all of this is going on beyond the knowledge of the public? i reply that i do not want to get into politics or the specifics of the matter and besides the machines are not under government control. stevie always tries to steer his callers into political channels but raoul the call has never taken such bait. politics acts to conceal the realities it is

at best a metaphor. it is interested in the suppression of issues
and not their articulation something which i would not get into
on the air because of the general mental inferiority—although
i have conceded their courage and individuality—of stevie's
callers. finally i decide that it is time to go or stevie decides it
is time to go the good host never letting you know when you
are being manipulated unless he wants you to know. the five or
six callers drop off like fruit from a vine and only stevie and i
are left in the singing emptiness of the strand that connects us
through the heart of the city from west ninety-third to east
sixty-fourth street dead river to river waste on both ends. i wish
you a good trip, stevie says, you will call in and tell us how it was
will you not?

'i have not yet,' i say, 'i have been a caller to your show *the
wasteland* for three years and two months and have never
mentioned my space flights until now. i wish to keep most of this
confidential.'

i do understand that, stevie says. you are freako. you are
farout man you are wild, raoul.

'so are you stevie,' i say, 'so are you my friend,' and we disconnect then; to put the phone down after so long is to be empty
and alone my ear craving for its contact the way the cupped
hand of a lover may shrivel for lack of a breast—but i do not
wish to get into the even more difficult issue of sex here—and
i put on the radio just in time to hear myself saying in seven-
second lag *so are you my friend* and a long pause even a sigh
from stevie. it is too much, he says, this is some night. i have
some friends. i will play a record now. while i look for a record
why do we not think of what has been heard tonight and what
we have learned.

that is stevie, pedagogical. i join him in thought, thinking of
what we have learned tonight what the true sense of it all is
until the thunder of the music begins to pour out of the receiver
and then disconnecting it is the music itself that i allow to carry
me my ship to the dark and departed spaces the rolling balls the
incontestable fire of the planets above, mercury, mars, venus or
the moon i am carried and so my voyage begins.

v i

there are some who will say that this story is not about actual
events but is merely a clever attempt to show that traveling to
mars or venus is no more absurd or strange or wonderful than
talking to stevie in the night the two of us linked by invisible
wire, there are some who will say that i have merely tied one
mystery to another mystery to show that all of life is an implaus-
ability and that i never really went to the planets at all but this
would be untrue and would show that the readers are stupid
and missed the point for i did indeed carried by the music begin
my voyage then and it is going on now even at this moment my
first and terrible voyage to venus because of course i did lie to
stevie . . . although i had had the method before i had not had
the courage to use it now for the first time until at last through
declaring myself on the air i found the strength to make the
commitment because otherwise stevie and the listeners would
have known that i was weak and carried forth by that i continue
on my strange and terrible journey. in one sense i owe it all to
stevie and *the wasteland* and in another sense i owe it nothing
but the resolution of this is strange and by the time i return to
earth with the look of eagles in my eyes will seem unimportant.

TOM REAMY *is an electronics engineer from Texas best known in the science-fiction world for the elegant amateur magazine* Trumpet *that he has published sporadically over the past decade. During a recession in the aerospace industry five or six years ago Reamy turned to professional writing, working for a time on the periphery of the motion-picture industry, then turning to science fiction. His work has appeared in several of the magazines and such anthologies as* Nova *and* Orbit, *and now he makes his* New Dimensions *debut with this evocative, haunting tale of the distant future, in which new species have come to inherit the earth and man is obsolescent.*

■

DINOSAURS

The bluebaby swam suddenly in a tight circle. The maneuver caught the others by surprise and their outstretched arms failed to make contact. Gleeful thoughts rippled between them.

But, even in victory, the bluebaby had tired of the game. It swam downward, shutting out the joyful thoughts of the other bluebabies as they continued to race about. It paused near a dreamer and poked among the stones until it found one to its taste. It deposited the stone in its mouth and listened idly to the dream.

It was supposed to be a very special dream, but the bluebaby found it tedious and dull. It had listened on a number of occasions since its hatching in the spring and found the dream never changing.

The dream was about the surface. In the dream the surface was green and thick and liquid flowed in large grooves. Two-legged surface creatures moved about haphazardly and lived in odd structures. The dream made the bluebaby impatient and it couldn't understand why it kept returning to listen.

A dreamer without a dream had attempted to explain it. The dreamer, with a faint note of envy in his thought, had explained that it was a very special dream because it was about the time before the world; before there were dreamers (or bluebabies, either); when there were only surface creatures.

If it was before the world, the bluebaby questioned, how did the dreamer know anything about it?

The thought of the dreamer without a dream was amused. That's the reason it is a very special dream.

The bluebaby swam away in search of a more exciting dream and paused suddenly.

There was something on the surface. It sensed a spot of heat where a surface creature was remaining in one place.

Curious, it swam upward.

◆

Flan raised the edge of the breather slightly and scratched the corner of his mouth with a stubby finger. He took one sip of water from the tube snaking to the pouch under his arm and leaned back against the gravel dune with a sigh. He let his muscles relax almost completely; his rest would be a short one. A few bits of gravel dislodged and rolled down the slope of the dune with soft clicks. Flan was unconcerned. His own movement had caused it.

He dropped his hairless head back against the cold gravel and looked at the sky. The stream of debris from the fractured moon stretched horizon to horizon like bits of broken glass. Flan tried to imagine how it had looked a million years ago, when it still was whole, but couldn't.

He raised a pale hand and jiggled the breather, settling it more comfortably over his mouth and nose. It smelled of ancient breath; breath so ancient the exhaled molecules had become a physical part of the plastic and metal. And the pack snuggled under his chin was definitely making an audible noise. He had thought so for years but had dismissed it as imagination and apprehension. How much longer would it last? A hundred years? Two hundred? It didn't seem to really matter. Already there were many, many spares.

The cold crept quickly through the surface suit and into his bones. He wrapped the cloak tighter about him and hunched his shoulders against his neck, shivering slightly. The odors of the cloak were as ancient as those of the breather. His effort had little effect. When he was younger, when obstacles were trivial and easily overcome, the cold had bothered him not at all. Besides, it was hardly *cold*, only early autumn. Flan sighed again, admitting his years. All fourteen of them.

But he had sired the child.

He had sired the only child that year. No shame on him or Triz. Seven in all; two surviving; the new one not yet old enough for naming—but in a few days. He had long ago decided on the name for the new son.

He thought of the other, his first born: Sith, the arrogant, prideful young pup. Prancing and displaying the instrument that would produce a child every year—maybe even two at a time. Poor Sith—eight years old and still childless. Naturally, he put the blame on sweet, hapless Brin. He knew he had no real reason for disliking Sith other than his own peevishness, but Sith wore his glory not well.

Flan slipped his fingers into the small pouch he wore on a cord around his neck and felt the warmth of the whispering stone. His fingertips caressed it for a moment, then slid it into his hand. It was circular and flat, thicker in the center and tapering to a rounded edge. It was half as wide as his palm, white, and faintly translucent like porcelain. It began to whisper.

Flan had seen others. There were always a few lying around. They had a simple beauty and the children liked to play with them. But this one was different. He had found it when Sith was a baby; picked it up where the child had left it lying. It had grown warm in his fingers, seemed to mold to his hand, though it had not changed its shape in any way. It had not begun to whisper until years later.

No one knew the purpose of the little discs; they were pretty stones that amused the children. Even Old Frel, an ancient of almost thirty years, who had a theory about everything, could not produce one for the stones. There had been interest and curiosity when Flan told of the way it warmed in his hand, but it remained cool in the hands of others and the interest waned. He had not mentioned the whispering because he knew that only he could hear it.

He huddled in his cloak, resting against the gravel dune, and listened to the whisper. It was, as always, maddeningly on the edge of understanding.

Flan felt an almost imperceptible movement in the gravel.

His rest had been shorter than he expected. He put the stone back in the pouch and the whisper died away. He stood quickly, with no noticeable effort, and stretched to his full four-foot height. He rolled the heavy muscles in his shoulders, working out the kinks. He checked the direction machine strapped to his forearm and walked away toward the north.

◆

Gray-blue chitinous claws like small shovels probed tentatively at the warmer area where Flan had been sitting. Finding nothing but rapidly cooling surface gravel, the claws withdrew from sight. Then the gravel bulged and rolled away as the bluebaby poked its head up to see the source of the warmth that had attracted it.

The bluebaby's eyes were small and limited but they caught Flan's receding figure. It watched curiously, nose-deep in gravel, until distance made detail a vague dark blur. It thought of following but knew the surface creature moved too rapidly. It had never seen one quite like it, but it did seem to be very similar to the ones in the dream.

The bluebaby poked among the surface stones with hard wide fingers and selected one with a greenish tinge. It popped the stone into its mouth. Another blue head emerged silently nearby. The thoughts of the two bluebabies compared the flavor of surface stones to those below and agreed that, while the surface stones might be the tastier of the two, the awesome *openness* was somewhat disturbing. The other head sank from sight.

The bluebaby looked again in the direction of the surface creature but could see only a small dark spot moving in the distance. It scratched absently at the fine wiry tendrils that had only recently begun sprouting from the joints of its horny body. The itching grew uncomfortable. It sank and swam away in the gravel sea, feeling the movement of the stones bringing delicious relief. The bluebaby's digestive system was already at work on the greenish stone, breaking it down, releasing oxygen and water and other nutrients for the healthy young body.

◆

Flan's stride was not hurried, but it ate away at the distance, bringing him nearer to the People and the summer Home, nearer to Triz and the child. His feet crunched at each step, sinking slightly. The gravel sea stretched to the limit of his vision in every direction, undulating in low dunes like frozen ocean waves. Flan knew the word *ocean* but found difficulty in grasping its meaning. He topped a dune and saw the thin white line across the flat northern horizon. He had made good time. The sun was only at twenty degrees in the west, small and white. He had over six hours before it set, but already the night wind was stirring his cloak. He hastened his step though he knew he would be there in two hours, long before the wind grew too strong. By sundown a man would be unable to keep his feet in the gale, and a few hours later the gravel dunes would begin to shift.

Flan passed the wreckage of the air bus. He hardly noticed. It was a familiar landmark on the southward trek in the autumn as well as the northward trek in the spring. The air bus wasn't exactly *wrecked*, not smashed, twisted, or ruptured. It was simply inoperative, lying half submerged like an immense windowed lozenge. It had shifted almost a mile to the south since spring.

Old Frel, a spinner of tall tales, claimed to remember riding in it as a child, claimed to have been riding in it when it crashed. Flan neither believed him nor disbelieved him. Who was to know if Old Frel spoke truth or fancy? No one else was nearly as old. But the story faintly disturbed him, nevertheless. He wished the shifting dunes would cover the air bus, as they did some years, but permanently. No one spoke, but eyes looked at it, thoughts of what it would be like if the trek were made by air bus rather than afoot passed through their minds. It was unwise to think back on better times.

The stone in the pouch around his neck began to whisper, softly, urgently, unintelligibly. It seldom whispered when he wasn't holding it in his hand, but there were times and places where it did. The air bus was one of those places. He hurried on, not wanting to hear because he couldn't understand.

The white line of the receding glacier was more pronounced. Already the gravel was growing coarser. Soon it would be smooth flat rocks, then tumbled stones as big as his head, then solid rock. The teaching machine, or memories of memories of the teaching machine, said the gravel sea was growing larger. Something about the glacier and the wind—the memory was wispy. It would reach the Home . . . when? A thousand years? Ten thousand?

The wind caught at Flan's cloak and cracked it like a whip. He reached to the breather and flipped the goggles up, covering his eyes against the dust and sand beginning to blow. He pulled the hood over his hairless head.

Less than two hours later he saw the Home. It was a low black blister set in wind-scored granite, made of a substance immune to the elements, intended to be immune even to time. It was ten feet across with a flat surface at the top; it was only the doorway to the Home.

Flan stepped onto the blister, moved to the flattened top, and clutched his cloak against the wind. The Home recognized him. The flattened section lowered. Now free of the wind, Flan released his cloak and sank through a long tube. The tube closed above him, cutting off the moan of the wind. He felt warmth. He lifted the breather from his face and filled his lungs. He smiled.

The downward movement stopped. The tube wall rotated. He stepped out to the greetings of the People. They crowded around him, anxious for news, though it never varied. Their naked hairless bodies were firm and healthy. Only Klor and Blod had noticeably swollen bellies. There would be at least two new children next spring if the sickness did not strike.

Flan removed the cloak and breather, putting them in the racks with the others. The People waited as he put the direction machine carefully in its case and emptied the water pouch, returning the water to the central store. He ran his hand from his throat to his crotch. The surface suit split open and peeled back. He stepped out of it, naked. Of all of them, only Flan wore any type of adornment: the whispering stone in its pouch around his neck.

Triz smiled at him proudly. Her breasts were back to their normal size but her belly was still flat. Flan sighed inwardly. She was too old for another child. She was sixteen, two years older than he, but still beautiful.

The child peeked impishly from behind her legs. He grinned hugely at his father. Flan's face split with pleasure. He knelt and the child ran to him. Flan grabbed him in a hug and lifted him giggling and squirming. Triz came to him and put her arm around him. The People smiled.

"How fares the gravel sea?" asked Thol, a young man in his prime and the happy cause of Blod's swollen belly.

"As always," Flan replied. "I went as far as the first way station. The bluebabies are still active. All is normal."

They nodded and drifted away. Triz said nothing but pressed her body against him. He felt her sorrow and shame with his skin. He touched his cheek to the top of her smooth head with love and understanding, and without reproach. She had mothered seven. She should feel pride, not shame. It was not her fault that she grew old. The child huddled quietly in Flan's arms, watching them with solemn eyes.

Triz slid her hand across Flan's chest and down over his hard belly. Flan felt the heat following her hand and then the pressure. Triz held the swelling in her hand and was satisfied. She had to keep trying, though the conception time was past. With the child cradled in one arm and the other around Triz, Flan moved through the long gray corridor to their sleeping room.

They lay on the sleeper. Triz opened to him. The child sat beside them, watching and examining. After a bit the child laughed and said, "Look, Father!" He tugged at Flan's arm. They looked and smiled. The child pointed to his little manhood, hard and erect. "Will I have many children, Father?"

They hugged him to them. "Yes, my son," Flan murmured in contentment, "many children." The child would have all of Sith's beauty, if only he avoided Sith's arrogance.

They lay together with the child between them. He lay quietly, exploring the contours of his mother's face with his fingertips. Finished with that, he settled back and looked at the gray featureless ceiling.

"Father?"

"Yes?" Flan muttered drowsily.

"When will the trek begin?"

"Soon."

"How soon?"

"As soon as the bluebabies have gone to sleep."

"What are the bluebabies? Have I ever seen one?"

Flan smiled to himself. He remembered asking almost the same questions. "No. The bluebabies are horrible, wicked creatures who live in the gravel sea."

"Why are they horrible and wicked?"

"Because they will grab you and pull you under."

"Why?"

Did he know why? Was there a memory of a memory? "Because they are horrible and wicked. Are you hungry?"

"Yes."

"So am I. Triz?"

"Yes. I'm ready for food."

They left the sleeping room, made a short detour to walk through the cleansing machine, and entered the big room. Flan punched the delivery button of the food machine three times. Three gray cubes slid out. He gave one to Triz and one to the child and kept one. The child bit into his with tiny sharp teeth and grinned when a crumb stuck to the end of his nose. The water machine ejected three containers at Flan's touch. They sat in the exercise machines, nibbling the food and sipping the water.

The others drifted in, smiled greetings, got food and water, sat in the exercise machines. The machines purred almost inaudible purrs. Sith entered with Brin. His handsome face was clouded. He wouldn't look at her. Brin's eyes were downcast and her lips were pale. Her fingers worried each other and strayed occasionally to her childless belly.

Flan watched them, unable to understand Brin's love for his churlish elder son. But he did, deep inside. Brin was shy and gentle and lovely. She had been overwhelmed by Sith of the merry eyes and impudent grin, by his powerful young body, by the promise of his large manhood. But the promise was unfulfilled and the eyes were no longer merry. Flan suspected he was cruel to her.

Food time was conversation time as well. As the end of the stay in the summer Home drew near, the conversation was almost always the same. Flan only half listened. It was for the children. This time for the child.

"I see no reason why the trek is still necessary. Why can't we spend the entire year here, or at the winter Home?" The question had always been asked, as far back as Flan could remember.

"I like the winter Home best. Everything is nicer and it has color. It isn't all gray. It's larger and more comfortable."

"Why didn't they make two teaching machines? Why didn't they put one here?"

"The winter Home has many things not found here."

Old Frel chuckled. "The teaching machine could tell us why there is only one teaching machine."

"If we only had the knowledge to repair it."

"We do have the knowledge," Old Frel muttered. "It's in the teaching machine." The others pretended not to hear.

"We might as well wish things were back the way they used to be; when there were no bluebabies; when there was no gravel sea; when the whole world was covered with vegetation and the air was thick and rich and the People lived on the surface, covered the surface in great cities; when there were pools of water miles across. We can wish that just as easy as we can wish we knew how to fix the teaching machine."

"But that's just myth. The teaching machine is real."

"Some storyteller, like Old Frel, made it up as a fancy. That's all it is. How could there be pools of water miles wide? Where would all the water come from?"

Someone chuckled. "And how could the People have been so many? There aren't enough food machines. It's only a myth."

"The People have always been as now."

"And always will be."

"Always."

The child had heard the myth before, but the idea of not making the trek was a new one. "Why can't we stay here all the time?" he asked, putting the conversation back on the subject.

"The teaching machine said we must not." A memory of a memory.

"Why?" the child repeated.

Flan smiled. "There are things we must do without knowing why."

"I stayed here through the winter once."

Old Frel's voice silenced the others. It was a new note, an electric new note. The silence hung as heads turned and eyes narrowed. Only the faint purr of the exercise machines was heard. Was this another of Old Frel's fancies?

"Why have you not told of it before?" a voice asked, soft, but loud in the silence.

Old Frel looked not at the others but at a memory. "There seemed no need. But now, every year the voices to abandon the trek grow louder and more insistent, and I feel this trek will be my last. Before the crash of the air bus, the trek seemed to be over in an eye-blink. The sun moved not at all between leaving and arriving. Now the trek takes many weeks of walking. Sore feet have become more important than the old ways."

"What happened?"

"The air bus crashed. It ceased to function and fell into the gravel sea. Many were killed. Many were injured. Even then, the hundreds of seats in the air bus were not filled. I was very small, but I remember. We left earlier then. There was no need to fear the bluebabies when we flew through the air like gods.

"The crash sprang open a locker filled with breathers we knew nothing about. Had it not been for that, all would have died. We were afraid to stay in the air bus, afraid we would be covered when the winds rose in the evening. We came back here. There was nothing else to do. The bluebabies were every-where. Many of the injured were dragged under when they paused in one place too long. We spent the winter here."

He was silent for a moment, his eyes far away. "As autumn came to an end, the wind blew all the time. It was too cold to bear. It was impossible to go outside, even in the middle of the day. When winter came the winds grew worse. The cold was unbelievable. It was difficult to keep warm even in the Home. The night winds . . ." He paused. His voice grew lower. "The wind during the day was the same as the wind, now, at night. The night winds made the Home tremble and moan. The walls, the floors, everything shook. The vibration was constant. And the noise. There was never silence.

"The next spring many more had died. Some went into the tunnels to escape the sound of the wind and were never found. Some took their own lives. Some were found killed, we never knew by whom. Some, though living, were never . . . right again. When autumn came again, when time for the trek came again, we walked. There were those who correctly interpreted the way-station chart. Now the memory of it is gone, and there are those who wish to stay."

It was several minutes before anyone spoke. "What's to prevent us staying in the winter Home? The winds don't blow there. It is far from the gravel sea. The vegetation makes it possible to stay outside for a while without breathers."

"In the summer the crawlers mate."

"Yes. We couldn't go outside while the crawlers mate. We'd have to stay inside the Home all summer, but there would be no wind, no vibrations, no sound. It was the sound and vibration, wasn't it? It was the wind?"

Old Frel nodded once. "Perhaps."

◆

The bluebaby felt languid. It swam in the gravel sea. The mantle of steely fluff growing from the joints of its body made movement awkward, but the itching of the growth made movement necessary. The bluebaby accepted its dilemma without question.

It swam near a clutch of eggs and listened to the incoherent thoughts flowing from them. It paused. The thoughts were small and formless, soft and selfish, sweet and indulgent. The bluebaby smiled a thought at them, then moved away when the two breeders hovering over the clutch grew nervous. They knew the bluebaby was no threat to their eggs, but breeders were always nervous and fretful until the spring hatching. The bluebaby thought idly of the coming time when it would be a breeder. The thought made it uncomfortable. There would be no swimming, no frolicking with other bluebabies, no freedom. From spring to spring there would be nothing but attention to the clutch.

The bluebaby had once expressed this apprehension to a

dreamer. The dreamer had told the bluebaby fondly to put such thoughts from its mind. When the time came to be a breeder, it would want nothing else. And did the bluebaby not want to be a dreamer? Everything came due in its time and its place. Now, go on with your games. I am about to begin a dream and I must decide upon one that is grand and worthwhile.

The bluebaby had left the dreamer unsatisfied. It hadn't made the thought at the time, but it wasn't too sure it liked the idea of being a dreamer any more than it did being a breeder. Now, it swam near a different dreamer encased in its impenetrable shell and listened a moment to the dream. But the bluebaby was restless and itchy and the dream seemed inconsequential.

It thought again of the peculiar surface creature and swam upward. Its head poked into the scream of the night winds. It saw nothing but the creeping dunes.

◆

Flan lay in sleep, touching Triz, touching the child who slept between them. The sleeping room monitored them, adjusted the temperature here up a degree and there down a degree. The room's almost sentient circuits hummed in soundless contentment. It was capable of contentment in its own way—as well as regret. Regret that the cycle was ending, that its units would be out of its care until the next cycle began. A unit turned in its sleep. The room adjusted the temperatures in less than a microsecond.

The whispering stone in its pouch slipped from Flan's chest as he turned and lay loosely on the sleeper by his neck. It spoke, not to Flan, but to another part of itself miles below the surface.

It hears but does not understand, it said.

Keep trying. The unit seems nearer understanding as time passes, it replied.

Too much time passes. This unit grows closer to the end of its existence.

It is the only hope.

It is not my original unit. Its pattern is similar but too differ-

ent. Too different. It does not understand.

It must. Time passes.

Time passes and they are so few.

So few.

Growing fewer.

The new ones increase—the new ones in the gravel sea. Their vitality increases and their number grows larger.

The gravel sea grows larger.

The units have lost their history.

They cease to function so quickly.

So do I.

Yes.

I am dying.

Yes.

My death will not matter if the units are no more.

Yes.

Without them I have no purpose.

Yes.

Without me they cannot survive. I have lost my voice in Shelter 23. I cannot communicate with them. The unit must understand. It is the only hope. They need me.

Yes.

I need them.

Yes.

The exchange ended. It was not a conversation precisely but the continuation of an introspection that had lasted millennia. It took no more than a nanosecond.

Flan turned again and woke, disoriented. More and more the whispering stone was in his dreams. He lifted the pouch, upending it. The stone slid into his hand. He felt its urgency and strained to understand. It was no use, but . . . sometimes . . . almost . . . understanding was like a phantom seen from the corner of his eye, a sound just outside his range of hearing.

Triz and the child were still sleeping. Then he remembered, knew why he had awakened so early. He put the whispering stone back in the pouch. This was the child's naming day.

The People gathered in the big room. The occasion was not as festive as it might have been. There was only one child to

name and the knowledge dampened their spirits. They tried
not to show it. Not from their own sadness would they tarnish
the shining moment for Flan and Triz and the child.

The child was led in by his parents. They were swelled with
pleasurable pride and could not avoid smiling at each other and
at the gathering. They were greeted by murmurs and nods of
respect.

Flan lifted the child to the naming platform and stood behind
him. He held the child cradled against his chest and smiled. Triz
sat at the child's feet. The child was nervous and bashful but hid
it with a small arrogance. His naming day was an important
time in his life, second only to the birth of his first child. He
stood proudly but, nevertheless, clutched at his father's arm.
The People stood quietly, all eyes on the child, waiting.

Flan slipped his arms from around his son's waist. He held his
arms up and out. "There is a name for the child," he said in a
singsong voice. A faint hum issued from the throats of the People. "The name for the child has been found." The hum grew
louder. "The name is . . ." The hum cut short and the People
stood in silence.

"The name for the child is *Roon.*"

The hum returned, louder, joyous. The People smiled and
nodded and murmured the name. Flan stepped away from
Roon. His son was no longer a child. Roon fidgeted nervously
and cast one quick glance at his parents. Triz joined Flan. Roon
stood alone.

Old Frel approached Roon and held out his hand. He touched
Roon's genitals and said, "Roon."

Roon blushed.

One by one, the others did the same, walked solemnly to
the boy, touched his genitals, and repeated his name. Halfway through the ceremony Roon's excitement brought an
erection. The People smiled. Flan hugged Triz to him. It was
a good sign.

The childless ones returned to touch again, hoping. Even Old
Frel returned.

◆

The bluebaby swam restlessly, unable to settle into the sleep. All around others were snuggled in their balls of fluff, clustered near the dreamers, sharing the dreams through the long winter. Breeders huddled at their clutches, insulating the eggs against the iron cold that would come.

The bluebaby scratched absently at its side, although the itching was growing less as the tendrils grew longer. It caught an inquiring thought from a dreamer, the one it had expressed doubts to before, the one that had still not decided on a proper dream. The bluebaby thought a greeting but did not wish to hear of what would be, did not wish to hear its restlessness would pass, did not wish to hear wise platitudes from a dreamer.

It swam to the surface and poked its head into the bright, brittle stillness of midday. It searched the gravel sea with small dim eyes, but nothing moved. It remembered the surface creature's speed, moving entirely on top of the gravel.

The bluebaby, on sudden impulse, emerged completely into the open air. It tried to imitate the creature's movements, but it was not equipped for walking. It floundered clumsily and looked up. Sheer terror overcame it. It was about to fall into that vast nothing, fall until the end of time. It was suddenly back beneath the surface and didn't remember how it got there.

Every day it came to the surface but never saw the peculiar creature. Nor did it venture out again farther than its nose.

◆

The naming ceremony had lasted long. Songs were sung, stories were told (Old Frel was the best), and then the People had moved to the surface with the midday warmth. They basked in the waning sunlight and gloried in open space while the children raced about in games. Roon had been self-conscious at first but soon joined in.

Triz had remained below for a while, then joined Flan and spoke to him quietly, out of hearing of the others. Now he hurried through the corridor, past the occupied sleeping rooms, past the many unoccupied ones, past the vast room where the air bus had berthed. He walked gray corridors he had not seen since he explored them as a curious boy. He passed the sighing room where the air machines made breathable atmosphere. He passed rooms with purposes he could not even imagine. The stone around his neck whispered as he passed some of the rooms, louder at some than at others, and loudest of all at one section of corridor. It whispered so loudly he paused, but then hurried on.

Flan knew his destination. Everyone had been there, but once explored, no reason existed to return.

It was a large area where the corridor terminated. Other tunnels opened at intervals on the other side, black unlighted tunnels. Flan had entered the darkness of one as a boy, but a thumping heart and clammy skin had ended his penetration after a dozen steps.

Two strips of metal on the floor ran parallel into each tunnel. Flan did not know the reason for the rails, nor did he even speculate that a reason existed. Had he been told of the time that had passed since they had been used, he couldn't have grasped it. The time was so great that even the inviolate metal of the rails had darkened.

Brin, small and lovely, stood in the doorway of a sleeping cubicle. No one knew why sleeping cubicles were necessary in this extreme end of the Home, but several were there, tiny and austere and functional.

She stood with her head down, looking at her feet. He walked to her, concerned and puzzled.

"Brin?" he said. She raised her eyes quickly and lowered them just as quickly. "Triz said you wanted to talk with me. Why here? Why not outside in the sun with the others?"

Brin stood for a moment without answering, then whispered something he could not hear. She repeated it more clearly at his question. "I do not want Sith to know," she said. Then she sobbed silently, her hands hanging loosely at her sides.

Flan took her in his arms and made soothing murmurs until her tears stopped. She snuffled and pushed him gently away, her eyes again shifting to the floor in embarrassment.

"Has Sith been cruel to you, Brin?" Flan asked softly.

Her eyes rose to his with pleading swiftness. "Oh, no. Not the way you mean."

He said nothing.

"Sith is not cruel. But his . . . silences and his looks are more painful than beatings." Her voice sank to a whisper he could hardly hear.

Flan released his breath in an impatient sigh.

"I know you dislike Sith," she said in a small tortured voice. "Most dislike him, but you are wrong. I love him. I love him more than my life."

"That is foolish. He does not deserve your love, Brin."

Her hands clenched into small fists. "You are wrong. Sith is beautiful. Sith is gifted. Sith is bright. Sith is golden. Sith has a right. It is only . . . he is tortured because he is childless. For three years I have been empty. Sith deserves many children."

"Others are childless. They are not lost in cruel rage."

"Sith is special."

"Perhaps Sith is at fault. Not you."

She stood as stiff as stone, her eyes closed and her lips pale. Flan knew why she had called him to this forsaken place. He knew and said nothing.

Her lips quivered before she spoke, her eyes still closed. "I do not believe my golden Sith could be with such a flaw, though Triz suggested it also. I do not believe it, but in my love and desperation I will grasp at any hope."

"There is danger. Sith has too much pride."

"I know. Sith must never discover the child is not his. The knowledge would be worse than childlessness." She looked at him quickly. "However, I do not believe there will be a child. The flaw is mine, not his."

"Why did you choose me?"

"Because Roon was the only child produced this year. Because . . . Triz suggested it."

"Is it your wish, or do you only follow Triz's suggestion?"

"I must give Sith a child."

He looked at her small pinched face, at the pain and pleading in her eyes. He did not speak. He knew from the tingling in his thighs and the pressure at the base of his belly; he knew his answer was visible.

When Brin had gone, giving him only one shyly smiling glance, Flan sat in the sleeping cubicle feeling relaxed and lethargic. The corners of his mouth curled slightly. It might be good for Sith if he did find out but, no, Brin would be the one to suffer. Perhaps Sith was tormented enough; perhaps if there was a child he would find a compromise between his arrogance and his despair.

Flan sighed and stood, stretching his arms over his head and rolling his shoulders. He clenched the muscles in his thighs and buttocks and felt suddenly restless. He took the whispering stone in his hand and heard its meaningless voice urgently commanding.

"I do not understand," he said aloud.

He passed by the dark tunnels, caressing the warm stone with his thumb, sliding his feet on the smooth coolness of the metal strips. He stopped and looked in, hesitated, took a few steps into the darkness. Childhood tensions caught at him and he turned back.

In the corridor the voice of the whispering stone grew louder, even louder than before because Flan held it in his hand. He stopped and looked at the walls. Both were featureless gray. A frown creased the skin above his nose. Behind one wall was the air-machine room. He turned to the other. He had always supposed, when he thought about it at all, that it concealed nothing but solid rock. He took a step toward it. It looked the same as it had always looked. He listened to the whispering and placed the tips of his fingers against the wall. It felt no different than any other wall in the Home. He spread his fingers until his palms rested flat against it. Still there was nothing, but he knew, he thought he knew, the wall was important.

He stepped sideways and let his hand slide on the gray smoothness. Then another step. He released his breath and stepped back, letting his hand drop. It was then he felt it, as his hand slid downward on the wall, just before it broke contact. He bent over and looked closely at the spot level with his chest.

There was an indentation there, a rectangle as big as his head recessed no more than a millimeter. It seemed no different than the rest of the wall and was almost impossible to see. He touched it again, running the tip of his finger around the edge. He put his hand flat against the rectangle and felt nothing.

Then—his vision was swimming and his ears were ringing—then, he placed the tip of his finger *there,* and again *there,* and once more *there,* and back again to the first place.

He understands.

No. He only follows blindly.

He touched *there* and *there* at the same time. The rectangle sank inward another half inch.

Flan gasped and jerked his hand away. And, without knowing how he got there, was pressed flat against the opposite wall of the corridor.

The wall in front of him slid to one side with a gritty sigh.

Flan stared into a great room filled with machines. They climbed to the high-domed ceiling in stair-stepping tiers, solid to the top, quiet, sleeping, their glassy eyes dark. The room was steeped in silent gloom; and in the center was a sphere, a globe, a vast round ball covered with pinpoints of light: blue, red, and amber, with violet lines crisscrossing as if it were encased in a net.

Flan looked for a moment, then went to get the others.

The People stood with craned necks, the eyes of the adults only slightly less goggled than those of the children. The globe towered above them like a mountain. They milled around it, trying to see it all.

"Do you see up there?" Flan said. "That white light? It's the only white one there is."

They backed away to get a better look because it was above the curve of the sphere. Yes, they agreed, it was the only white light. Flan listened to the whispers and felt the stone warm in his hand. "Old Frel," he said softly, "you know the way-station chart."

"Yes." Old Frel stepped beside him and looked at the white light.

"Look at those small lights below the white one. Are they the same as the way-station chart?"

"Yes," Old Frel said doubtfully. "They look the same, but there are lines and too many lights."

"Just the small lights." The others were gathering around and nodding agreement. Roon started to his father with his mouth half open in question, but Triz stopped him and held him at her side.

Old Frel dipped his head once. "Yes."

"The white light I think is here, the summer Home. Follow the way-station lights as if we were making the autumn trek. It leads to that larger light that must be the winter Home."

"But," Old Frel protested, "the light is amber. It is amber like the way stations that have something wrong with them."

A violet line from the white light to the amber light suddenly brightened. It glowed for a moment, then went out completely. The People looked at each other. Then another line brightened, from the white light to a blue light farther around the globe. The line remained.

Will they understand?

Wait.

Flan moved away from the others and watched the blue light. Nothing changed on the globe. He looked back at Old Frel and saw agreement glittering in the ancient's eyes.

"No," Old Frel said, coming to him. "It's too far."

"The machine is telling us to do it."

Old Frel shook his head. "It is twice as far as the winter Home. We could not make it walking. If the air bus hadn't crashed . . ."

No. No.

Another violet line brightened. It led from the white light around the globe in the other direction.

Far below the gravel sea impulses flashed through semisentient circuits unused for millennia. In the room at the end of the corridor where Flan and Brin had met, one of the darkened tunnels was suddenly lighted. Two hundred miles away a long narrow vehicle moved into the lighted tunnel. It looked something like the air bus but had only one window at the front and rode the metal rails on magnetic skids and something that was almost antigravity. It passed the speed of sound in seconds.

"Look!" Sith pointed to the new violet line and they all followed his finger. A green dot moved on the line, moved rapidly toward the white light of the summer Home.

The whispering stone sang. "The tunnels," Flan said softly.

"The dark tunnels at the end of the corridor."

He understands.

Wait.

The others looked at him. "We must travel to the new Home in the tunnels."

Cybernetic relays closed here and opened there. The impulses flew joyously, for they were capable of joy in their own way. Then there was an unthinkable sifting of impossible dust. The impulses derailed, were shunted to the wrong circuits, relays closed at the wrong time, opened at the wrong time, microscopic memory cells went insane.

Magnetic currents in the rails fluctuated. The rocketing vehicle's skids impossibly touched. Sparks flew like a meteor storm. The vehicle yawed and struck the tunnel wall as the lights went out.

Flan ground his teeth and pressed his hands against his ears. The whispering stone screamed, once, briefly, unbearably, and then was still. The green light moving along the violet line flickered and darkened.

The People waited at the end of the corridor, watched the dark tunnels. Flan waited in the room with the great globe, but the whispering stone did not whisper again.

Triz came to him in the following days. She waited with him silently and then finally she spoke. "The trek begins, Flan."

"We must go through the tunnels," he muttered.

She was silent again for a moment. "No. We could not bear the darkness. They tried. Come, Flan. We must go."

He went with her at last and left the silent white stone lying on the floor.

◆

The bluebaby felt torpor creeping through its body, but the sensation did not produce warm lassitude and a desire to curl up in the steely fluff. It only made the bluebaby uncomfortable. It was the only one who had not entered the sleep, the only one who swam about sluggishly and irritably. More and more it caught the inquiring thoughts of the dreamer who had not found a dream, but it refused to answer.

It kept swimming, although the completed growth of fluff made movement clumsy, because it dared not rest, dared not let the sleep creep upon it unbidden. It found an especially delectably rusty stone but did not enjoy it. The stone lay in its stomach with dead weight. The digestive process had halted for the sleep. The bluebaby regurgitated and pushed the stone away.

It swam to the surface—and saw them!

The surface creatures moved by a short distance away, many of them. The bluebaby subdued the lethargy that slowed its limbs and dived. It made a swoop and returned to the surface. Excitement flowed from it with such strength, two nearby breeders awoke and crouched with spurs poised to defend their clutch.

The bluebaby watched, wondering if the one seen earlier was among them. It couldn't tell. They all looked alike except for variations in size. All were wrapped in loose flat things that stirred with the rising night winds, and all wore things over their faces. They moved in an irregular line that clumped and thinned sporadically.

The bluebaby followed.

◆

Flan glanced occasionally at the direction machine strapped to his forearm. The indication glow remained steady with a brightness that should mean the way station would come into view within minutes. Triz walked beside him, matching his pace without effort. Roon walked at his side. The boy was tiring but never complained. He clung to Flan's cloak as they topped a large dune.

The way station lay ahead, poking its smooth black top just above the surface of the gravel sea. The others reached the top of the dune and sighed loudly and pleasurably at the end of the first day of the trek. They scooted down the other side, moving a little faster, moving with lighter feet.

The way station was one of many scattered over the vast

expanse of the creeping dunes no more than a day's walk apart, put there in the same distant past the Homes were built. It floated on the gravel sea, anchored in place, kept level by its machines. Most had never known living things, never exercised their purpose after the day the workmen departed. The machines of the way stations purred in solitude, keeping them afloat, keeping them anchored, keeping them level. Inside, the air machines produced breathable atmosphere, the food machines and water machines stood waiting.

Except for a few. On the large charts in the Homes, several way-station lights had gone dark and others had changed from clear blue to amber and red. The second way station on the trek was an amber light—the air machine no longer functioned. The People used it anyway, sleeping in their breathers. It was uncomfortable and awkward but not worth the lengthy detour. A detour was necessary near the end, four extra days of travel to skirt a darkened light on the chart. The flotation-anchoring machines had malfunctioned. The way station was awash, lost forever in the gravel sea.

The People entered in small groups, as many as the descending tube would hold at one trip. They stripped away the uncomfortable surface suits, the irritating breathers, stretched unconfined bodies, jostled and laughed in the one cramped room. They patiently waited turns at the small toilet, ate the gray cubes from the food machine, sipped at containers of water, and wished for relaxing exercise machines.

Many returned to the surface, escaping the confinement for a while. Rested and with full bellies, they wanted the freedom of space for as long as possible. Flan sat with Triz. He thought regretfully of the promise of the globe in the forgotten room and didn't understand. He put his arm around Triz and pulled her to him, putting the whispering stone from his mind.

They nestled comfortably in the loose gravel, watching Roon and the other young ones play a game of chase and touch. Roon would be ready to mate when he reached five years or, if he was lucky and developed quickly, at four. Already he was the constant companion of young Glur, the daughter of Slef and Klin. Flan hoped Roon would select a mate younger than himself—

if any females were produced in the next couple of years. When the female was older, the reproducing years were shortened. If Triz were his own age or younger there would be a chance of two or three more children. Now, there would be no more. He pulled Triz closer to him. She turned her eyes from her son to Flan. Her breather moved with her smile. Flan would not interfere with Roon's decision. Never once had he regretted mating with Triz, even if there would be no more children.

◆

The bluebaby floated nose-deep in the gravel sea, watching the antics of the surface creatures. The light wind ruffled the thick fluff around its head. Some of the creatures, the smaller ones, raced about with great activity. Others reclined on the surface. As the wind rose, some of them entered the black bubble.

The bluebaby slipped below the surface and moved closer. It swam slowly and carefully, not wanting to disturb the creatures. When it emerged again the swiftly moving small ones were quite near. Their activity was not unlike its own romps with other bluebabies, though without the grace of swimming. It marveled at the rather incredible agility and speed with which they moved despite their clumsy limitations.

Roon ran in a great circle to avoid Glur's touch. She was at present concentrating on contact with Jird, who was an easier target. This time he would win the game. Roon crouched behind a dune, hoping to be forgotten until after Jird had been touched.

He huddled against the low dune, breathing rapidly from exertion. He was tired and happy and content. The excitement of his first trek was very satisfying. (Although it was actually his second; he had been too young to have more than the vaguest memories of the first in the spring.)

Unease slowly rippled through Roon's contentment. He frowned behind his breather but could find no cause for his apprehension. He craned his neck slightly to peer over the dune. All was as it should be. None of the others seemed disturbed. He felt faint prickles on the back of his neck and decided to return even if it did mean losing the game. As he rose from the ground he turned and looked behind him.

At first he thought it was a round blue stone slightly larger than his head, but then he saw the eyes. They were two black smudges in horny sockets, just barely above the level of the ground. And they watched him.

Roon gasped and took a step backward. He had never seen a bluebaby, but he was sure it was one. But the bluebabies were supposed to be asleep. The southward trek didn't begin until they were asleep, and the northward trek was completed before they awoke.

The blue head sank into the gravel without a trace.

Roon turned and ran. He had taken two slithering steps up the dune when the chitinous blue claws closed around his foot.

Roon screamed but the breather muffled the sound. It was doubtful that the others would have heard anyway above the noise of the rising wind.

But Glur saw him rise above the dune and drop down again. She smiled behind her breather. So that was where he was hiding. With exaggerated stealth she crept around the dune and pounced.

No one was there. Only the edge of Roon's breather protruded from the gravel sea.

◆

The bluebaby pulled the surface creature down with some difficulty. It squirmed and threshed with great determination. The bluebaby also had some difficulty moving it through the loose gravel. If the creature would swim . . . but it had stopped moving altogether.

The bluebaby stopped and examined it. Something seemed to be wrong with it. Besides its cessation of activity, its outer covering was leaking fluid. It felt the creature and was surprised at its softness. The outer covering seemed filled with pulp. The bluebaby suddenly became concerned and dragged the creature quickly to the surface. It pushed it completely out and

watched it for signs of activity, but there was none. It continued
to leak fluid.

The bluebaby felt a great sadness and sank slowly into the
gravel. It swam downward, willing the sleep to come, but it
would not. A hollowness grew in the bluebaby. It swam toward
the dreamer without a dream with many confused questions.

The dreamer thought comfort at the bluebaby; comfort and
regret and understanding. The surface creatures are harmless,
fragile things. They should not be bothered.

I meant it no harm, the bluebaby thought in remorse.

I know. The young are curious and unwise. The surface creatures are able to live only on the surface. To bring them under
means their death. You must never do it again.

What is death?

The dreamer thought amusement at the solemnity of the
young. You are not mature enough to grasp such a concept.
Wait until you have become a dreamer. You will have time to
think of such things. Now is the time for youth. Everything will
come due in its time and its place. But the bluebaby insisted and
the dreamer thought it was like being hatched, only the opposite, and would think no more.

The bluebaby swam away unsatisfied and wrapped itself in
fluff near a dreamer with other bluebabies. The sleep came
quickly, but the dreamer's dream seemed to involve surface
creatures with leaking fluids.

The bluebaby was the first to awaken in the spring. The
others still slept in balls of fluff. It swam quickly to the surface,
leaving its steely fluff scattered through the gravel sea, shortly
to decompose. It poked its head into bright day and looked at
the black bubble floating there. No surface creatures were in
sight. It swam around the bubble, touching it, feeling its faint
vibrations. Had the creatures returned already? It swam to the
dreamer without a dream.

The surface creatures had not returned. It was not time, but
it would be soon. Why had the young one awakened so early?

I must see them again, the bluebaby thought. My sadness is
still with me.

It went to the surface many times every day, but still the creatures did not return. It watched the clutches hatch and the new bluebabies swim away. Would they too destroy surface creatures? It wanted to tell them, to warn them, but their thoughts were only for frivolity. Perhaps they would never know without doing it themselves.

It watched the breeders, free of their clutches, shed their husks and emerge as new dreamers. They quickly encased themselves for eternity. It listened to their tentative inexperienced dreams and swam away restlessly.

The time for the return of the creatures had long passed, but they had not returned. Midsummer arrived before the bluebaby abandoned its vigil. It swam to the dreamer without a dream.

It was only the second time within the dreamer's memory— the dreamer was young—that the surface creatures had failed to pass over. Before that they moved through the air. The dreamer pushed aside the bluebaby's queries about moving through the air and thought on the surface creatures' failure to return. After a few days of deliberation, it decided. Yes, it was a perfect subject for a dream. It began the dream immediately.

It was a great dream and lasted nearly a thousand years.

DONNAN CALL JEFFERS, JR., *is the grandson of the poet Robinson Jeffers and lives in Carmel, California, in the heart of that turbulent and beautiful coastal strip that his grandfather celebrated in powerful and passionate verse. At the moment his ancestry is the younger Jeffers' chief claim to literary fame, for, although he has been writing since 1963, he has had nothing published yet except some poems in a local magazine and the short story you are about to read. But this is not as serious as it may sound, since at last report he was still a few months short of the legal voting age and preparing to enroll as a college freshman. He tells us that his chief interests are "fiction of almost any kind, especially my own; Aubrey Beardsley; Ronald Firbank; good rock, especially Bowie; Satie; Mesoamerican art and archaeology; any and all mythology." His hero figure is Orpheus, and he hopes "someday to be a starving author; soon after a well-fed one." This soaring and lyrical story is an auspicious beginning, I think.*

■

MASK

Through the Orosor domes falls starlight, past green and purple mists. I stand here with my mask in my hands, my mask on my face, and wait. Something is coming. :O Maryss! I still love you:

—*Iav'ni Sar'niavt'iav, the star-singer was born on the*
—*world Shoon when the world Shoon was young and young;*
—*L'hia danced red and orange and the night was all-black,*
—*true-black, black-black. Iav'ni Sar'niavt'iav, the star-*
—*singer was born at L'hiard; L'hia-son was Iav'ni Sar'niavt'iav.*
—*Sun's son, sun-singer, he played the* fhuha*'s strings, he*
—*sang the stars into the sky.*

I met a museum dealer from Cordelain this evening, fresh off the strand-follow from Earthome, with his mind all ancient-cluttered, and wearing a mask like a dolphin in steel and red-stone. I don't like dolphins.

He said my mask was an Hellenic god, was 'tousle-haired Apollon, Huakinthos, Narkissos. Orpheus, maybe.' I knew what he was talking about, as I was born on Earthome, in Ellis. But when I was on Earthome, I wore the same mask, and it was my face. Here on Thyannir, it isn't.

Later I saw Khor'a N'akhors'khor, a ssun friend from Sal'r Kwoord and Shoon. My friend Khor said he thought the mask was a human analogue of Iav'ni Sar'niavt'iav. I do like Khor.

> **Orpheus the harper was by birth a Threix, from the*
> **barbarian lands north of Hellas, where all the great*

> **musicians are born. But Orpheus, son of Apollon and the
> **Muse Kalliope, was the greatest singer of all. When he
> **played and sang, the people would gather about him, and
> **the birds and beasts, and the trees would uproot themselves
> **from the earth to listen, and the very stones on the
> **ground would roll to his feet.

My mask: a young man's face of beaten gold, with all the calm of Tutankhaten's burial mask, but with a pensive smile and a gaunt beauty alien to the Khem. Beryl in the eyes; platinum spun for hair.

My face: three years ago: ditto the above, but make it live.

My face: now: the left half has been melted in a crucible, the nose has a great, rightward dent, the eye in it is perpetually half-closed and not mine, but blue and grown in a vat, the ear is a small, misshapen lump. A stripe of hair that falls across the eye that is not mine, is not mine either, it is black and coarse. I have no great love for this face of mine. :It is not mine!:

> —*Iav'ni Sar'niavt'iav, star-singer, sang the stars and*
> —*planets out of the night, and waited. When the sons of*
> —*the sun, the ssun of Shoon, took their dancing kites into*
> —*the all-black, black-black, Iav'ni Sar'niavt'iav went,*
> —*world by his-created-own world.*

Tierrdileonn is one of the most beautiful (to my taste) worlds in Triplex—Nouv Imperialle di Earthome has it, to her unjoy. Unfortunately, it is also a world choked with nightmare.

For the ssun, they remember Iav'ni Sar'niavt'iav, and that at the collapse, those ssun left on Tierrdileonn managed to kill themselves off, when all the other colonies prospered.

For humans, we have genocide. Humans discovered a flourishing nonmechanistic culture of indigenous sentients, the leonn. We killed them all, for their furs, as their Earthome namesakes almost were. Not many people live on Tierrdileonn. Guilt is hard to bear. But for those few, entertainment is needed, more frequently than most places, and I'm popular.

For me, I have my own especial unfavorite nightmare. Like this: The gly-mattress ripples under me and I am almost asleep.

Vaguely, I hear the door to the hostel suite open, and close, then the sound of plashing water in the cubby. It is too much trouble to awake fully.

I feel water dripping on my chest. My Maryss stands above me, her spun-ice hair dripping, melting. She smiles a strange, Maryss-smile with teeth the same color as her hair, her skin. Her eyes flash red.

Flashing gold, a strange faceted thing describes an arc to my belly. It is warm there. It throbs. I cup my hand over it and it throbs at me.

Maryss, wet, coils onto the bed with me. Her hand on mine. She lifts it, her other hand takes the gold thing. It flames on me as her fingers near it; it burns as they grasp. Strangely, simultaneously as it pains, a throb of sensual pleasure spreads out from it.

Her hand on my lips. She kisses my forehead. I kiss her fingers. She positions herself above me, around me, one hand on my shoulder, the other cupped between her shallow breasts, the nipples of which, palest pink, stand out in nubs. Gold gleams between those fingers.

'Cheeta, my love,' she says, not looking at me, addressing some nebulous, perfect Cheeta, the ideal of me. He is not present. So she could be speaking to me. It feels otherwise.

She writhes the fingers around the gold. 'What is it?' I ask.

'A reward for you, and me,' she says, dreamily, then, awake, 'I found it in the ruins. I'm not sure what it is.'

I close my eyes.

The hand on my shoulder moves under my neck, she leans her elbow on my chest and breathes in my face.

Pain. Screamingly
  Pain
 !Pain!
  ain!
   in!
   !ni
   !nia
!niaP!

She has (shrieking) put something warm and (screaming)

throbbing and burning hot on my eyelid. I feel my face melting
away, boiling down my skull.

But at the same time that it (HURTS!) hurts, there is a great
thrilling, a sensitivity of all my nerves, and half the (PAIN!) pain
is the unbearable stimulation as we move together.

                    Hundreds of
Screaming
                    years later, as the
Crying
                              skin of me ignites and
                                                      the
Burning
bones of my skull melt, and all through me
                    PLEASUREPAINPAINPLEASURE
fight it out, I open my eye to see Maryss, glowing white hot, her
eyes blinding pink, and through the unmelted ear I hear her
screaming as loudly as she can and I myself as well, and our arms
are around each other as tightly as they can, crushing, and a
final crashing burst of
                    PAINPLEASUREPLEASUREPAIN
and spirally blackness hides me, lit only by a towering phos-
phorescent fountain
    regular spurts: pleasure—pain—pleasure—pain
                    PLEASUREPAINPAINPLEASURE
and is the end.

When I woke, Maryss was gone.

They gave me a new eye, and filled in a scalp-spot where it
had been burned out, but was all they could do. So I am no
longer beautiful Cheeta, but Panther the Singer.

I love you, love you::hate and fear, Maryss:

   **Orpheus went to Kolchis, on Argo, with Iason. He charmed*
   **the ever-waking dragon to sleep, that Iason and Medeia*
   **might take the golden fleece. He was the singing hero.*

I fell in love on Aresshu five years ago.
I do like the stars.
There is a whisper in my ears, the rustle of silk behind me.

I turn. She stands there, all white and wrapped in white silk, and white hair hanging down her back, and silver masking her eyes.

:No, I won't believe it's you, Maryss, go away:

I have to believe, for it is her voice that says, 'Cheeta, you aren't beautiful any more.'

'O thanks, thanks so much.' I turn away.

:I hate you, hate you::love and desire, Maryss:

The fingers of one hand are ice as they pull at my second-skins, which fall off. The fingers of the other hand (the whole hand is) are aluminium, that tink!s on my mask, before it falls clang! to the floor. Naked I turn to her, and as calmly as it can, my voice says, 'I do not love you, Maryss.'

'I know,' she says. She touches the throat of her gown and it crumples down around her; she drops her mask, she drops a hand. She is still white, and her eyes are still pink.

—*Iav'ni Sar'niavt'iav came to Khuth'thlalli* (Tierrdileonn,
—*Ornoti, human) from the true-black, his glittering kite*
—*falling fiery to rest. There were females there, brought*
—*by another kite, and their dances were crude, their music*
—*monotonous. The females hated.*

I am telling my fingers (they won't listen) to take Maryss' throat and crush it. She kisses my lips and stands, all white, and says, 'Farewell,' and walks away, pausing only to snatch up the aluminium hand, which she buckles to her stump.

'No!' :Is that my voice?::I've only got you back, don't go away!:

I don't how, I pull myself up and stumble after. She looks back and runs. I run too. I am not fa-ast enough. I a-am too slo-ow. She's get-ting away.

Through metal- and plax-lined corridors we run, and monstrous domed chambers with the killing air of Thyannir watching us. And we come to strand-follow central, and Maryss, laughing now, throws a kiss—off her metal hand—and is in a cubicle. And by now gone. Gone.

**Orpheus the singer loved Eurudike, a nymph of the waters,*
**and wooed her with his harp and voice. She came to him,*
**and they were wed in the old ways of the Mother of All.*

**But one day, when they were yet a month together, a*
**keeper of bees lusted for Orpheus' lady, and fleeing*
**she was slain by a serpent in the grass.*

:Maryss Zilandfyr:
::Gone:: says the web of Orosor, Thyannir, Slu.
:I *know!* Where?:
::Simbra::
:Give me the pattern:
With the pattern for Simbra in my mind, I enter a cubicle.
The web sends aiding tendrils into me and I stare at the Thyan-
nir-pattern on my door, willing it replaced by the Simbra-
pattern. After a time, it is.

Quite chastely clad in second-skins of palest blue, Maryss
greets me. She stands in front of the booth across from me,
holding tightly to its door. :I want you, come here: 'Shoon,' she
says, and the door closes behind her.

   —The females hated. Iav'ni Sar'niavt'iav stood on an upcrop
   —of black-black basalt, near the shimmer-wings of his kite,
   —and he sang, and the true-black, all-black was thrust
   —through with fire-stars, and the females listened. They
   —heard; they hated. The black-black was filled with new
   —stars; the song was ending. They heard; they hated.

:If I can find it, I have the Shoon-pattern in my mind. Ah,
there it is. My credit is good, is it not, O lord machine? May I
use your strength, machine? Will you send me where I want,
machine, while you stay here? Nothing personal, but I hate
having you wander around in my head, machine. Ah, well, off
we go:
A building to human geometries and aesthetics set, depending on your views, like a finely cut diamond in a crude and
barbaric setting (human), or an absurd, off-world plant growing
crazily, not quite undesirably, in an intricate dying sculpture
garden (ssun); as a general rule I prefer the ssun view, despite
my ancestry: strand-follow central, Shoon, L'hia.

I had thought it unlikely I would see anyone I knew—except
maybe :hopefully: Maryss—even though I am one of the few
human artists appreciated by the ssun, and am friend to many.

Shoon is still mostly unpopulated, rediscovered as it was only thirty Earthome years ago by a Ch'skiiiyaliii migration. The only permanent inhabitants are aristocracy from the empire, though that has been dead and gone these twenty-five millennia. The center of ssun civilization is still Sal'r Kwoord. Yet, right over there is Khor. :Is it only yesterday afternoon I saw him?:

'Greetings, Khor'a N'akhors'khor,' I call in my bad tseun. He turns and lifts his vermilion-dyed feeding limbs, and says, in lingua di earthome—he is unfailingly polite—'An unexpected pleasure, Pant'hiir.' Polite. He wouldn't call me Cheeta.

'Why are you here?' I ask. :He doesn't need mechanical augmentation, he can strand by himself::the wanderers gave *us* strand-follow, but we need help to use it; we gave it to the ssun, and they don't; why?::why is he here?:

'Why are *you* here?' he replies.

Not wishing to be enigmatic, but it hurts, I say, 'Maryss.'

The tentacles on his feeding-limbs flare outward in a ssun affirmative. 'Yes, she is with the Noiv now.'

:Unexpected? No::I will never understand tseun—'Noiv' is a title, but an untranslatable verb, as are 'ssun,' 'Shoon,' and 'L'hia.' It's a good thing they are so good with lingua, or there would be no communication at all::What is happening, happening, ing, innngggg?::We call the Noiv 'Prince in Ruins,' but what does it really mean, mean, ean, eeeannn?::Is this death, or am I only fainting?::What is Khor saying, I barely hear it, 'The Noiv will accept her request'? What request?::happening, ing, ingingginginnnggg::dying, dying, dyingingginginginnngggg::::::::

**Orpheus the singer took the descent to Haides, he charmed
**Kerberos the dog, who let him pass, he charmed Charon, who
**ferried him without fee, he charmed dread Plouton the king
**and Persephoneia the queen, and the judges of the dead.
**Entranced in his music, Plouton relented and gave back to
**Orpheus Eurudike, on a condition.

I think that I am asleep, for where else could I be? I am inside an almost-sphere formed of mirrors, and half the mirrors show Cheeta's face, half Panther's. There is no light, yet I see; my

eyes are closed, yet I see. My skin and flesh have been stripped
from me: strange organs cluster in my ribcage, veins and arter-
ies loop about my limbs. Plax and metal tubes from nowhere are
hooked into various appropriate apertures. I am asleep; I am
dead.

:Where are you Maryss?::where are you Khor?::where are you
fussy museum dealer from Cordelain?::where is Cordelain?:-
:Thyannir?::Earthome::Sal'r Kwoord?::Shoon?::all the worlds
I've seen and not?::where am I?::where am I::where am
Iiiiiiy:::::::

I am asleep; I am dead.

—Iav'ni Sar'niavt'iav ended his song; the black-black, all-
—black, true-black danced with his new stars. The females
—gazed at him; their feeding-limbs danced with hunger. Iav'ni
—Sar'niavt'iav the star-singer did not see. He stepped down
—from the great basalt to his kite. The females began to
—sing. Their song did not raise up stars. He listened.
—They sang; they hated. They danced; they hated. They ate
—Iav'ni Sar'niavt'iav's face from his head.

My mother is dead, how can I be born?
And yet, this must be.
The flesh is growing back along my bones. Dirty newborn
pink, laced with flash-red capillaries, it creeps inward from my
toe- and fingertips.

All the mirrors show Cheeta, now.

:Am I asleep?::Am I dead?:
:dyinginginginnnggggg:::::::

**Hermes Psuchopompos led Orpheus, the Erinus led Eurudike,
**and they took the road up from Haides. The condition
**that Plouton had put on the singer was: not to look back at
**his lady till they both should reach the upper world. As
**Hermes led him, Orpheus did not look back, though he could
**not be at all sure that Eurudike was in truth behind him.
**As he reached the gate to the world of the living, he heard
**the Erinus cackling behind him, and he turned, suspecting
**treachery.

:Living, maybe?:

'K'heyt'ah? Wake, K'heyt'ah.'

:Can't. I'm dead::Who is that? It's ssun, but Khor would never call me Cheeta. Who is it?:

'K'heyt'ah, it's time to wake up.'

:No:

'K'heyt'ah!'

:O, all right:

(From the grave, hoarsely) 'It's too bright. Can't open my eyes. Turn down the lights.'

It becomes darker, and I can see. Khor stands next to my bed. 'Welcome back,' he says.

'You called me Cheeta—?'

'Yes.' He does something, and the back of my bed rises. A mirror forms in front of me. :I've had enough of mirrors!:

And it isn't me reflected in the mirror, it isn't Panther.

—*All the stars heard Iav'ni Sar'niavt'iav's cry, their*
—*creator's cry; L'hia heard his cry. For the star-singer*
—*the stars sang. All together, in a glorious sweep of*
—*melody, the stars sang, and with their singing, they*
—*formed a new face for Iav'ni Sar'niavt'iav, more beautiful*
—*than ever before seen. The singer travelled to many more*
—*worlds, and created many more, and when he died, his last*
—*song blossomed into the constellation of 'Iav'ni Sar'niavt'iav*
—*the Singer.'*

The face in the mirror is mine, Cheeta's. There are no sags and wrinkles, the nose is straight, both eyes are open and both are green, the hair is all the same color. When I lift my right eyebrow, it lifts its left. When I smile, it smiles back. It is my face.

'How?' I ask.

Khor says, 'Mer'yazs.'

As if on signal, Cheeta's—*my!*—face smooths out of the mirror, and there is Maryss.

She tries to sound flippant, and can't. 'Sorry for the inconvenience and the follow-my-leader, and all that, Cheeta. I did *mean* to do it, but not so much as it did. It was, you see, the *hand*. Which I got rid of. And now you're all right, and Cheeta, and I'm glad.' The *imago* begins to fade, still holding out the empty palm of her aluminium hand, and faintly she says, 'I love you,' and is gone.

I am fearful that I do, and yet I must say, 'I don't understand.'

Khor turns away and his voice-cavity squeezes shut in a ssun grimace. 'Remember the gold she was found on Khuth'thlalli—Ah, Tierrdileonn? You might call it a drug. Something ssun haven't used for a long time, but it works as well for humans. It will heighten the sensations of the sexual act to an almost unbearable degree, for both persons. But on one person, it at the same time causes great pain, and has the same effect it had on you—destroying, melting, deforming bone and flesh.' He pauses and looks at me. 'To the other person, it grafts to the skin. And it wants to do the same again and it makes its carrier feel it. Why Mer'yazs had to amputate her hand. Very strong to do that. Stronger for what she has done now. Be thankful, K'heyt'ah.'

**Orpheus looked, and Eurudike fled his gaze back to Haides,
**and he was again alone. He was found by the followers of
**the mad god Dionusos, and when he would not play for them
**in the manner they wished, they slew him and threw his
**head into the sea. Dionusos, in smallest recompense,
**placed Orpheus' harp among the stars as 'Kithera.'

'Where is Maryss?' I ask, knowing.

'You understand,' says Khor, then clamps his voice-cavity entirely closed. He does another thing, and another *imago* forms: two mirrored spheres, within one, my skeleton with its flesh growing back, in the other Maryss.

'You do understand. We have not been here enough long. Our sciences have gone different ways since we lost Shoon. Some of these machines do not all we want.' He abolishes the *imago*. 'This, that Mer'yazs asked, does not. It needed her strength to heal you. It killed her. She's dead, K'heyt'ah, she's dead.'

'No!'

:Yes!::Maryss, why?::I love you, love you, love, loooovve::::::::

'Yes,' he says it gently.

:NO-O-O-O-O-O:

:Orpheus, that I have lost her, now the mainades, where are the mainades to slay me? Where are they, ey, eeeeyaaa*AAAA*a ao-o-o?::::::::

Of the dozen contributors to this issue of New Dimensions, *only four—Farmer, Tiptree, Malzberg, and Effinger— are reasonably familiar to regular readers of science fiction. Two—Randall and Gotschalk—have appeared in previous issues of* New Dimensions. *Two—Reamy and Pollack—have had stories published in other anthologies recently. And the rest—Girard, Jeffers, Tincrowdor, and Marshak—are reaching print for the first time in a widely distributed publication. Eight new writers out of twelve, which is probably as it should be in a book that calls itself* New Dimensions; *and I find it cause for optimism that there are so many good new writers suddenly making the science-fiction scene. Of* DAVID MARSHAK *I know very little more than you do; his story came in, as most submissions to* New Dimensions *do, unsolicited and unheralded, and my request for biographical data brought this cryptic reply: "I was born and raised in the Windhamite Colony in central Alberta. I defected from what I know now to be the remains of a once brave 19th century utopianism at the rather late age of 28 and have spent the last half decade aging a hundred and some odd years. One previous publication, a story: "Carcinogenia," in the* Winnipesaukee Journal." *So be it. The story must speak for the man, and it does so quite impressively.*

■

168

David Marshak

■

WATER

(6–23–4AF(2022 AD)–23.1)

The last hour of the day always brings me back toward wondering. Always, at least, before—before these last three months —before the winds, that day— Yes Sam, you ask us why we keep these earthnest time structures, now organically meaningless, because their meaning derives from physical changes in the ecosphere of the earthnest, physical changes beyond the control of people—I wonder if Joshua will ever believe that people could actually accept such conditions? Here in the shipnest, so much of what we've brought with us from the earthnest feels so—incredible, nonsensical, threatening to collapse and yet touching on remote wonder, and— What is a day but the temporal measurement, elapsed time, of one turning of the earthnest on its axis?

Sam wants us to get started on his time-use project. He's raised the issue at almost every meeting in the last year. Let's throw the whole structure of earthnest time reality out, he argues. And I giggle, not at his idea but at his use of language. Throw it out. Surely by now we've learned, as a species, that we just can't throw anything out. Out where? All we can do is move it from here to there. And to do that, we've got to use some energy. Sam doesn't appreciate my amusement. He's more concerned with what he calls action. In my idea, all we do is active. Otherwise we're not doing it.

Why assume that our present system of time use is necessarily the best one? Sam asks rhetorically. Let's get rid of these ancient assumptions. We're no longer bound by the simple motion

169

of any planet. Why continue to act as if we were? Right now we're behaving only according to habitual patterns. We don't know the best way to deal with our time. We don't even have any consensus or empirical criteria defining what our goals are in this regard. Why not? Now is the right time for action. We've got to start discovering what we want to do with time use, so that we can eventually learn how to do it. Or at least how far we can move in that direction before we run up against the biological limits of the organism. And then we can always consider attempts at directed organismic change, if the ends are worth it.

Here Sam shakes his huge, curly-haired head once, throwing off the weight of changing us all, and lets a narrow smile drift onto his face. That's all at a distance, he says. All I want us to do now is to agree to begin. Here's the question. What are our goals in regard to time use? I can't do this work alone. That would be irresponsible. We've all got to work together. To the extent that we act consciously and knowingly, we control what happens. To the extent that we accept what is without examination, the universe controls us. Control is here in our hands, sisters and brothers. We can't go on pretending that our hands are empty.

Sam sticks out his wide hands when he comes to that last line. Flat, palms up. They look empty to me, but I know what he sees in them. Sam likes to make speeches. He's good at it.

Of course, there's no consensus yet about starting this work. Too many of us are comfortable with things as they are. And there's so much else to do. I have another reason. Ties to the earthnest will decay and dissolve as soon as we allow them to do so. We must consciously order this process, looking backward as well as forward. Once the inner feeling of something is lost, it's gone.

(6–24–4AF–22.7)

Two nights in a row—For the last few months, I haven't even walked past my recorder station, since—I can't recall the day —Let me see—3–28–4. Yes. Amazing that I could forget it, so amazing and so easy to believe, knowing me. And now I'm at work two nights in a row. Duty must be licking around at my wounds. Training. And now, drowning in that awareness, I won't work. Just a shred of a tantrum. I'd rather go float in nullgrav and sing between my closed eyes.

(6–26–4AF–23.1)

We were circling the fourth planet in the Antares system, 7–3–3, when Joshua, then three and a half, asked me, Papa, where did we come from?

What is our promise, bound to an exploding fragment of order? I asked MASCOM but didn't bother to wait for a print-out that wouldn't come. Then Antares was a giant red coin burning across a wide angle of the space visible to us from its system. And burning in my black hand. A careless trip over dangling ion transmutation tubes, at six years, had burned a coin into the flesh of my left palm, a glowing circle the exact color of Antares, blood fire.

The speechless sages of the fourth planet welcomed the visit of our small tribe with wild tremors of ecstasy. With our arrival, they had achieved the fulfillment of their prophetic mythology. People coming to their home from the stars to share with them the fruits of the valley, the river, and the light, and then, after the visitors had returned to the stars, rebirth in the home of Antares, return to unity with Antares, everywhere the center of warmth, the heart of joy, the boundless field. Escape from Beta Antares, a tiny yellow dot beside her twin's vastness. Yellow, the empty fist, madness, isolation, individuality, linear being.

I never claim accuracy for my attempts at the interpretation of alien realities in terms of probability predictions. Che insists that my claimed inability to do so results not from the nature of my work but from my negative attitudes toward the power of probability prediction and my resultant unwillingness to master the use of the necessary techniques. He says that his field, health care, is as complex as mine, and he has no problems with probability. Why don't we trade roles for six months and see how we do? he asks. I tell him that I'm still weighing his offer, and how can he say that I don't like probabilities? I set them up on all my interpretations. Fifty, fifty. Either I'm right or I'm wrong. Che shakes his seventeen-year-old shiny bald head and wanders back to his kitchen.

I never claim accuracy, but what I believed would happen on Antares four after our departure involved species behavior on the part of our friends that would appear to us to be mass suicide, like earthnest lemmings, while those experiencing the behavior would perceive an apocalypse, an end-of-time reunification with Antares, a return from matter into energy. Fearing that our observation might interfere with this religious process, I worked hard to convince the tribe to allow our caution to triumph over our curiosity. This one time, at least. Sam argued that exactly that sort of policy, if allowed to prevail in our meeting, would soon lead to our demise, because we needed to let our curiosity guide us. Otherwise we would stagnate in the swamps of earthnest tradition. I argued respect for the rights of aliens. Sam agreed, as always, to go along with the consensus.

(6–27–4AF–23.2)

To whom am I speaking in this record?

I ask that question often. To myself? To my sisters and brothers? To my grandchildren? To a distant future? My father, the only precedent I know in this role of shipnest poet, always spoke as I have done in this sentence—always explaining, clarifying, restating, as if the reader cannot be assumed to know anything about us. Not Joshua did this, but Joshua, my son, such an age and such a look on his face, did this. My father and I never really discussed the poet's role. Prior to the fission, I assumed that he would continue as poet for a good many years, and so, I didn't question him, even after I began to keep my own record at age ten, as Edward had instructed me to do. Micah, my father, let me watch him work, but he always seemed too involved in his speaking for me to interrupt. He was a man familiar with both rapturous and mundane concentration in his working hours. And during the tumultuous days of the fission, we were both too absorbed in our own decisions to find time to talk about the poet's role. I think Edward wanted it to be that way. He wanted each new poet to find his own path.

I've read Micah's record many times. His work is good, his style consistent. My own style changes. When I do follow his precedent, it often feels strange, for such a style requires that I separate part of myself from the rest.

Here I am as Micah.

We are seventeen. Our youngest, Mark, child of Zoya and Alex, born on the fourth planet of Antares, is almost a year old now and starting to talk like a good reinventing language system tape. When we brought him into nullgrav for the first time, he astonished us all. He didn't waste even a moment in fear. At once he was flying like a veteran spacer. At six months, flying baby fat. And before we could loosen our instinctive grips on the handholds after more than six months on the 1.1 grav planet, all the other children, Joshua, the oldest at three years, Leah, the youngest besides Mark at two, and Lao, Shasta, and Marie between them, were flying around with him, spinning around and over, laughing and gurgling and cawing. Within half an hour, everyone had readjusted, and Thomas and I went down to level one to drive the shipnest out of its long orbit of Antares four.

Again as Micah. The shipnest has three levels, each six by two km. One, the functional area, including MASCOM and its terminals, social and body function areas, work areas, labs, the farm, the navigation and control area, is at 1.0 grav. Two, the old power source area, redesigned as a forest and field after the invention of star drive, at 0.5 grav. Three, the nullgrav play area. A complete picture is stored in each MASCOM lobe. I enter this skeletal description into the record every once in a while only because Micah did it every month. Without fail. An orderly man, my father.

(6–29–4AF–23.0)

Miriam was talking about Mark's immediate adjustment to nullgrav again tonight. We ate dinner together atop the mat-weed knoll near the southeast corner of level two, with our son, Joshua. After the meal, he went cartwheeling off to climb trees, and Miriam started telling me about the work she was doing in regard to Mark's behavior. She'd have me call her speculations theories, but I'm wary of any attempts to use scientific methods. My training as poet was specifically designed, by Edward, to compel the internalization of certain types of profound balancing prejudices against the more ineffable powers of behaviorial and, to a lesser extent, physical scientists. I know Miriam to be an excellent philosopher-psychologist. My attitudes toward her work are necessary for the survival of our tribe. The poet must act as a balance. I call her theories guesses, because if I were to allow them the status of theories in my head, I would then have to grant the possibility and desirability of obtaining empirical evidence about them. I have no wish to know empirically. Empirical science rests on causation constructs. Cause and effect is deadening to real knowledge. Cause and effect is not reality but rather an ancient human model imposed upon the flux of reality for the sake of psychological well-being. Cause and effect has its rewards in terms of power over nature. Granted. But the price you must pay for that power is an intense constriction within a mechanical cosmos. And you know, in a cosmic sense, less than you did before.

The cosmos I know is magical.

Miriam explained that Mark, as an embryo, had experienced almost eight months of shipnest existence prior to our landing on Antares four. During that time, Zoya, his mother, whose skill as farmer is so great that she need only allocate as much time to her work as she wishes, chose to spend most of her days and nights on levels two and three. Mark took to nullgrav so readily, Miriam said, because it was a homecoming for him after all those heavy months on the planet. He's our first real nullgrav child, you know?

Her last words were a question, a grinned one. She knew very well that I wouldn't know in that way. Exploding her smile, she rolled over onto her stomach, lying stretched out against the sweet-soft mat-weed, soft blue heavy water harmony feel against her brown skin, extending her spine farther and farther out, pushing and stretching becoming reaching, closer and closer, filtering out more and more static from her cortex, getting down into the heart flower of her animal brain, to be one with all of one. Miriam always says that she has trouble getting into a consciousness of cosmic harmony without feeling my vibrations near. I know that's only her fear speaking.

(7–1–4–22.9)

I can't really feel what things are like in the earthnest, I complained to Miriam this morning. I want to feel what it's like there, to know where we're coming from, to be able to see what's happening in us that's new. I communicate with at least one earthnest individual every week or so, let that person know me so that I can know him or her. But the more I feel the earthnest person opening, the more unreal the communication between us seems. I'm sure they feel it, too. And MASCOM doesn't help much either. I've worked my way through all the data about the earthnest that Edward stored in MASCOM, all the films and sensory gestalts. I can't get into them enough to find their meanings. I don't feel my connections with them. Just take the concept of city for an example. How could so many people live so close together? Don't they ever want to know what it feels like to be alone in open spaces?

Miriam closed her eyes in concentration, and I waited.

I was trying to see my first home, she murmured after a long minute of silence. The hillside trees that stuck out over the pond like crooked fingers, blazing red bark in the sunset of a cold, clear day. Lines of fire in the water, shifting red on deep black. These are the words of it, but I can't visualize that memory any more. That was my last one. I can visualize pictures of the earthnest that I've seen in sensories, MASCOM's pictures. But my own pictures are gone now. I'm trying to remember when I lost the picture of that memory—That bothers me, Isak. The connections cut. Mark was born on Antares four, and I was born in the earthnest. Sometimes I feel like the last linkage, gradually being torn apart. I talked to Sam about it once, but all he could suggest was his damn probe.

She scowled. Miriam doesn't always trust the clinical techniques of her own discipline. That's an old prejudice, I've learned from my study of earthnest psychology. MASCOM probably instilled it in her.

The probe is a strange phenomenon. For aliens, it is what its name says it is. Probing reveals brain structure and functioning. For us, probe is a misnomer. Wash is more accurate. The removal of the symptom from the mind. Pinpoint amnesia.

(7–2–4–22.7)

What do we do about the individual in the shipnest?

We all want to be together, to shatter our identities together into dazzling waves of phased resonance, like dancing to the smooth flight of gulls, their serial cries cranking up higher and higher, wings flapping like machined whips against the drowning press of gravity. And the gulls fly.

And we all want ourselves to be selves.

I talk about many things that don't exist objectively here in our reality. Gulls only fly in MASCOM sensories. Once when I was younger than my present twenty years and my exuberance was less hassled by reality structures, I boasted to Miriam from within a honey of exaltation, I can talk about anything. Anything I can conceive of I can put into words for someone else to hear. In words, I can be everywhere and everybeing.

Those passions amuse me now. And I can see one side of the universe smiling with me. But no more.

(7–3–4–23.1)

I will always wonder about what happened to us on Antares four. There was no communication between individuals on that planet, at least none that I could discover. All communication was between the people and Antares, the spirit of all, the heart of joy. In our six months on the planet, not one member of our tribe ever communicated with anyone or anything of Antares, except myself. Antares, the spirit of all, brought into my head clear and simple answers to the questions I asked. The questions that have continued to circle around my head ever since we left the Antares system (for example: what's going on here?) never surfaced while I was on the planet. I know Antares, the spirit, had everything to do with that.

Antares asked me to stay on the planet for six months, and so we did. We were in no hurry. Life there in the midst of the rapture of another species was good.

Every other week Sam asked me if I were still hallucinating personal communication with a giant red star. Sam plots behaviorial graphs for each of us in 100,993 variables. The markings are then evaluated and digested into a composite which, if you accept the validity of the discipline, yields 90 percent predictability in terms of the given individual's future behavior. Of course, Sam only programs. MASCOM does the work. Sam told me that from a reading of my weekly composites during the six months that we lived on Antares four, he had to demand that I immediately accept probing. To use blunt language, he said very heatedly, I was going mad.

I listened to what Sam had to say, calmly, and then ignored it. It's Sam's job to analyze and predict our behavior, but we don't have to accept his predictions. And there's no compulsion to consign ourselves to his expertise. He has to get us to deal with him. And if we don't—

Sam uses level three more than any of us, except the children. He likes to roll over and over for hours. That's the only play he allows himself.

(7–4–4–22.9)

The way we communicate with the earthnest seems to be unique to our situation. It doesn't work when both parties are in the home system, and we can't do it among ourselves here in the shipnest, although Sam assures us that we could learn how if we wished to do that. Thomas disagrees. He says it must be a function of the curvature of space. We have to be far enough away to be close enough to communicate. And what exactly is it that we've labeled communication? It's always different. What it usually involves is an experience of an earthnest person as if you were that person, while you know that that person is experiencing you in a similar way. But within that general description, variation is apparently infinite. Reported experiences range from achieving an awareness of an amoeba to conducting a long and rational conversation with an earthnest psychologist. The duration of communication in clock time is always short, a few seconds or minutes at most. But the subjective time is always much longer, hours or even days. We can communicate with the earthnest at will, but only if an individual there is open to communication. We think they can do the same, although we've never been able to verify that in communication.

Edward once called it religious communication, the communication of being.

When our starship first left the home system, no one expected the crew to be able to maintain any kind of contact with the rest of the species, except for a shiny spoonful of professional primitives, crystal ballers, psychotics, and saviors. The starship would be gone for many generations. Our mothers and fathers, who embraced the challenge of the cosmos, accepted the realities of isolation as well. They would never again be with any of their people, except those of the shipnest. And they were so prepared. But Edward refuted the assumption of isolation only four and a half years later, when the shipnest was poised to enter the system of Proxima Centauri.

Edward was already an old man, when the starship was launched on 3–19–2001AD. His broad back was still straight, but his arms were down and weary. A handful of the youngest pioneers had opposed his inclusion in the crew. He's almost eighty years old, they had argued like reasonable young men. What good can he be to us? We'll just have to recycle his corpse in a few years. But they had lost, because Edward knew exactly why he had to come with them. And he had the power to insist on his inclusion. Many of his colleagues attacked him for unconscionable vanity. He agreed with them and smiled.

Edward died a week after we achieved an orbit of Proxima, but before he left us he composed two time capsules for us to hear at specified times in the future. That's what drew me into this recounting. MASCOM called us together to hear the first one this morning after breakfast hours. And now I understand what Edward had had in mind back at the beginning. The original prospective crew for our shipnest was very young. There was no one over twenty-four years. Edward wanted several older people on board, people who would die at appropriately spaced intervals. We could not be allowed to apply our imaginations to the reality of death. I can just imagine hearing

Sam and Che telling us that death was not real but rather only self-fulfilling prophecy, not the good end of the cycle of life but something gross and unnecessary. Edward could not allow us that kind of tragic lies, he said. You must know the way of your fathers. And you must not have any opportunity to breed truth into myth. Make your myths always on firm ground.

Edward had managed to bring two middle-aged men aboard with him, to set the right timing in his clockwork of death. My father was the older of these two. I am the only cross-generational child.

This recording isn't objective history, if there is such a thing. Edward was my teacher. I report the past as he saw and recorded it. For good and bad. I go through it again now and then to remind myself of our roots to him. And there's a lot to learn in his writing. Yes, writing. He refused to use recorders.

I was only three and a half years when we entered Proxima orbit, but I can remember that day as accurately as I can drive this starship. Edward was telling me about Prometheus, when he suddenly broke off in mid-sentence, wide-eyed and shook with wonder. Even he wasn't expecting it.

I was just on earth for a whole day, he said more to himself than to me, but I was here all the time and it was only a moment. The water was cold and clear, I swam across the lake, and then I climbed up the northern cliff, the blue sky. I was back in the mountains in Wyoming where I used to go to be alone. But I was someone else. And he was here, in me—Edward sat there shaking his ancient head in shock until I gently touched his hand with mine, as if I wanted to wake him up. Then he spoke to me. Isak, he said, this is fantastic. We can communicate with the earth.

After the breakthrough, it was easy. Once Edward had taught us how to concentrate, everyone could do it. We used to communicate with the earthnest much more than we do now, but ever since the fission, we just don't feel the need. And the mystery is gone. It's as natural now as it was miraculous the first time. And there was a great deal of resistance to the miracle. Micah was particularly stubborn in his adherence to ancient, earthbound demands of possibility, when Edward first revealed his discovery to the tribe that day.

Micah said that he had to stand against Edward this time no matter how much he, as an older man, wanted to believe in the reality of this incredible communication. He knew Edward too well. They had come a long way together, and he knew that Edward's mind could carry loads that most others couldn't even get a good grip on. I know that's the lord's truth, Micah insisted, but the very power of his mind can also induce into our minds an acceptance of this phenomenon as reality, when, in truth, it is only the invention of an old man's heart. It's from that grain of cloth that he brings us this communication with a planet four light-years distant. And can anyone else do it except Edward?

Yes. We all could. Even me, and I was little more than a baby. The first born in space. That's how I got to be the poet. And the son of the poet.

(7–5–4–23.4)

Sensories are beginning to bore me. And all of us, I think. Maybe we should begin to think about weeding out some of the earthnest ones and replacing them either with alien sensories or with other data. Yes, Micah, I can hear your criticism of this entry. Sensories is slang for sensory gestalt programmed experience. You slip into a tube on level three where there is an absolute minimum of stimulation of any kind. You get into a simple trance state, and then MASCOM takes over, providing your head with sensory input from a preselected program. One of my favorites used to be watching the northern lights on a calm, cool summer night in a valley in the Canadian Rockies, smelling the fresh pines and hearing the rippling of rapids. But now even that bores me. I think its part of a widespread turning away from the earthnest that's shared by all.

(7–6–4–22.9)

Sometimes my eyes roll and swell and tear like the pictures of violent storms rolling over the vast seas of the shadowed earthnest. My eyes are like the seas. And I fear the blindness of a black day under starlight. My mother went blind under fierce pressure. I fear what I will see when I can no longer see with my eyes. The tribal faces from antiquity, animal deities scratched into cave walls. My grandmother was blind at birth. All these terrors sometimes bead together into a consciousness that's funny beyond quick relief. When Sam hears me laughing like the scratching of spacetime with the sharpened claws of a chalk cat, he rushes to soothe me. He says that he can help me, and I resist. I know how his probe works. And I know that it does work, very well indeed. But I don't want it to work on me. Why, druid Isak? My reasons all tie into the focus of myself. I am here to keep a record of our tribe in my life and to apply a visionary force to our history. For more than four years I've done that. I've done a good job. I want to continue. And I'd rather lose some of my peace to fears of blindness than surrender my authentic mind to the probe.

(7–7–4–22.7)

For the sake of MASCOM's peace of mind, I am the designated leader of our tribe. I don't really know what a leader does other than talk to his brothers and sisters about what's going on and what should be done. I've read in the films about earthnest leaders, and I've even communicated with a few. They all seem to be smashed idols, falling endlessly into their own traps.

(7–8–4–22.9)

I've been reading through my record of the month of the fission. In his writings on history, Edward talked about how important he thought it was for the poet to be involved in a process of continuous study of the tribal history, to keep what had been recorded fresh in his mind so that he had a good sense of perspective when he wrote new history. That makes sense, although I have to admit that my study is far from continuous. The best way I know to achieve that objective is to enter that part of the history that I'm studying into my record again. That keeps me involved in a creative process.

Thomas developed the unified field star drive in the last month of the year 2018AD.

It was as easy as sleeping at work, he told me. Out here. And yet I don't think it would have ever been put together by anyone who was born inside the earthnest. It belongs to our variation of experience.

Thomas was born only a week after I was.

All our heads were spinning when we first heard about the new star drive. Now it seemed that we could instantly go anywhere that we could conceive of. The drive relied on a power that was mathematical, not material. The only limits were those we set in our heads.

There's so much in the universe that's beyond the grasp of our conception as yet, Thomas was explaining.

We can learn—

Yes, we can, Thomas agreed slowly. But there's one other limitation to the use of the drive that I don't believe that we can overcome. At least it doesn't seem possible given what I know about fields. Once you use this drive to go somewhere, you can't use it to get back to where you came from. It doesn't work. I don't know why, but you just can't do it.

Right now, he explained hesitantly, we're only a little more than nine light-years from the earthnest. According to my best calculation, given the demands of the drive and the characteristics of the shape of spacetime in this locality, that's just too close. You see, if we want to use the drive now to go away from the earthnest, we can't expect to use it to go back there. Ever— Thomas caught my eyes through the chaos of our shattered tribe, shock blanking almost every face, and we both knew what we had to do.

After long railing days of confusion and sorrow, we found a hard decision. A harsh but necessary one. The twenty-six men and women of the original crew, our mothers and fathers, would return to the earthnest in exploratory capsule two, via star drive. They had lived in the starship for seventeen years, and now they wanted to go home. This was their unanimous choice. The rest of us, their eleven children, would go on in the shipnest. We were already home.

It was a necessary fission.

We communicated Thomas' discovery of the star drive back to the earthnest as soon as Thomas could fashion his equations into an unmistakable message. We wanted the earthnest to send out many more starships to join us in our exploration of the universe. All they had to do was to install new drive units in old intra-system ships. There's so much to be done out here, we told everyone that we could communicate with. Come and join with us. And our parents helped to argue our demands when they had returned to the home planet. But the leaders weren't interested in our visions. They took our parents as parade heroes and told us to learn the value of patience. They didn't want to act hastily in this matter, they told the earthnest people. They didn't want to keep sending out starships that could never return. They didn't want to overtax their limited resources. And more and more.

We couldn't comprehend their response. Maybe they didn't really understand, we rationalized like zookeepers. So we worked hard at desperate communication for two days to explain it to them again. The way the drive worked, how we saw the wonders of the universe waiting before us, how we couldn't begin to turn our backs on it. We were ready to use the drive. Our decision was irrevocable.

They repeated their plea for caution, more examination and analysis, more complete cognition, don't do anything you'll be sorry about. That night, we all grieved in self-imposed isolation from them. Even Samuel joined us in meditation.

The next morning, we went.

(7-9-4-23.1)

I awoke this morning without wondering. Sam says that we will all soon cease to wonder, because we will lose the fear to know, the terror beneath our old motivation to knowledge. And we shall find new reasons to learn. Very soon, he assures me. The evolution of our species is so accelerated within our environment, the telescoping of thousands of years into a few is far beyond my ability to perceive its manifestations in any specific forms or to organize that perception. We've cut ourselves loose, Isak.

I hear what he says, but I don't feel any changes of that sort. Miriam and I talked about having another child. No decision. After dinner, Sam told me that he had looked through the record I had kept during the past few weeks. In fact, he said, all of the entries since you started work again.

Inside our shipnest, everyone has free access to everything. We have no secrets. No hidden faces.

Sam said that he found my work to be very good, very rich, very precise. But didn't I think I was leaning into negatives a bit much? I don't see a representative share of your joy in the record, he commented. And, Isak, you're one of the most intensely celebrant of life of us all. You know that. What sort of history are you trying to make? You have to deal with that question openly, Isak. Intent. Your intent affects us all. You're the biblemaker. You've got to know exactly what you're doing, and why.

I didn't need to hear more of his threads to see his weaving. I think I understand all of Sam's numerous stimulus-response strategies. When you love psychologists, you learn how they work. Sam truly believes that what we are doing here will eventually result in the creation of a new human species. A Homo much more wise and free than poor old sapiens. He is certain that we can only succeed, because nature is with us. We are nature. He wants everyone to share his belief, and I don't. I see us trapped inside our own genius. We're stranded. Nothing in the universe is ultimately concerned with us, except ourselves. When will we learn not to delude ourselves with grandiose pride?

I believe I shall be immoral long enough to program MAS-COM to return this entry only to me or my successor.

(7–10–4–22.9)

I keep writing about the past, even when I've already written about these things many times before. I can't seem to escape this dysfunctional repetition.

I tried to write a story this morning, with a hand stylus. A story about greed and fevers, about sores and dislocations and the times we have passed beating back toward a new fantasy of innocence.

We don't like to scar our children (I wrote), but they learn how we do it anyway. They learn with grace. And now when

they're learning, we've stopped growing in flesh and what can
we say to them of life processes? We're dying into wisdom and
idiocy, insight and blindness. I'm not even saying as much as I
can remember, and I'm less than twenty-one years into it. If we
could understand the birth of life on the home planet. If the
concept of causation were not a sham. If we could laugh at
spacetime and give birth. And we have. I'm one—

I stopped. The rest of the words were empty.

(7–11–4–23.1)

You don't need a wealth of identification with all sorts of
specious, ancient lines of tradition to be, to know who you are
and where you fit into things, Sam was explaining. All the
earthnest psychologists were so consumed with these myriad
and irrelevant questions of identity in social and cultural perspective. We don't need to bother with much of that absurdity
here. We've got too much else to do dealing with experience
absolutely new to our species. The real heavens at our fingertips, eh, Isak? The reality of infinity. And all we have and all we
need, as individuals, is what we are now. Here. This moment.
No matter what lies earthnest people liked to believe to gauze
the jagged edges of their lives, that's all you ever get anyway.
Anywhere. Here and now. Everything else is a symptom.

(7–12–4–22.9)

The second time capsule from Edward was delivered to me
this morning by MASCOM as a sealed print-out. Edward had
requested that I read his message aloud to the tribe in meeting.
When all had gathered in the circle, I broke the message seal,
and a little wind rolled out over our heads.

A slight breath from the dead, Miriam whispered. And Louisa
giggled nervously beside her.

Yes, Zoya agreed with Miriam. A bit of fertilizer.

Thomas protested that he couldn't understand how Edward
could have programmed that effect into MASCOM. How could
he get our computer to create a mass illusion in us? he asked.
He wanted to demand an answer to his question from MAS-
COM at once, but Alex and Jomo prevailed on him to wait for

the reading. Yes, he mumbled, I'll wait. Later he told me that MASCOM would not respor.d to his queries. He was very upset.

Did you get any response at all? I asked.

Yes, he replied. MASCOM said it didn't have the slightest idea of what I was talking about.

That's probably the truth, I said. And Thomas just looked at me. He didn't believe that.

Edward's capsule went like this: Hello, my children, no longer children. I have only a few things to say to you. I have never tried to give anyone the only way toward anything. I see no value in that sort of limitation. It seems to me that there will always be many good ways to do things. What follows is only one way, but one that I like. You have never lived on earth. In many ways, you are new. On earth, people were becoming more and more lost in the palm of ego, when your parents left on this voyage to the stars. They were becoming more and more removed from the spiritual essence of their own lives. I don't know if you can comprehend that sort of separation. Think of the distance between parable and reality, increasing. Of necessity, you are already whole. You must teach yourselves and your children never to lose that wholeness of being. You must always remember to do exactly what people on earth were forgetting to do. Live your own lives well. Affect your own lives and the lives of those around you. Deal with your personal reality, where goodness is recognizable and love is obvious. You have been born into a tribal family. This is an ancient form of human social organization. It can work well for all but will do so only as long as the balance between open and closed elements in your society is right. It is a delicate balance. You can't demand it, force it, program it, administer it, or fake it. The correct balance must come from the people you are, the ways you live with each other and with the universe. Only good people can create a society properly open and closed, hierarchical and mobile, changing and stable, secure and challenging, and free to become. This is a paradox in form. You will be the parents of new worlds of humanity. This paradox is your challenge. It is for you to create the future of us. And to be good.

There was another short message directed only to me. Isak,

Edward had written, I couldn't resist the urge to leave you with direction, warning, and prophecy. How did I do?

I smiled and cried.

(7–13–4–23.3)

I use the language of science constantly. You have to use it if you live in a starship, always in space and yet out of it. I know that I don't understand the realities that seem to compel our particuliar mode of existence anywhere nearly as well as I could. And sometimes I feel this ignorance as a budding callus buried deep inside my brain, pressuring me, bending me into isolation, tricking me into misunderstandings of our condition as to drift and nuance, like the dead finger stripped bare of flesh, now insensate bone. Yet I have no wish to learn these things, and sometimes I wonder if that's not a druid passion I'm echoing, an old lust for unbroken faith.

This whole concern doesn't touch Miriam. She knows a lot more about these things than I do but not nearly enough to satisfy my yearning romanticism. She tells me that she believes in the necessity of specialization. There's so much material in every discipline, Isak, she says, more in any one discipline than anyone can handle even adequately. We all struggle with that. And it's the same old story of explosion. The more we know, the more there seems to be to learn. I don't know about what you want, Isak. You're not interested in writing a summa for space man, are you? Now tell me the truth—She giggled to put away my fears and swung upward in a lazy arc. We can all fly on level three. It's an old human dream come true. We can't do anything but.

I left Miriam to her exercises and flew over to play freeze tag with Louisa and Jomo and the children for a while before I went down to level one to prepare dinner. It's my turn. I may be ignorant, but at least I can cook. Joshua knows that. He can always tell right from the first mouthful when I've had my hands in the preparation of a meal. And he's always right. I don't know how he does it unless he's got his own track into my mind. Sam and Che agree that that's definitely a possibility. Everything seems to be a possibility here, but we won't know for sure until Joshua's ready to tell us about it.

(7–14–4–23.8)

We discovered an earthnest-type planet in the five-planet system of a central core star in a tiny galaxy 3.46×10^9 light-years beyond core Andromeda in the same relative direction from the earthnest. When we broke into orbit of the planet, we called everyone to look. It's a beautiful planet. To my eye, it's quite similar to what we know of the earthnest, greens and blues in abundant delight, brown and yellow and crimson, land and sea and white clouds in blue sky, and only one moon.

The people of the planet were very surprised to see us when we landed a capsule outside a small village. Their most knowing seer (I have to use that term for lack of a more accurate translation. You can never get a good translation in this universe, it seems. Only telepathic communion) wasn't, however. He said that he had been expecting us. In fact, although his planet was settled with more than five thousand villages of approximately equal size, we had landed near his. Under his guidance, he explained with a smile. My people, he went on, think that you are of our galaxy. I shall have to correct that impression. There is no longer any travel across space in our galaxy. For many thousands of years we were part of an organization of peoples involving ten thousand planets. All people in our galaxy knew of all others. Those who were backward in development were given assistance that they could join with the rest. But ever so slowly, as water cuts stone, the peoples decided to take life back toward its sources. To go back in, when there was nowhere else to go out in harmony. We returned to the separate lives of our own planets. Here on earth we live in happiness and in peace.

I explained how we had come to his planet. As I spoke about the fission and our necessary exile from the earthnest, the old man startled me with a torrent of pealing laughter, clapping his hands and shaking his head.

He said that he had to chuckle with wonder at the odd and different ways that intelligence had evolved in our very same universe. This reality was the central truth one found in a study of the old records of his earth, too, he said. Everyone, not only every planet but almost each and every individual on every planet, had known such strangely different truths before his galaxy had joined itself as one. Now, he assured me, on this earth, we are all simple people. We all know the same simple truth.

The seer started to tell me how we could cross back over the star drive field to return to where we'd come from, until I proved to his satisfaction that I didn't understand what he was talking about. I went to get Thomas.

Later in the afternoon when the planet's star nestled on the tops of the leafy trees on the horizon, the seer asked that I come to eat the evening meal in his house. This would be a great pleasure for him. Bring your son, too, he called out to me, as I started to walk back toward the capsule. If you don't, we'll both have to act our ages. When he smiled like that, I could see a vision of the father-of-all in his old, wind-and-water-worn face. He was beautiful. I had to discard my fears of age for a long time.

(7–15–4–23.4)

We didn't return to the earthnest today, although we could have done that very easily and been back here for breakfast.

There's no hurry, Miriam said in meeting, and not surprisingly, we all agreed with her. I suspect there will never be much hurry.

We did communicate the news about drive reversal back to our parents as soon as we could.

(7–16–4–23.6)

This morning the seer tried to tell me more about how his galaxy had disbanded back into single worlds.

We were tired of the cancer in our structure, he said with a tinge of sadness in his voice. The whole would not stop demanding growth, expansion, new members. We had to destroy the whole galactic being to rid ourselves of the cancer. There was no other way. When we were finally ready for annihilation of the whole, we brought everybeing in the galaxy into the same point—center of consciousness—to create anew the primordial atom—to evolve into new beings—to create/recreate the old/ new consciousness of individuality—to become complete as separate and distinct beings now/again—

That's the best translation that I can manage. As I look at the words, I know they're almost without meaning in our language. And I'm saddened by my weakness.

The philosophers of the galactic whole, the seer continued, would argue that now we are so much less than we could be. Each of us could be one with all else in the galaxy. As separate individuals, our consciousness is so diminished that we are not even aware of potential for cosmic unity. That's what they would say. Unfortunately, the price of such unity seems to be a cancerous need for growth. Ah, he smiled, most of us know of these things of the past only as myth. We don't care about the philosophers of old times. We know a good life.

After a light midday meal, the seer led us to a lake. We buried ourselves in the free flowing water like sweet dreamers in the last instant of sleep. Cool, soothing water pressed against every mm² of skin. Sweet clear water. The old man swam through the water with the strength of a starship. Joshua and I learned how to swim quickly. Later this afternoon, I asked Thomas if we could build a lake on level two of the shipnest. He said that he saw no reason why it couldn't be done. Only why would we want to do it? I took him swimming in the lake, and he understood at once.

(12–13–4–21.6)

Are you ready to leave this planet? Samuel asked me this morning, wiping the sweat from his stubbled chin with a bronzed palm. If you aren't ready, Isak, I suggest that you conduct a thorough evaluation of your emotional attachments to this planet. We're not going to stay here forever.

I replied that, of course, I knew that. We had only been here for five months. We spent that much time on Antares four, and isn't this a much finer place?

He nodded like a bloated camel. You are a poet, he said. This planet is one hell of a paradise for you. I've seen you pour out energies on this planet until surely you must run dry. And yet, you don't. I'm amazed at the way you're extending yourself. And Joshua, too. But the rest of us are ready to explore again. We live in a starship, Isak. I don't think you should forget that.

Are you sure you speak for everyone? I asked.

I'm not trying to, Isak. Talk to them yourself. They'll tell you. If you'd been in the shipnest for more than a few running minutes at any time during the past two months, you'd already know.

Samuel was right. I should have known that he wouldn't have spoken about it if he wasn't certain. I keep forgetting that he isn't like me.

(12–14–4–23.1)

This was our last day on the planet of the seer. We swam in the lake and ate from the vines, as we've done so many other fine days. We relaxed on the trampoline and read aloud to each other from the literature of the last years of this galaxy before the return to separateness. Then Joshua and I kissed the seer and left. He's almost five years now. And he was ready to go.

(12–15–4–23.1)

This night we watched a war on a nearby planet. With our screens set at top power, we could see everything. A mole on a soldier's chin, split by a needle arrow. A mad soldier shooting at shadows. Twenty soldiers on their bellies by a slow-moving creek, poisoned. We watched one soldier run for hours to carry secrets to the other side, sinking ever lower toward the trail as his minutes blurred into a skeleton of fatigue. When he finally crawled into a clearing that was his destination, the guards wanted to shoot him. But he talked fast, and they dragged him to the porch of the general's house. They made him lie down with his face flat against the boards, hands tied behind his neck, while they looked around for an officer.

This part will probably take a long while, Sam commented from behind me. From the looks of their uniforms and what that implies about the psychology of their organization, these guards will undoubtedly have to go through channels to get any attention from a general. And that takes time. These damned organizations, Isak. Bureaucracies. They rule the earthnest still, you know. Years and years after everyone has agreed on their obsolescence. They just don't know how to escape from them. And I don't know how anyone puts up with their incompetence. But of course, it's all in the training. If we'd been planet-bound, we'd do it, too. Gladly, I bet.

Later, I watched the traitor face the enemy general. They clasped each other by the shoulders and kissed each other's cheeks. I was the only one watching them.

(12–16–4–23.1)

It's a good thing that MASCOM keeps a record of us in conjunction with mine. Otherwise there'd be months missing all over the place. I wonder if that might not be good. Missing months to give whoever reads this record an object of fantasy. Fill in the missing months—

(12–17–4–23.1)

I went spacewalking today for the first time in many months. Into the suit and out through the triple locks. I had forgotten so much of it. It's very nice. You're at the top, you're at the bottom, you're everywhere in the universe and here. And you can remember to know how it felt. You can take a memory back inside with you.

"We are on the outside of things here, because here there is no inside."

This is the message I found revealed during my spacewalk. It was flashing ahead of me, and I had to lunge, almost out of control, to catch it. I'm keeping a collection of these revelations. Someday I hope to piece them all together into one good joke.

(12–18–4–23.2)

Micah believed in one lord. It's all over his record. One god who wasn't in the universe but was beyond it. A god who spoke to those who believed in him. That's reassuring. One of my parents brings me blindness and the other, deism. I wonder how he couldn't feel that holiness is in everything, that every-thing profane in the universe is everything sacred.

(12–19–4–23.1)

I answered Joshua this morning. I told him that we had come from water. Always running out into symbols when we can get away with it.

(12–24–4–22.3)

"I almost set my house on fire last night."

"They always show the same ones on Christmas Eve."

"I hear me every night, and he sounds the same."

"There was blood on my sheets this morning when I woke up so I knew I was gonna cut myself soon."

"The name's Billy. Griddle up on four."

"Annie was a baby in my swing, a roll of fat, her mother gave her a nipple, sweet core and warm milk in one, you can run and you can run, but you ain't never gonna make it."

"Once upon a time, there were three fish in a pan, outside time was the rule."

These are the kinds of communications we've been receiving from the earthnest for four days now, never experiential, always verbal. And the communication is only in our direction. They come down into our heads with a line or two, direct hit, and then they break off. We have no real conception of what might be going on there. Only a few guesses. Sam and Alex spent a whole day trying to squeeze some data from an analysis of the "Annie" message. That's the longest one so far. They ran it through every model bank they could fox MASCOM into drawing up, every semantic drill and every behaviorial schematic. But there was absolutely nothing they could make of it.

Maybe they're involved in some sort of global process of ego disintegration, Sam suggested when we gathered in meeting to talk about our alternatives.

Who could be doing it? Louisa asked. If it were being engineered, then don't you think that someone would have to keep an old consciousness to run the show? We should be able to communicate with him. Or them.

They might be shielded from us, Sam replied. Or it might be mechanized, if that could be done. It all seems so wild. I've kept an ear on developments in the earthnest, and no one's been talking about anything like this, no one that I had any access to at least. And why would anyone want to do it? No, sisters and brothers, it's got to be a natural process, an evolutionary step. I can't think of anything else that would explain the data that we've received from the earthnest other than an actualization of the old childhood's end myth. It was a prophecy, too, you know. A prophecy of complete breakdown involving all the mental processes that we know about in the organism. A crumbling in totality. A universal species psychosis.

But in the prophecy, wasn't the breakdown followed by the emergence of a new consciousness?

Yes, it is. A higher consciousness, Sam replied gravely. In the prophecy—But prophecy always deals in rebirth—

The unspoken question spread through everyone's head. Does reality do the same? There was small talk of going back to the earthnest to find out. Brave words on the fringe, dimmer lights and hotter air. We're so much into our own life. Are we afraid the psychosis might touch us?

(12–26–4–23.1)
It's passed now. No more communication. We're staying out here.

(12–29–4–23.1)
I look at Joshua and I see that he is learning to understand what he can do now. Look into the darkness and feel safe and alone.

(12–31–4–23.9)
The end of the year. Nothing.

(1–25–5AF–23.1)
Louisa has been talking about looking for a good planet to settle down on. She knows how to start the necessary search, but she wants help.

How long are we going to go on like this? she asks, circling her hands like equal gears. I want to try a simpler life, she tells us. I don't want to be an explorer forever. Sometimes even explorers ought to stop in a good place and make something from their own lives that they're never going to find. We wouldn't be tied to that planet. We wouldn't lose the shipnest. We could gain so much—She stares at each of us one by one, trying to pour out her feelings into ours.

I want to be where there's life in a free environment, she goes on. Where plants and animals don't have to stay in tanks and cages and starships in order to survive. I know that you can all say that I'm making an irrelevant distinction. Life belongs wherever it can go and survive, you'll say. According to the logic we've all been programmed to use, that's right. But I'm sick of that logic. It's becoming more and more destructive to everything that I feel is good.

Joshua took me aside after dinner and asked me why Louisa was so upset. He's very close to her. He's close to everyone in the nest.

She wants to live on a planet for a while, I told him. She's tired of living in a starship.

Why, Papa?

I think she's beginning to feel separated here from what she feels she really is. She feels we're just wandering around the universe, because we've got nowhere to go, where we really want to go and be. I'm almost ready to agree with her. What do you think about it, Joshua?

Oh, I like it here, Papa.

(1–26–5–23.1)

Man can be whatever he can make himself to be, Sri Aurora wrote. Everything is natural in possibility. Any way that man can change himself can be good. Anything can happen. Evolution will not stop. Everything man does is evolutionary. It must be so be it.

Micah accepted the Aurora credo as the one human document that made perfect sense. So did Edward. Aurora's truth was poured into me like the flood of a cloudburst overwhelming a dry gulley in the heart of the desert. Now I don't know about the burden of those waters. The credo doesn't feel so good here.

It leaks pride. And I do know that I feel with Louisa.

Maybe this case only involves us as individuals. Reacting. There may be no general human concerns at stake here. But there always are. Edward said that. You can't ever escape them. Nobody understands that here.

(2–14–5–15.3)

Sometimes I slip into a deep trance state, trying to feel what blindness will be like.

(2–26–5–4.7)

Today will be a day of celebration. I refuse to be a part of it. It's not a right feeling—

(3–9–5–5.2)

I ramble around and do nothing. I don't even keep much of a record. And they all look at me—

(3–19–5–13.2)

The winds are coming back—Now I'm beginning to understand about those months last year, between 3 and 6—The winds will bring me the truth—

(3–21–5–12.3)

All the winds. I'm here. The spirit of Antares deep inside my head. I know it's been there all this time, waiting to come out when—The spirit wants me to—Damn. Louisa's here, down the way. She's looking at me. Staring. Now she's screaming for Miriam. I'm not going to let her—

(3–21–5–23.1)

Samuel, closing the record of Isak.

Placed Isak into condition 2589S, suspended metabolism, 16.5.

Authority: consensus of meeting, no alternative.

Precipitation: threatened safety of others, again, 12.4.

Case record: first manifestation of psychotic behavior in claimed communication with "spirit of Antares," 7–15–3, 7–

17–3, 7–18–3; recurrent dysfunction, refused to leave Antares four until 1–3–4, refused treatment; recurrent dysfunction 8–3 through 3–4; breakdown into violent antisocial behavior, 3–28–4; probe treatment, authorized by consensus of meeting; return to consciousness with 96 percent successful implanted memory, 6–22–4; continued follow-up verbal therapy 6–4 through 12–4; apparent satisfactory recovery, 12–1–4 (projected satisfactory recovery date, 100 percent accurate); signs of relapse, 12–30–4, 1–25–5; insistent refusal of treatment, does not work; meeting refuses authority for probe, 2–14–5; breakdown imminent, 3–6–5; meeting again refuses authority for probe, 3–9–5; breakdown, 3–21–5–12.4

Prognosis: suspended state will be maintained until corrective treatment designed.

Role: record to be kept by Joshua.

PHILIP JOSÉ FARMER, *of course, is the brilliant and ferociously original writer whose work has been delighting and/or infuriating science-fictionists since the dazzling novella "The Lovers" appeared in 1952. He has collected an assortment of trophies along the way for such remarkable works as his "Riverworld" books and his controversial novella "Riders of the Purple Wage" and has won a reputation for scholarship as well with his biographical studies of such mythic figures as Tarzan and Doc Savage. This is only his second appearance in* New Dimensions; *would he were seen here more often.*

What little we know of LEO QUEEQUEG TINCROWDOR *comes from Farmer, his collaborator and friend, who informs us that Tincrowdor was born in 1918 in New Goshen, Indiana, but spent most of his childhood and early youth abroad. His father, a civil and electrical engineer, built power plants and dams in such places as Easter Island, Brazil, Egypt, Mozambique, India, Siberia, Alaska, and Arizona. His mother, a schoolteacher, tutored him during these travels. His father was an aficionado of Melville, which accounts for his son's middle name. Tincrowdor teaches painting and the history of art at a university and produces about thirty paintings a year, most of which he sells at high prices. These are based on a theory which he calls the "Tollhouse Effect" but which he admits is probably invalid. While lecturing on art in Peoria, Illinois, he became a friend of Farmer. Farmer was so intrigued by him that he put him, with his permission, in a science-fiction story. This is a series titled* Stations of the Nightmare. *The first of its four parts appeared April 1974 in* Continuum 1, *published by Putnam and edited by Roger Elwood.*

■

Philip José Farmer and
Leo Queequeg Tincrowdor
∎

OSIRIS ON CRUTCHES

I

Set, a god of the ancient land of Egypt, was the first critic. Once he had been a creator, but the people ceased to believe in his creativity. He then suffered a divinity block, which is similar to a writer's block.

This is a sad fate for a deity. Odin and Thor, once cosmic creators, became devils—that is, critics—in the new religion which killed off their old religion. Satan, or Lucifer, was an archangel in the Book of Job, but he became the chief of demons, the head-honcho critic, in the New Testament. The Great Goddess of the very ancient Mediterranean regions, named Cybele, Anana, Demeter, depending on where she lived, became a demon, Lilith, for instance, or, in one case, the Mother of God (and who criticizes more than a mother?). But she had to do that via the back door, and most people that pray to her don't know that she was not always called Mary. Of course, there are scholars who deny this, just as there are scholars who deny the existence of the Creator.

Those were the days. Gods walked the earth then. They weren't invisible or absent as they are nowadays. A man or a woman could speak directly to them. They might get only a divine fart in their faces, but if the god felt like talking, the human had a once-in-a-lifetime experience.

Nowadays, you can only get into contact with a god by prayer. This is like sending a telegram which the messenger boy may or may not deliver. And there is seldom a reply by wire, letter, or phone.

In the dawn of mankind, the big gods in Egypt were Osiris, Isis, Nephthys, and Set. They were brothers and sisters, and Osiris was married to Isis and Set was married to Nephthys. Everybody then thought that incest was natural, especially if it took place among the gods.

In any event, no human was dumb enough to protest against the incest. If the gods missed you with their lightning or plagues, the priests got you with their sacrificial knives.

People had no trouble at all seeing the gods, though they might have to be quick about it. The peasants standing in mud mixed with ox manure and the pharaohs standing on their palace porches could see the four great gods, along with Osiris' vizier, Thoth, and Anubis, as they whizzed by. These traveled like the wind or the Roadrunner zooming through the Coyote's traps. Their figures were blurred with speed, dust was their trail, the screaming of split air their only sound.

From dawn to dusk they raced along, blessing the land and all on and in it.

However, the gods noticed a peculiar thing when they roared by a field just north of Abydos. A man always sat in the field, and his back was always turned to them. Sometimes they would speed around to look at his face. But when they did, they still found themselves looking at his back. And if one god went north and one south and one east and one west, four boxing the man in, all four could still see only his back.

"There is One greater than even us," they told each other. "Do you suppose that She, or He, as the case might be, put him there? Or perhaps that is even Him or Her?"

"You mean 'He or She,'" Set said. Even then he was potentially a critic.

After a while they quit staying up nights wondering who the man was and why they couldn't see his face and who put him there. But he was never entirely out of their minds at any time.

There is nothing that bugs an omniscient like not knowing something.

II

Set stopped creating and became a nasty, nay-saying critic because the people stopped believing in him. Gods have vast powers and often use them with no consideration for the feelings or wishes of humans. But every god has a weakness against which he or she or it is helpless. If the humans decide he is an evil god, or a weak god, or a dying god, then he becomes evil or weak or dead. Too bad, Odin! Rotten luck, Zeus! Tough shit, Quetzalcoatl! Trail's end, Gitche Manitou!

But Set was a fighter. He was also treacherous, though he can't be blamed for that since the humans had decided that he was no good. He planned some unexpected events for Osiris at the big festival in Memphis honoring Osiris' return from a triumphant world tour, SRO. He planned to shortsheet his elder brother, Osiris, in a big way. From our viewpoint, our six-thousand-year perspective, Set may have had good reason. His sister-wife, Nephthys, was unable to conceive by him and, worse, she lusted after Osiris. Osiris resisted her, though not without getting red in the face and elsewhere.

This was not easy, since Osiris' flesh was green. Which has led some moderns to speculate that he may have come in a flying saucer from Mars. But his flesh was green because that's the color of living plants, and he was the god of agriculture. Among other things.

Nephthys overcame his moral scruples by getting him drunk. (This was the same method used by Lot's daughters many thousands of years later.) The result of this illicit rolling in the reeds was Anubis. Anubis, like a modern immortal, was a "funny-looking kid," and for much the same reason. He had the head of a jackal. This was because jackals ate the dead, and Anubis was the conductor, the ticket-puncher, for the souls who rode into the afterlife.

Bighearted Isis found the baby Anubis in the bulrushes, and she raised him as her own, though she knew very well who the parents were.

Osiris strode into Memphis. He was happy because he had just finished touring the world and teaching non-Egyptians all about peace and nonviolence. The world has never been in such good shape as then and, alas, never will be again. Set smiled widely and spread his arms to embrace Osiris. Osiris should have been wary. Set, as a babe, had torn himself prematurely and violently from his mother's womb, tearing her also. He was rough and wild, white-skinned and red-haired. He was a wild ass of a man.

Isis sat on her throne. She was radiant with happiness. Osiris had been gone for a long time, and she missed him. During his absence, Set had been sidling up to her and asking her if she wanted to get revenge on her husband for his adulterous fling with Nephthys. Isis had told him to beat it. But, truth to tell, she was wondering how long she could have held out. Gods and goddesses are hornier than mere humans, and you know how horny they are.

Isis, however, had to wait. Set gave a banquet that would have turned Cecil B. De Mille green with envy. When everyone ached from stuffing himself, and belches were exploding like rockets over Fort Henry, Set clapped his hands. Four large, but minor, gods staggered in. Among them they bore a marvelously worked coffer. They set it down, and Osiris said, "What is that exquisite *objet d'art,* brother?"

"It's a gift for whomever can fit himself into it exactly," Set said. Anybody else would have said "whoever," but Set was far more concerned with form than content.

To start things off, Set tried to get into the coffer. He was too tall, as he knew he'd be. His seventy-two accomplices in the conspiracy—Set was wicked but he was no piker—were too short. Isis didn't even try. Then Osiris, swaying a little from the gallons of wine he'd drunk, said, "If the coffer fits, wear it." Everybody laughed, and he climbed into the coffer and stretched out. The top of his head just touched the head of the coffer, and the soles of his feet just touched its foot.

Osiris smiled, though not for long. The conspirators slammed the lid down on his face and nailed it down. Set laughed; Isis screamed. The people ran away in panic. Paying no attention to the drumming on the lid from within the coffer, the accomplices rushed the coffer down to the Nile. There they threw it in, and the current carried it seaward.

III

Some gods need air. Others are anaerobic. In those days, they all needed it, though they could live much longer without air than a human could. But it was a long journey down the Nile and across the sea to Byblos, Phoenicia. By the time it grounded on the beach there, Osiris was dead.

Set held Isis prisoner for some time. But Nephthys, who loathed Set now, joined Anubis and Thoth in freeing her. Isis journeyed to Byblos and brought the body back, probably by oxcart, since camels were not yet used. She hid the body in the swamps of a place called Buto. As evil luck would have it, Set was traveling through the swamp, and he fell over the coffer.

His face, when he saw his detested brother's corpse, went through the changes of wood on fire. It became black like wood before the match is applied, then red like flames, then pale like ashes. He tore the corpse into fourteen parts, and he scattered the pieces over the land. He was the destroyer, the spreader of perversity, the venomous nay-sayer.

Isis roamed Egypt looking for Osiris' parts. Tradition has it that she found everything but the phallus. This was supposed to have been eaten by a Nile crab, which is why Nile crabs are forever cursed. But this, like all myths, legends, and traditions, is based on oral material that is inevitably distorted through the ages.

The truth is the crab *had* eaten the genitals. But Isis forced it to disgorge. One testicle was gone, alas. But we know that the myth did not state the truth or at least not all of it. The myth also states that Isis became pregnant with a part of Osiris' body. It doesn't say what part, being vague for some reason. This reason is not delicacy. Ancient myths, in their unbowdlerized forms, were never delicate.

Isis used the phallus to conceive. Presently Horus was born.

When he grew up he helped his mother in the search. This took a long time. But they found the head in a mud flat abounding in frogs, the heart on top of a tree, and the intestines being used as an ox whip by a peasant. It was a real mess.

Moreover, Osiris' brain was studded with frog eggs. Every once in a while a frog was hatched. This caused Osiris to have some peculiar thoughts, which led to peculiar behavior. However, if you are a god, or an Englishman, you can get away with eccentricity.

One of the thoughts kicked off by the hatching of a frog egg was the idea of the pyramid. Osiris told a pharaoh about it. The pharaoh asked him what it was good for. Osiris, always the poet, replied that it was a suppository for eternity.

This was true. But he forgot in his poet's enthusiasm his cold scientist's cold regard for cold facts. Eternity has body heat. Everything is slowly oxidizing. The earth and all on it are wrapped in flames if one only has eyes to see them. And so the pyramids, solid though they are, are burning away, falling to pieces. So much for the substantiality of stone.

Meanwhile, Isis and Horus found all of Osiris' body except for a leg and the nose. These seemed lost forever. So she did the best she could. She attached Osiris' phallus to his nose hole.

"After all," she said to Horus and Thoth, "he can wear a kilt to cover his lack of genitals. But he looks like hell without a nose of any kind."

Thoth, the god of writing, and hence also of the short memory, wasn't so sure. He had the head of an ibis, which was a bird with a very long beak. When Osiris was sexually aroused, he looked too much like Thoth. On the other hand, when Osiris wasn't aroused, he looked like an elephant. Usually, he was aroused. This was because the other gods left him in their dust while he hobbled along on his crutch. But Isis wasn't watching him, and so he dallied with the maidens, and some of the matrons, of the villages and cities along the Nile.

Humans being what they are, the priests soon had him on a schedule which combined the two great loves of mankind: money and sex. He would arrive at 11:45 A.M. at, say, Giza. At 12:00, after the tickets had been collected, he would become the central participant in a fertility rite. At 1:00 the high priest would blow the whistle. Osiris would pick up his crutch and hobble on to the next stop, which was, literally, a whistle stop. The maidens would pick themselves up off the ground and hobble home. Everybody else went back to work.

Osiris met a lot of girls this way, but he had trouble remembering their faces. Just as well. Humans age so fast. He never noticed that the crop of maidens of ten years ago had become careworn, workworn hags. Life was hard then. It was labor before dawn to past dusk, malaria, bilharzia, piles, too much starch and not enough meat and fruit, and, for the women, one pregnancy after another, teeth falling out, belly and breasts sagging, and varicose veins wrapping the legs and the buttocks like sucker vines.

Humans attributed all their ills, of course, to Set. He, they said, was a mean son of a bitch, and when he whirled by, accompanied by tornados, sandstorms, hyenas, and wild asses bearing leaky baskets of bullcrap, life got worse.

They prayed to Osiris and Isis and Horus to get rid of the primal critic, the basic despoiler. And it happened that Horus did kill him off.

Here's the funny thing about this. Though Set was dead, life for the humans did not get one whit better.

IV

After a few thousand years people caught on to this. They started to quit believing in the ancient Egyptian gods, and so these dwindled away. But the dwindling took time.

Female deities, for some reason, last longer than the males. Isis was worshiped into the sixth century A.D., and when her last temple was closed down, she managed to slip into the Christian church under a pseudonym. Perhaps this is because men and women are very close to their mothers, and Isis was a really big mother.

Osiris, during his wanderings up and down along the Nile, noticed that humans had one method of defeating time. That was art. A man could fix a moment in time forever with a carving or a sculpture or a painting or a poem or a song. The individual passed, nations passed, races passed, but art survived. At least for a while. Nothing is eternal except eternity itself, and even the gods suddenly find that oxidation has burned them down to a crisp.

This is partly because religion is also an art form. And religion, like other art forms, changes with the times.

Osiris knew this, though he hated to admit it to himself. One day, early in the first century A.D., he saw once more the man whose back was always turned to him. This man had been sitting there for about six thousand years or perhaps for much longer. Maybe he was left over from the Old Stone Age.

Osiris decided he'd try once more. He hobbled around on his crutch, circling on the man's left. And then he got a strange burning feeling. The man's face was coming into view.

Straight ahead of the man was what the man's body had concealed. An oblong of blackness the size of a door in a small house lay flat on the earth's surface.

"This is the beginning of the end," Osiris whispered to himself. "I don't know why it is, but I can feel it."

"Greetings, first of the crippled gods, predecessor of Hephaestos and Wieland," the man said. "Ave, first of the gods to be torn apart and then put together again, predecessor of Frey and Lemminkäinen. Hail, first of the good gods to die, basic model for those to come, for Baldur and Jesus."

"You don't look like you belong here," Osiris said. "You look like you come from a different time."

"I'm from the twentieth century, which may be the next-to-last century for man or perhaps the last," the man said. "I know what you're thinking, that religion is a form of art. Well, life itself is an art, though most people are imitative artists when it comes to living, painters of the same old paintings over and over again. There are very few originators. Life is a mass art, or usually the art of the masses. And the art of the masses is, unfortunately, bad art. Though often entertaining," he added hastily, as if he feared that Osiris would think he was a snob.

"Who are you?" Osiris said.

"I am Leo Queequeg Tincrowdor," the man said. "Tincrow-dor, like Rembrandt, puts himself in his paintings. Any artist worth his salt does. But since I am not worthy to hand Rembrandt a roll of toilet paper, I always paint my back to the viewer. When I become as good as the old Dutchman, I'll show my face in the mob scenes."

"Are you telling me that you have created me? And all this, too?" Osiris said. He waved a green hand at the blue river and the pale green and brown fields and the brown and red sands and rocks beyond the fields.

"Every human being knows he created the world when he somehow created himself into being," Tincrowdor said. "But only the artist re-creates the world. Which is why you have had to go through so many millennia with a phallus for a nose and a crutch for a leg."

"I didn't mind the misplaced phallus," Osiris said. "I can't smell with it, you know, and that is a great benefit, a vast advantage. The world really *stinks,* Tincrowdor. But with this organ up here, I could no longer smell it. So thanks a lot."

"You're welcome," the man said. "However, you've been around long enough. People have caught on now to the fact that even gods can be crippled. And that crippled gods are symbols of humans and their plight. Humans, you know, are crippled in one way or another. All use crutches, physical or psychical."

"Tell me something new," Osiris said, sneering.

"It's an old observation that will always be new. It's always new because people just don't believe it until it's too late to throw the crutch away."

Osiris then noticed the paintings half buried in the khaki-, or kaka-, colored dust. He picked them up, blew off the dust, and looked at them. The deepest buried, and so obviously the earliest, looked very primitive. Not Paleolithic but Neolithic. They were stiff, geometrical, awkward, crude, and in garish unnatural colors. In them was Osiris himself and the other deities, two-dimensional, as massive and static as pyramids and hence solid, lacking interior space for interior life. The paintings also had no perspective.

"You didn't know that the world, and hence you, was two-dimensional then, did you?" Tincrowdor said. "Don't feel bad about that. Fish don't know they live in water just as humans don't know a state of grace surrounds them. The difference is, the fish are already in the water, whereas humans have to swim through nongrace to get to the grace."

Osiris looked at the next batch of paintings. Now he was three-dimensional, fluid, graceful, natural in form and color, no longer a stereotype but an individual. And the valley of the Nile had true perspective.

But in the next batch the perspective was lost and he was two-dimensional again. However, somehow, he seemed supported by and integrated with the universe, a feature lacking in the previous batch. But he had lost his individuality again. To compensate for the loss, a divine light shone through him like light through a stained-glass window.

The next set returned to perspective, to three dimensions, to warm natural colors, to individuality. But, quickly in a bewildering number and diversity, the Nile and he became an abstraction, a cube, a distorted wild beast, a nightmare, a countless number of points confined within a line, a moebius strip, a shower of fragments.

Osiris dropped them back into the dust, and he bent over to look into the oblong of blackness.

"What is that?" he said, though he knew.

"It is," Tincrowdor said, "the inevitable, though not necessarily desired, end of the evolution you saw portrayed in the paintings. It is my final painting. The achievement of pure and perfect harmony. It is nothingness."

Tincrowdor lifted a crutch from the dust which had concealed it all these thousands of years. He did not really need it, but he did not want to admit this to himself. Not yet, anyway —someday, maybe.

Using it as a pole up which to climb, he got to his feet. And, supporting himself on it, he booted the god in the rear. And Osiris fell down and through. Since nothingness is an incomplete equation, Osiris quickly became the other part of the equation—that is, nothing. He was glad. There is nothing worse than being an archetype, a symbol, and somebody else's creation. Unless it's being a cripple when you don't have to be.

Tincrowdor hobbled back to this century. Nobody noticed the crutch—except for some children and some very old people —just as nobody notices a telephone pole until he runs into it. Or a state of grace until it hits him.

As for his peculiarity of behavior and thought—call it eccentricity or originality—this was attributed by everybody to frog eggs hatching in his brain.

EFFINGER *again, with an odd and sinister fable that is not quite as cuddly and Disneyesque as the first few sentences might lead one to believe.*

■

CHASE OUR BLUES AWAY

Wacky Mouse had a deeply ingrained sense of responsibility. He was intense, sincere, and sensitive, but that proved to be not enough. Wacky Mouse loved us, but he couldn't help us when we needed him most, and so he's gone. Our street is quiet now, no one roaming up the block from Lake Shore Boulevard to Westropp, drawing us laughing from our homes with accordion music. We sit in our living rooms and think, wishing that Wacky Mouse would come back. We know that he never will, that both he and we ruined that. There is nothing left now for us to share but arguments; he failed, and so he couldn't stay among us.

Wacky Mouse used to come to us every summer for as long as I can remember. No one on the street can recall a year when he didn't visit, and those recollections go back well before the Depression. So we knew that Wacky Mouse himself was very old (if, in fact, it was always the same Wacky Mouse every year. Some people have suggested that this wasn't so. I don't remember any clue that there might have been more than one). He was short; I remember that he didn't stand as high as my waist even when I was in elementary school, so Wacky Mouse must have been less than two feet tall. He was made in the style of his contemporaries: Mickey, Mighty, Ignatz. He wore tight blue shorts and a thin gray shirt or sweater. He didn't have hands, exactly. Like Mickey, he had four fingers clothed in what appeared to be white gloves but which were actually unremovable. He walked on tan ellipsoids that were more foot than shoe. His head was thin and pointed, accentuating the rodent association. His eyes were 1930s style, black ovals with wedges of white intruding along the lower left side of each. He had a nose like a black Ping-Pong ball and huge, stiff black ears.

Wacky Mouse used to sit with us against the backstop in the schoolyard. The backstop was old, too, made out of wood and covered with peeling green paint. Wacky Mouse told us about before they built the backstop, when boys and girls playing kickball would let the volleyball roll past them all sometimes and into 149th Street. Of course, if Wacky Mouse were there it had to be summer vacation, and no crossing guard could get the ball for them. Wacky Mouse would do it, skipping across the sidewalk, leaping the tree lawn, somersaulting over the red brick street, coming to a stop where the ball rested against the opposite curb. He would do tricks, like pretending that the ball was stuck fast to the ground, or "accidentally" kicking it out of reach every time he stooped to pick it up. We would watch and laugh until it hurt, but whoever was on base would make up a rule about stealing while the ball wasn't on the pitcher's mound, and if we wanted to stop him we could appoint our own catcher. The bickering would grow until no one was watching Wacky Mouse any more. He would pick up the ball sadly, knowing how kids were, and he'd walk back and tell us that we had agreed before that there would be no base stealing. Usually the kid on base would get mad and quit. Sometimes that was me.

Wacky Mouse was the sort of person that you could tell your problems to. He listened to all of us, no matter how old we were. When we had fights about paying the penalties in Monopoly, he taught us to put it all in a pool for the first player to land on *Free Parking*. When we were older he helped us through first-year French, his squeaky voice doing horrible things to the diphthongs. He advised us about baseball, cars, and teenage drinking. About girls he told us, chuckling, "Just wait a while." He'd have gladly helped our parents with their problems, too, but the adults on the street didn't trust him. I asked my mother to invite him to supper once when I was about eight years old. The affair was ghastly; Wacky Mouse's tiny body was lost in his chair as we sat at the table. He tried to talk with my father, but Dad just stared at his plate in embarrassment. My mother left the table at every opportunity, to "check on things" in the kitchen. At last Wacky Mouse tried to save the evening by doing his famous milk bit, urging me to drink plenty of it just as he did. He held his white-fingered hand out and said "Heeeere it *comes!*" just the way he does in all of his cartoons, but no glass of milk appeared. About seven-thirty my father told him that I had to go to bed, which wasn't true. Dad shook hands with Wacky Mouse at the door and gravely told him to come back again. Wacky Mouse never did. I suppose he had dinner with every family on the block; it must have gone the same in the rest of the homes, too, because we never talked about it.

Isn't it a shame the way our silly lives change? You hear often enough someone bemoaning the loss of the childlike innocence or whatever, but that's not quite it. The friends I had back then weren't so unblemished. The only thing that I have lost in getting older is my youth. The feeling that, if not tomorrow, then as well next week. No deadlines of any importance, and all of forever to go before we had to be home. Wacky Mouse, where are you now? A wetbrain in one of the closet-sized rooms of the Greenwich Hotel? How do you hide that famous two-foot mouse figure, sitting in Nedick's dunking doughnuts?

Wacky Mouse came close to personifying the *Zeitgeist* of 147th Street. No one ever moved out of a house on 147th Street between Westropp and the Boulevard. Even though Wacky Mouse caused the adults great concern when he appeared during the summer months, he held them together with a special sense of magic that no one could want to lose. Wacky Mouse, though available to everyone all year long on the screen at the Commodore, was peculiarly *ours*. We shared in this special favor, children and adults, and although we never discussed it with our parents I know that they, too, had the same warm feeling of belonging. There was a clannishness among the children from 147th Street that no one else—bully, parent, or teacher—could compete with. For years we matured in a private realm of security.

Wacky Mouse grew to be more than a familiar cartoon character and then more than just a friend. Thinking about it now, years later, I can see that Wacky Mouse was the sort of myth figure so important to young children. He was our own Br'er

Rabbit or Mister Toad. But beyond that he fulfilled the proto-religious longings we all felt as our awareness of the scope of life grew.

We spent a good deal of time trying to decide exactly what part Wacky Mouse played in our lives. The clearest example of this that I can recall happened when I was in sixth grade, eleven years old. Bobby Hanson, my best friend, and I were walking through the school's garden. We stopped by the goldfish pond, as we did every afternoon after school. Sure enough, in a little while we heard the plop of a frog jumping into the water. We both smiled.

"I have a poem," said Bobby.

"Really?" I said.

"Yes, a haiku. 'How many splashes/of Basho's frog have you heard?/Are you still asleep?' "

"That's pretty," I said. "Who's Basho?"

"A friend of Wacky Mouse," said Bobby. "Wacky Mouse told me about him last summer."

"I think Wacky Mouse would like the poem. Are you going to tell it to him next summer?"

"Sure," said Bobby, "if I still remember it."

We talked about our cartoon friend for a while as we watched the goldfish swimming in the pool. Bobby said that he thought Wacky Mouse was much more complex than we realized.

"Sometimes Wacky Mouse seems to me to be a manifestation of Will," said Bobby. "Pure *Idea,* in a form that we can relate to without fear but with respect."

"Like a burning bush," I said.

"Right. If Wacky Mouse had come to us as another kid, we'd never listen to him."

"But as Will he'd be incomplete. Mere will isn't enough to effect itself on the physical plane."

"That's true. And Wacky Mouse is unusually successful in his teaching. So apart from the essentially creative but powerless aspect he has a subsidiary self that carries out that will. This is the Wacky Mouse most familiar to us, because he must thoroughly understand our motivations in order to encourage us along the lines he thinks best."

"So we have two Wacky Mice," I said, laughing, "and nobody else even has one."

"No," said Bobby quietly, "I think we have three."

"What is the other one?"

"This is purely subjective, you understand," said Bobby, staring across the garden toward the playground, "but I feel that there is a third part of his personality that communicates the humanized Agent's conception of the Will's desire. Just as the Agent takes the purely abstract *thought* from the Will and makes it concrete, this third Function must take that concretization and make it human, tailoring it for each of us individually."

"That sounds like a suspiciously metaphysical process," I said doubtfully.

"There's no way of proving it, but there must be an interceding factor."

"The Dove Descending," I said. Bobby grinned at my understanding.

This is the way we all theorized about Wacky Mouse's purpose and origin. Of course, we were much too shy to ask him directly, but I feel certain that he was aware of our questions and secretly pleased. Sometimes he would catch one of us staring at him wonderingly, and he would laugh and take us all to the School Store to buy us milk.

This is how we thought of Wacky Mouse in the days of our artlessness. Those warm moments couldn't last forever, of course; if we had a special shell of warmth, then we had a special difficulty in hatching into the adult world. After the failures that everyone accepts in maturing—beyond the failures of one's self, the failure of faith, of politics, of education—we were compelled to deal with Wacky Mouse's continued role in our individual lives. How were we to relate to him after the summer sandbox days?

One afternoon in August a couple of years after my discussion with Bobby Hanson I was playing softball in the playground. I was sitting against the backstop waiting for my turn to bat. For some reason I was paying little attention to the game; instead, I was watching some primary kids on the swings all the way across the schoolyard and some of the first-semester sixth-graders playing First Bounce or Fly against the red brick wall of the school. When the kid before me in the line-up struck out, however, I didn't need to be called. As I walked to the plate Wacky Mouse put his arm around me. It was thin and uncomfortably bristled as it circled my legs behind my knees. I bent down to hear his whispered plan.

"Bunt," he said seriously. There were two out and the bases were loaded.

"Bunt?" I asked him. I wanted to hit a grand slam.

"Yes," he said, looking up and doing his Saturday-matinee smile (dissolve to: Continental Productions presents *Wacky Mouse* in . . .), "they sure won't be expecting it!"

I was disappointed, but I wouldn't argue. As I stood there beside home plate, before I shouldered the bat, I wished that I had a large glass of milk. I stared across the schoolyard. I saw that two big kids were trying to get the ball away from the sixth-graders playing First Bounce or Fly.

The first pitch bounced between the pitcher and the plate. I settled myself back in the batter's box, waving the bat tentatively toward the pitcher, pointing it out over center field where the big kids had taken the rubber ball from the sixth-graders. The big kids were throwing the ball high up on the school building. It came down too hard for the sixth-graders to catch and bounced too high for all but the two big kids. The sixth-graders stood around helplessly, shouting, "Hey, c'mon, give it back!"

I bunted the next pitch toward the pitcher, who grabbed the ball and tagged the runner from third, who was too confused to run. I didn't even go down to first base. I grabbed my glove from the girl who played right field and I took her place. As I trotted out I noticed that the two big kids had left the sixth-graders and were heading for our diamond. They walked between me and the kid playing center field. I felt cold with worry.

"Hey, we gonna play?" asked one of the big kids.

"There's two of us. One on each team," said the other.

"We gonna let these big kids play?" someone shouted.

"No," came the answer from several frightened kids.

"They're gonna take the ball away," said Bobby Hanson.

Wacky Mouse stood completely still. He didn't say anything; these kids were strangers. I figured that they came from the parochial school. Whenever we had any trouble with kids we didn't know, we assumed that they came from St. Jerome's. So far the big kids hadn't noticed Wacky Mouse. One of them went up to the girl who held the bat. He took it from her.

"Let us hit some, okay? We just want to hit a couple," he said.

"They're gonna take the bat away," said one of us.

"He's gonna hit the ball and we won't be able to find it," I said.

Wacky Mouse did a strange thing. He smiled his famous smile and, waving his arms and gesturing comically, he walked toward the big kid with the bat. The kid didn't see him yet, but the other one holding the softball on the pitcher's "mound" stared in amazement. Wacky Mouse got very close to the batter, then pantomimed slipping and falling on a banana peel. The big kid heard him and turned around. "Oh, my God," he whispered. Wacky Mouse was still clowning, looking for the imaginary banana peel and dusting himself off. He turned around and bent over. The big kid grinned and aimed a kick, just as Wacky Mouse intended. "Wacky Mouse, look out!" we all shouted.

The big kid looked bewildered. He hesitated. Wacky Mouse stood up straight and smiled. We knew what was coming. So did the big kids. Wacky Mouse looked around at all of us, and his expression made us all happy again. "Heeeere it *comes!*" we screamed with him. He held out his hand, but again no glass of milk appeared. The big kid laughed and swung the baseball bat at Wacky Mouse, hitting him across the chest and knocking him down.

We all gasped in horror. The big kids were frightened, too. They dropped the bat and ball and ran from the playground. We went to see about Wacky Mouse, but before we reached him he was up and dusting himself off again. He was doing somersaults and making funny faces, but we didn't laugh. He tried even harder to make us smile, but we couldn't anymore. We didn't blame Wacky Mouse for not chasing the big kids away. It wasn't that, exactly; we knew that it wasn't his job to guard us all the time. But suddenly we sensed that the real crises of life needed more than his simple approach. For a few more days we all showed up at the schoolyard, but it wasn't the same. The older ones of us stopped coming soonest, and in a short while everyone was avoiding the playground. Wacky Mouse was gone well before school began in September.

Wacky Mouse, dearest of memories, now that I'm out of college I'd like to meet you again sometime. Take you uptown for a drink. Buy you dinner and talk about what we've been doing. I always wanted to ask you what happened to that straw boater you used to wear in your earliest pictures, making you look like the rodents' Maurice Chevalier. Wacky Mouse, you know you made us glad. We laughed so hard our stomachs ached. We waited all year for the summer, when you'd come and we could forget about Miss Warren and the condors of Peru. Now it hurts to see your films at the Commodore. Come back, Wacky Mouse. The sun is always bright when you're in town.

This is another of those unsolicited and unexpected manuscripts from an unknown writer—but JAMES GIRARD *is no novice, as the depth and thoughtfulness of this exploration of the nature of synthetic human beings demonstrates. He lives in Kansas, where he majored in creative writing at college; he has a master's degree from the graduate writing seminars at Johns Hopkins University; he has worked toward doctorates in American studies and in anthropology without completing either. After four years as a newspaperman in Topeka, he has taken an editorial position at the University of Kansas while he works toward his long-term goal of a career as a writer, editor of fiction, or teacher of creative writing. He has had two stories accepted by* Kansas Quarterly *and one by* Fantasy & Science Fiction *and will, I expect, be seen again more than once in* New Dimensions.

■

James P. Girard

■

THE ALTERNATES

I

There came a morning, finally, when I found myself sitting at the edge of the beach, mumbling to Fred-1 about behavior analogues, as if he were my last friend, as if he were the person I'd hoped he would be by this time.

Actually, what I was sitting on was more cliff than beach, hanging a few feet over the water. Breakers reached high enough to slap my bare feet occasionally, and, out beyond the waves, now that the sky was light, I could see seabirds of indeterminate color worrying a school of fish. Over on the leeward side of the island were real cliffs and a real beach, but I liked the windward side because of the spray—which was exactly why the Alternates disliked it and why Fred-1, more familiarly known as Freddy the First, sat behind me, well away from the water's edge, in one of the little watertight cabanas that looked like outhouses.

The door was open, which meant that Freddy realized he was far enough away from the ocean not to need the cabana's protection, but it made him "feel better" to sit inside it: one of Scanlon's affective behavior analogues at work, simulating an instinctive fear of rust.

"Tell me about your sports and games," I shouted at him.

Freddy turned up his volume, which is not the same thing as

shouting, and said, "We have the rules and techniques of approximately ninety types of . . ."

"Why approximately?"

"There is some dispute about certain activities. Some argue that judged competitions such as figure skating and exhibitions of the body are not true sports. Others feel that such activities as professional wrestling and roller derby do not qualify."

"Yeah, okay. But you play some of them?"

"All that we can. Some aren't practical because of our physical characteristics; others we haven't the facilities for. But, for example, there is a Ping-Pong club in the village, and it issues regular schedules of matches, and even . . ."

"But why?"

"This provides a systematic way of insuring opposition for those who wish to play."

"I wish I knew if your obtuseness is programmed," I told him. "I mean, why bother to play games at all? What do you get out of them?"

"It feels good," Freddy said, somehow inflecting his inflectionless voice to give the impression he was shrugging his unshruggable shoulders. "I suppose we have been programmed to present a generally positive affective response to such activities."

I sat up, feeling a sour taste building in my throat, perhaps from lack of sleep, and said, "Even the most intricate analogous approximations of human behavior that Scanlon can fabricate remain only analogues and only approximate." It came out sounding like the rehearsed little speech that it was.

"You've said that before," Freddy pointed out. "And Dr. Scanlon agrees with you."

"Yes, of course. It doesn't discredit him to say it. After all, he's already done far more than was expected of him."

"We were speaking of sports," Freddy remarked in an attempt at tact but with the tactless result of reminding me how subtle and complex Scanlon's creations could be.

I climbed to my feet with some difficulty, thanks to the stiffness left from the long night, and stretched and said, "The real question is this: Why don't you invent some games of your own

—games appropriate for your own physical capabilities and the island's resources? And you will say that some of those we have given you are adequate but that, if we wish, you'll be glad to whip up some new ones, synthesizing all the rules and structures from the existing ones. But, you will add, unless we ask you don't have any particular interest in doing so."

"That's essentially correct," said Freddy. "I would have said that it wouldn't occur to us to do so unless you asked."

He looked rather like the offspring of a Las Vegas slot machine and a Hialeah flamingo, with his bulky body and spindly legs of bright pink—a bandit with two arms, both retractable. I spread my arms and walked toward him, asking, "But now? Now I've suggested the possibility. Now you've heard of such a thing. It's occurred to you. Now might you decide to invent a game especially for Alternates?"

He didn't even appear to think it over.

"No. That possibility evokes no response, either positive or negative."

I sighed and folded my arms.

"Okay. What are your rationales for your positive response to game-playing in general?"

"First, repeated reinforcement of physical and mental potentialities for dealing with analogous survival situations. Second, enrichment of certain types of interpersonal relationships. There are other rationales cited for human enjoyment of sports and games, especially in Saricks, 1982, which lists . . ."

"Spare me." I wondered if Scanlon realized he had made the Alternates somewhat sycophantic. Probably he'd done it on purpose; it made them very easy to get along with.

"Any new ideas?" I asked. This was the same as asking Freddy to solve my problem by demonstrating that it didn't exist, but I liked to try it every now and then, like a man who works hard for a living but keeps buying sweepstakes tickets.

"Not a new idea as you mean it but a suggestion."

"Suggest away."

"I have observed that the expression that something is lacking in the Alternates is in actuality merely a statement of our capabilities relative to humans. The concept of lack may be inappropriate since we possess, in fact, far more data and greater physical and cognitive capabilities than any human on this island. Therefore, it seems more proper to say that we are in fact too complete, relative to humans, or, to state it negatively, that there is some lack in humans which we do not share. It may be that this lack is instrumental in what you term 'creativity.' "

I nodded, said thank you and goodbye and walked past Freddy's cabana, down the white dust road that led to the human village.

I I

When I was growing up, they had what they called a war on poverty, partly on my behalf. I was what they called culturally deprived—which was nonsense: My culture was rich with music and drama, fullnesses of life and conflict pouring out of the speaker I held against my ear everywhere I went, to shut out the dullness my other senses showed me. The radio kept me up with my generation, kept me informed of the doings of the mythic figures of my age (Yankees, Celtics, Packers) and kept me filled with hints of personal possibilities that made me ache inside.

This was the part of life that was as real to me as the weather, and it was hard to see how to make a life out of it all, until—somewhere in a hazy college career, en route between English and psychology, with no money to speak of and a newly acquired wife—I took a second look at anthropology and discovered that it had a gaping hole in it, just at the point where I had something to fill a hole with.

If you want to know the details, you can buy my book, *The Gods of Olympus,* if you haven't already. That's right: Dr. Theodore Saricks, the man who claims baseball is our national religion. Or something. Actually, I was interested in getting traditional anthropology to grapple with a complex, heterogeneous culture—to get out of the laboratory of New Guinea and Lapland. It seemed obvious to me that cultures differ only

in size and complexity—not in function—and that students of
Western culture, in particular, should stop pretending that language and institutions hadn't evolved any since Durkheim.
Looking around, for starters, I asked myself: Do the churches
really have anything to do with religion? They surely seemed
to be lacking the pervasiveness, power and sheer ecstasy of
religious behavior among, say, the totemists. So I looked around
for something else that might be serving the fundamental religious functions—something like a massive reinforcement ritual,
perhaps, with myth re-enactment, sacred ground and objects,
ritualized spectator responses, a sacred calendar, and so on. And
there they were, all around: football, baseball, rock concerts,
symphonies—the things we call sports and arts, not really knowing what they are or what they do for us but just enjoying them.
And if you find something like that in a so-called primitive
society, where do you put it? That good old catchall category:
religion.

Anyway, that's the way it seemed to me, so I wrote a disserta-
tion with a long and precise title, and, the next thing you know,
a publisher had paid me a lot of money to retitle it and put it
in hardcover, and the next thing you know I had lots of money
for the first time in my life and was making the TV rounds, book
in hand. And, the next thing you know, I was talking to the
directors of Project Companion.

And all because of a few remarks in the introduction about
the possibilities for a robot culture. Not finding the kinds of
approaches that appealed to me in the traditional literature of
anthropology, I'd gotten pretty heavily into some fringe areas
like computer theory and ethology, and, somewhere along the
line, I'd decided we had the technology to build man (the cul-
ture-bearing animal, you know) from the ground up. The Project, funded by someone with a lot of money and the conviction
that man could only be saved by exposure to a form of "alternate intelligence" (they'd been putting a lot of dough into dolphins, for example), decided to take me up on my claim.

Which is how I came to meet Dr. John Scanlon (credentialed
sociologist; self-styled "behaviorist") and how, later, I came to
find myself sitting on a miniature cliff at the edge of an island

in the South Pacific, holding an absurd discussion with myself and a pink-legged robot named Freddy, who, it had turned out, was much more Scanlon's creation than mine.

For Scanlon was also a man with some radical notions, not the least of which was his view that any behavior—*any* behavior—could be programmed if described specifically enough. He believed, in fact, that it would be possible, given the time and money, to build a robot that would act just like a man, in every essential detail. And he seemed to be proving it.

Whereas . . . well, what had become of my notion of a robot that would generate its own culture, becoming manlike from the inside out? Apparently the difference in approach was subtle enough to escape the attention of most of the scientists and technicians in the project, including its directors, who couldn't figure out why I remained dissatisfied with Scanlon's Alternates. What was my gripe? they asked. Weren't we producing a machine that acts and talks and thinks like a human? Well . . .

Anyway, I'd figured the humanities contingent would see the difference—and they did. The trouble was, they backed Scanlon, because, from their point of view, he was only creating an elaborate puppet, while I was bent on designing a machine with a soul. They knew what I was up to from the beginning, as I'd expected, but, unexpectedly, they opposed it. And what made things worse was that the humanities contingent included the *other* Dr. Saricks—Sarah, of art history.

III

So now I'd been up all night, with some small part of my mind wondering all that time where Sarah might be, though I was just enough afraid of seeming foolish to go looking for her. I could tell myself truthfully that our time scale on the island had gotten so skewed by work habits and tantalizing ocean nights that her being gone overnight didn't really mean anything. On the other hand, I couldn't tell myself very convincingly that it didn't still feel sad to be left by oneself in the private darkness of a Project cottage, with dim lights and voices rising from the other cottages all around.

Not that the company of Freddy the First had been much better. The isolation of the island had its merits, but what I really needed, I felt, was someone uninvolved with the daily doings of the Project. So I'd been waiting out the dawn, really, to have a talk with the Rev. Roger Michaelson, our resident philosopher, theologian and recluse, who had pitched his cottage out this way, away from the human village, right after the third Alternate died.

Near where Freddy and I had been sitting, the white road to the human village was cut by a narrow, shallow stream that zigzagged down from the island's "mountain range" (essentially, a big pile of rocks over on the leeward side). The stream itself was never more than a minor nuisance for the humans—especially since most of us went barefoot—but it was, by design, a serious survival problem for the Alternates, since moisture could literally kill them (quickly, through a short circuit, or slowly, through oxidation) and all the stationary energy sources —the Alternates' food analogue—were located on the side opposite the Alternate village.

In the Project's "primitive period"—before I'd been overruled by a majority vote to give them radio access to the World Information Bank at Alexandria—the Alternates (or rather some Alternate, subsequently imitated by the others) had devised a heavy, awkward, barely seaworthy raft, made of the native wood and caulked with sap. The unreliable raft had gone down, finally, causing the death of the two Alternates aboard. Another raft had been built—a virtual duplicate of the first— but before it could kill any more robots, they'd been plugged into the WIB, after which they'd promptly constructed a functional, wooden bridge, which Ray Pierson, one of the engineers, termed the "first wonder of the Alternate world."

Before that, however, in the last days of the "primitive period," when each Alternate had access only to his own experience and observations, plus whatever he might get second hand from one of his compatriots, there had been a third death—that of an Alternate named Robert–4—and the Rev. Michaelson, late of Cambridge, had promptly moved his cottage to the spot beside the stream where Robert–4 had been found, with the avowed purpose of "investigating the mystery."

The "mystery" lay in the fact that Robert–4's death was still unexplained in terms of mechanical or electronic malfunction; he had simply stopped working. He had been found, completely immobile and unresponsive, just by the bank of the stream one morning, across from a SES, but apparently undamaged. There'd been a thunderstorm the night before, so it had been thought at first that he might have been caught out in it, or suffered electrical damage (the Alternates lost radio contact with one another during lightning storms), but investigation had shown otherwise. Scanlon labeled it a "software malfunction," poked around a little bit, and then shrugged and let it go at that. There was plenty of functional hardware to work with.

Michaelson and I had had a lot of entertaining arguments about the nature of man and culture, back in the early weeks of the Project, a time when I looked momentarily for the dawn of Alternate culture—a dawn that never broke. He had never been quite as hostile as most of the other humanities people— nor had he ever shown much enthusiasm for Scanlon's miracles of programming. In fact, his attitude had seemed one of amused tolerance, and he had given me the distinct impression that he expected the Project to have no important outcome, except possibly for the arguments themselves. I'd lost contact with him, as I had with nearly everyone, including Sarah, when things started turning sour for me, and I'd taken his surprising interest in the Robert-4 matter as merely an excuse to separate himself from the rest of us and from the undercurrent of hostility that had entered Project discussions.

Now, as I came over a sandy rise above the neck of the stream where his cottage stood, I found him stretching away sleepiness in the door of his cabin, a heavy, bearded man dressed in undershorts and a T-shirt. At the same instant, flashes of light arose all around me, tiny bulbs set in metal poles planted in the sand —the Alternates' weather lights. When they flashed it meant there was a 99 percent chance of precipitation within the next twenty-four hours.

"There now," Michaelson said, sweeping an arm around at the blinking lights as I approached, "that ought to be creativity enough for any man."

Though I guessed he was being facetious, I shook my head and said, "No. Just straight-line logic. Precipitation is a survival threat, and they have direct access to virtually all the meteorological data in the world. I wouldn't be surprised if an ordinary computer could be programmed to forecast weather as well . . . if weather prediction were a survival matter for anyone with access to a computer."

Michaelson smiled and stretched again. Near his shoulder, beside the cottage door, hung a wood-burned sign reading "HEADQUARTERS—ROBERT THE FOURTH LEAGUE." I tapped it with a knuckle.

"Have you solved your mystery yet?"

"Certainly. Nothing to it." Then he grinned. "However, the semanticist in me insists on pointing out that mysteries, by definition, have no solution. Problems may be solved, but mysteries may only be . . . considered, meditated upon. However, it would be true to say that I have solved the problem of the mysterious death of Robert the Fourth, and the solution is this: Robert the Fourth was himself confronted with a mystery, whereas he was equipped only to recognize and deal with problems. He was, of course, unable to cope—went mad, perhaps— and ceased functioning. This raises, of course, yet another problem . . ."

"What was the mystery that drove him crazy?"

"Just so. Come along and I'll show you." He turned and led me along a flattened path in the sand between his cottage and the stream, to the elbow of the stream where I knew Robert-4 had been found. I half expected some sort of monument, but there was none. "There," Michaelson said, pointing. "That log."

Nearly at our feet was a long, thin tree trunk, doubtless uprooted by some storm, which had gotten wedged crosswise into the curve of the bank, trapping a tiny, stagnant, semicircular lagoon between itself and the sand.

"What about it?" I asked.

Michaelson shook his head sadly.

"In some ways, the Alternates are better philosophers, better observers of reality, than we," he said. "Though, of course, they can't avoid it. Ah, well. When you look at that log you see only a former tree. Robert the Fourth saw it as it is now."

"A dam, you mean?"

"Not bad. What else?"

I stared at the log, trying to figure what Michaelson was driving at.

"Come, come," he said. "What is it that crosses the surface of a body of water, connecting two points of land?"

"You mean a bridge? But the two points are on the same side."

"Irrelevant. Anyway, you might say the same thing, logically, of a bridge across a river. You *could* walk around it by going all the way to the source."

I shrugged.

"Okay, it's a bridge. Why should that drive an Alternate crazy?"

"In this case, because the Alternate didn't need a bridge. He already had a raft."

"So what? The Alternates do things different ways."

"Now they do. But . . . well, what kinds of software did you order up originally?"

I thought back, mentally ticking them off.

"Space, time and causality; an overriding survival directive; visual coding of data; generalized curiosity; an instinctual fear of moisture; some pain and pleasure analogues . . . that's about it."

"What about bounding?"

"Bounding? I didn't care."

"Yet you have to do it one way or the other; the universe has to be bounded or unbounded. I asked. In the primitive period it was bounded. Every bit of data stored by the Alternates at that time was fitted into a perfectly closed system, a perfectly ordered universe. And, of course, each new bit of data further limited the scope of that universe." He shrugged. "Some kind of anomie was inevitable. A bounded universe is fine when you're dealing with an ordinary computer, but not one that's roaming around in the real world."

I was nodding, thinking about it. This was news to me, something I hadn't thought about. I wondered briefly if Scanlon had done it intentionally, a part of some subtle sabotage plan. But that was unlikely; it was undoubtedly my own fault for ignoring the question. Some technician had probably just flipped a coin or something.

"So he wasn't prepared to accept an alternative solution to a problem he'd already solved," I said.

"Just so," said Michaelson. "He died of despair."

"Despair?"

"Of course. A rejection of the order one perceives in the universe, which is a rejection of God, which is a loss of hope, which is despair. As an anthropologist you must be aware that too much anomalous experience can lead to a similar reaction in humans. In Robert the Fourth's bounded universe, one anomaly was enough. Now, of course, the Alternates are living in an unbounded universe, since they have been hooked to WIB and have access to virtually all data, so that any reality is conceivable, because the world in its fullness is not ordered—or, at least, what order it has is not revealed in phenomena. In such a universe, of course, despair is impossible . . . as is hope."

I glanced at Michaelson, trying to read his expression through the thick hair on his face.

"And that suits you, in this case," I said.

He shrugged but didn't smile.

"Give me a moment to get dressed," he said, "and I'll join you for breakfast in the village."

While he stepped into the cottage, I wandered back toward the stream, where there were low, scrubby bushes sticking out of the sand, plus occasional stands of palm and bamboo. Out toward the road the land was smoother, except for a small stretch along one portion of the stream itself, where odd little flowers, looking something like tulips though multicolored, were scattered. The sky above the sea was no darker than before, but the weather lights still flashed all around, and I could see several Alternates, off toward the island's center, moving unhurriedly in the direction of their village. When Michaelson reappeared, we moved slowly along the stream bank toward the hump of the road and our own village.

When we were near the sea again I paused and asked him,

"You think this is all a dead end, don't you?"

Seeing I was asking the question seriously, he said, "Yes, I do. Your conception of it, anyway. Of course, there's no telling what Scanlon's model-making may lead to, though I find it all rather pointless, however entertaining."

I studied him a moment.

"But something about Robert-4 has settled all this in your mind," I said. "What is it?"

He sighed.

"Because it seems clear to me," he said, "that what protects man from despair in the face of chaos is his intuition of the actual order that underlies reality, even if it isn't apparent—his belief that things really do make sense, ultimately. The Westerner may ascribe anomalies to the presence of evil in the world, the Easterner to the illusory nature of what the senses reveal, the totemist to man's own incompleteness apart from nature . . . but all agree that there is some reality back of everything, something to believe in."

I shrugged.

"Cultures all have their different faiths," I said, "growing out of their different experiences."

Michaelson gave a deep sigh.

"I'm really not trying to argue for one true path," he said. "I'm only pointing out that humans have faith in an underlying order, which enables them to disregard apparent anomalies and to perceive truths which are not amenable to proof. But if you try to reprogram the Alternates to assume that there is such a reality, that there are such truths, all you're going to get are more Robert the Fourths, and much more quickly."

I stood in silence for a long time, looking out over the sea, trying to follow Michaelson's reasoning out to some point where I might find an answer to make to it, but I found I couldn't concentrate that well. It does make a kind of sense, I thought, perhaps that's all there is to it. I wanted my mind to come to grips with it, but there seemed to be too many personal and professional irritants intervening. I grew tired of thinking about things and decided to let Michaelson have what he clearly regarded as a victory.

"It's odd how we never the notice the ocean when it's all around us like this," I said at last.

Michaelson put a hand on my shoulder.

"Let's go get breakfast," he said.

IV

Perhaps my problem is that I always expect things to be simpler than they really are. That's certainly the way it was with Sarah, anyway. I accepted at face value her disavowals of her parents' middle-class values, her protests that she wanted no children, only a career and a mate who would let her pursue it. That's the way I felt, too, so it was something of a surprise when, in the third year of our marriage, Sarah told me bitterly, "You don't want a wife; you want a female roommate."

If I'd been from a middle-class home myself, perhaps I'd have recognized the pattern. Or perhaps I'd only have been more trapped by it. In any event, I don't think I'd have been quite as astonished when Sarah discovered that she really didn't want to be an art-history professor after all, that she really liked staying home and cooking and cleaning and generally bothering me, that children might not be so bad after all. I preferred to view it as a phase she was going through, perhaps in reaction to some of the rather extreme antimale views of some of her female-academe friends. Knowing they'd be only too happy to blame me for forcing Sarah back into the kitchen, should I assent to it, I chose to regard the whole thing as her problem, which she must work out. After a time, in fact, she stopped complaining about her teaching and she stopped talking about children, but she seemed to have lost some measure of happiness.

The trip to the island, in part, was intended as a chance to help her regain it, thanks to my underestimation, once again, of the difficulties that lay ahead. I honestly thought that the Project was overstaffed by far—that there was nothing to do but program the software I'd asked for into a computer with mobility, manipulation and binocular vision, then place it in an environment with survival problems and the means of solving them, and culture would inevitably blossom. I figured the Project for an expensive lark and a chance to get things right between Sarah and myself.

At first, in the primitive period, things even went as expected. The Alternates wandered aimlessly, driven at first by curiosity and then by hunger or pain analogues. They stored data and shared it to solve minor problems. And Sarah and I, caught up in the island and the sea and the expectation of success, wandered with them, among them, a part of their scenery and the data they were gathering. We swam and danced and postured and even gave little impromptu plays for them, while Scanlon and what I thought of as his large, superfluous staff languished in the village, playing computer games and agitating for something to do. But Sarah and I were as little concerned about their activities as the Alternates were about ours. Once we made love in broad daylight, on a secluded beach, and found later that three of the Alternates had joined us—but that they were apparently entranced by the sidewise progress of a sandspider dragging some morsel to his den.

Two weeks later it was clear that things were going wrong. There was the double "drowning," of course, though incidents like that had been expected. But then observers reported that no further change was taking place. The Alternates had solved all available problems and had ceased exploring, initiating new behaviors and communicating with one another. Robert-4 died. Scanlon's group pushed for more programming and I was badly outvoted on the compromise measure of giving them access to the WIB.

Even with that, though, it was becoming painfully clear that they hadn't a wisp of genuine culture.

"If they were intelligent animals," Joe Lincoln, our zoologist, pointed out, "they'd at least oil one another in the hard-to-reach places. But they don't."

Scanlon stepped in with an offer to help "smooth out this hitch in Dr. Saricks' project," and I relinquished effective control of things rather than face more votes.

Scanlon was a couple of years younger than I, and I had been a prodigy so far, at least beyond the doctoral level. I had thought of him as a bright kid, boyish and cheerful, charming but deluded in his views of human behavior. In our private conference which marked the shift in the Project's orientation, I saw for the first time the arrogant self-confidence that underlay his charm.

"You've been proceeding as if you took Genesis literally," he told me, grinning as if he meant me to take it as a joke. "Men didn't start off with free will, or whatever you want to call it. They must have been nothing but bundles of instincts at one time, like other primitive animals, and gradually evolved to nonprogrammed behavior. We need to start a little farther back —prime the pump a little, you see—and then gradually replace bits of the preprogramming until we reach the point where, say, a younger generation of Alternates has the freedom to build on or rebel against the behavior patterns of preceding generations."

I could hear how reasonable it would sound to someone who hadn't been following my own line of thought, and I knew I was licked, but I told him, "The only thing wrong is that we'd be creating their culture for them, in advance, then taking away the exterior compulsions, instead of letting them build their own, without our direction."

He dismissed it with a grin.

"As long as they end up with a society whose patterns are no longer instinctual, what's the difference?"

There wasn't any point in trying to answer that.

V

Sarah and Scanlon were sitting in the commissary together, finishing breakfast, when Michaelson and I arrived. If I'd been alone I might have sat somewhere else, but with Michaelson there I felt obliged to join them.

"I think we've got the love problem licked," Scanlon told me, by way of greeting, as we sat down.

I knew what he was talking about, but Michaelson didn't, and the look that flickered across his face drew a sharp giggle from Sarah. She slapped Scanlon on the arm, as if correcting him.

"Think what you're saying," she told him. "All of us in the humanities are afraid that's exactly what you're up to—licking the love problem and all those other annoying, unscientific human eccentricities."

Scanlon answered with more seriousness than the point deserved: "Eccentric behavior is just behavior as far as I'm concerned. I don't condemn any kind of behavior; I'm just interested in describing it systematically."

"The behavior analogue for love has been one of the tricky ones," I told Michaelson.

"I should certainly hope so."

"But not impossible," said Scanlon, brightening. "In fact, the key to it is simply the fact that the Alternates are already individuated somewhat in terms of appearance and idiosyncratic behaviors. None is exactly like any other. In fact, when you start adding up the permutations—especially figuring positive and negative potentialities for each—you get a very large number indeed, though finite, of course."

"Pardon me," Michaelson interjected. "It occurs to me that the Alternates are no more likely to be impressed by large numbers than by small ones. Haven't they the ability to extrapolate all possible permutations, given the pattern?"

Scanlon waved it off, grinning broadly.

"Sure. But this pattern isn't programmed in at a cognitive level—it's preprogrammed, as part of their fundamental software, which they don't have direct access to. It should all be a complete mystery to them."

Michaelson glanced at me and raised an eyebrow.

"'A complete mystery,'" he repeated. "Perhaps Dr. Scanlon is on the right track after all."

Scanlon gave me a piercing glance, then said to Michaelson, "You have to realize that we're talking about love as a defined complex of behaviors, which might not be the same thing you mean by the word. Basically, we're proceeding on the assumption that love consists of the sum of graduated positive and negative affective responses to idiosyncratic differences in individuals identified as potential recipients of love behavior." He waited for a moment, as if he expected Michaelson to say something, but the philosopher only stared at him, so he went on. "Specifically, then, we assign different positive and negative affective values, at random, to each individual characteristic and then preprogram those values into one of the Alternates. Each Alternate gets a different set of values, representing affective responses, so that one gets a big charge out of green torsos and long arms, while another can't stand that combination. And so on. The result is that each Alternate appears to each other Alternate as a complex sum of positive and negative affective responses. We assume, then, that each individual will seek to affiliate himself with the one that offers the best available combination of characteristics."

"Suppose the one with the best set of characteristics can't stand the other one at all?" I asked.

"Then the first one might have to settle for something less. But that's great, you see. We can't have enough problematic experience. Hopefully, we'll get unrequited love, love triangles . . . oh, whatever you can think of."

"Falling out of love?" Sarah asked.

But before Scanlon could say anything Michaelson asked, "What about procreation and sex? If the one, what about family relationships? If the other, what about things like homosexuality and prostitution?"

Scanlon spread his hands apart.

"At this point," he said, "those are largely hardware problems. I suppose eventually we'll make it possible for any two Alternates to reproduce themselves somehow by cooperating to derive mutual pleasure from the process."

"That's a typical male approach," Sarah said with surprising vehemence. "You're tying sex to procreation, making it completely mechanistic and giving them two sexes, one of which—"

"I didn't say anything about sexes," Scanlon interrupted, completely serious again. "I said *any* two of them. Anyway, these are things we really haven't thought about yet."

"I've thought about them some," I offered. "I think it might be a good idea to have two sexes, since eventually they're going to have to have some kind of 'natural' group identifications, to give them the capacity for class systems and division of labor and so on."

"Masters and servants," said Sarah, turning on me. "That's what your division of labor means: Somebody has to do the dirty work and somebody gets to give orders. So you're planning sexist robots. Why not racism too? Maybe they'll think of slavery."

"We may and they may," I said, finding myself glad to have her attention, even in the guise of hostility, and disliking myself for the feeling. "Come on. You know enough about anthropology to know that social injustice only seems unjust in a society that no longer has any use for it."

"I just have to feel there's something better," she said remotely, as if suddenly tiring of the whole discussion. Michaelson reached across the table and patted her hand but didn't say anything.

"Professionally, I'm afraid I have to agree with your husband," Scanlon said, then added, "But of course we all agree that such things are unjust in our own society. Frankly, though, I don't think you have too much to worry about. I have a hunch it's going to turn out that the Alternates are simply too logical to be able to rationalize such behavior the way man does. Perhaps this has been our problem all along in the Project." He gave me another pointed glance, but Michaelson picked up on what he had said faster than I did.

"You seem to be arguing," he said, "that the key difference between man and Alternate is the efficiency of the reasoning faculty."

Scanlon grew earnest.

"I'm only suggesting that what we call creativity may only be a kind of fanciful guesswork, springing from ignorance and inconsistency in the use of reason. You in the humanities are fond of pointing out that there's a thin line between genius and insanity. From my point of view, that's just another way of saying that sometimes it works and sometimes it doesn't—that the behavior itself is nonsystematic." He gave a little smile and turned to me. "Isn't that how magic works?"

"Magic," I quoted from some textbook, "is a way of attempting to do what one hasn't the technology to do."

"Or to solve what can't be solved," said Michaelson. "A mystery, in other words. Yes. All these things seem bound up together. Perhaps you are right, in a sense, Dr. Scanlon. Though, instead of saying that man is ignorant, I would say that man has a greater, intuitive knowledge of the world than the Alternatives can have, limited as they are to phenomena and logic."

Scanlon only grinned broadly and spread his hands apart. I understood then that they were both satisfied to have rejected my views of the matter—that they each felt they could live with each other's. Between them, whatever the philosophical differences, they had dismissed the notion that human culture and creativity might be duplicated in another form, without some kind of active outside intervention—be it behavioral analogues or God.

I sat for a while longer, listening to their small talk, then left the three of them there.

VI

It grew muggy toward noon and seemed hotter than usual, though out over the sea, to windward, we could see the dark clouds beginning to form up. I killed the rest of the morning doing laundry before I realized the storm would arrive just about the time I was hanging things out to dry, so I just piled them, wet, into wicker baskets and lay down for a nap, beginning to feel the effects of the sleepless night before.

Sometime during the late morning Sarah came in, but I pretended to be sound asleep and watched through nearly closed lids as she undressed and slipped into her bathing suit, then left again. The sight of her changing clothes awakened a touch of drowsy lust in me, making me think that not many weeks ago it would have been easy to touch her in such circumstances, to be vulnerable, but now we had gotten into our old unhappy patterns and I knew there was too much chance of being rebuffed.

But after she'd gone I couldn't get to sleep again, so I got up and put on some sandals (visibility is poor during storms and there are things you wouldn't want to step on barefoot) and went back outside, trying to think of someone to visit. But there wasn't anyone—so many of us, it seemed, given the opportunity, had turned into hermits, like Michaelson. It hadn't seemed strange to me before, but now it made me vaguely irritated at myself for being a part of it.

I went to the commissary and ate lunch by myself, then headed out toward the Alternate village, taking the long way around, to leeward. There was no road on that side, not even a path—just a sort of rocky plateau rising above the sea, cut by shallow, jagged ravines that ran out to the cliffs, above a broad, white beach that was not easy to get to. For that matter, it was hard country to walk in, all up and down, soft sand and pointed rocks. The Alternates kept to this side of the island, mostly, because there was less sea spray, but the broken terrain made movement so difficult for them that they had constructed watertight cabanas everywhere. You were seldom more than fifty feet from one.

I found Fred-1 and three other Alternates pitching horseshoes on one of the incredibly long courts they had set up, and I waited for a break in the game before asking Freddy if he'd join me for a talk. Scanlon claimed human consideration was lost on the Alternates (indeed, they seemed to take any human request as an order, unless it threatened survival), but I liked to imagine that they appreciated it.

"How much do you understand of the way your mind works?" I asked as we strolled out toward the sea cliffs.

"Only what is available to my retrieval system. I know there is some information that was preprogrammed—that I have no access to—but I don't understand this."

"Understanding the essential workings of our minds is also man's greatest unsolved problem," I told him, wondering how he would receive such a generalization.

"I think it's incorrect to say this is a problem for us," he said, "since we aren't attempting to solve it."

"You sure aren't ones to borrow trouble."

"How could trouble be borrowed?" Freddy asked. Idiomatic speech had always been one of the gray areas of the Project.

"In this case," I said, "it means seeking solutions for which no present need exists. Properly, I suppose, it's a matter of foresight—projecting future needs and acting to solve them now."

"We do that, but on the basis of probability. Does 'borrowing trouble' include situations of low-probability projected need?"

I nodded.

"I guess that's right. But how probably does something have to be before you worry about it?"

"Forty percent or higher. Fifty percent would be sufficient, logically, but forty gives us what is called an edge . . . correct?"

I shrugged.

"But you ignore everything below forty?"

"Yes."

"As far as I'm concerned, that takes away your edge."

I sat down on a smooth boulder only a few feet from one of the cabanas, knowing that Freddy would want to be getting inside before long. The air had turned perceptibly cooler while we walked, and there was a dark lid of cloud across the opposite half of the island.

"Frankly," I told him, "your notion of probability is somewhat simplistic—even archaic. There is a philosophical dimension to probability as well as a mathematical one. Am I right that your computations are based solely on logic and numerical frequency?"

"Yes."

"Scanlon has left out the concept of subjective probability, then?"

"No. I am acquainted with that concept, but it is not very useful to us. It is true that Dr. Scanlon feels that subjective probability refers to instances where humans make erroneous projections on the basis of insufficient data, but it is also true that this is borne out by the literature."

"Some literature," I pointed out. "I would challenge the word 'erroneous' for starters. Hunches often turn out to be correct."

"But not because they are properly data-based. If one projects a seventy-five percent chance of rainfall when in reality the probability of rain is ninety-five percent, the computation is erroneous, though the general prediction of rain is likely to be accurate."

"But only by accident," I murmured, shaking my head. It seemed to me suddenly that Scanlon had been creating the Alternates in the likeness of the earnest young graduate students who surrounded him back in California. "Despite Dr. Scanlon's obvious low opinion of humanity," I told Freddy, "the fact remains that subjective probability is a matter of some controversy in the literature."

"Yes," said the Alternate. "Dr. Michaelson and some others believe that the human mind is somehow not less but more efficient than ours and therefore capable of projecting what you call 'hunches' on the basis of data that exists but is not apprehended cognitively. This is similar to the belief in so-called psionic abilities, which is also mentioned in some of the literature. But substantial research indicates that Dr. Scanlon's view has the highest probability of being correct."

I smiled.

"On the basis of observed frequency?"

"Yes."

"So you assume the truth of Scanlon's view in order to support an argument in support of Scanlon's view. That's not even circular; it's tautological."

"What is tautology," asked Freddy, "but logic at its purest?"

I tried to think of some way to respond to that, but before I had the Alternate began moving away from me.

"Please excuse me," he said. "I have to get inside now."

"Sure." I waved a hand at the closing door of the cabana and looked out over the nearby cliff at the ocean, where everything had turned black, sea and sky. Out beyond the shelter of the island, breakers whipped and scattered along a double line of coral, but with the storm behind me and the island between, I could see that the water nearest the shore was relatively calm. I walked that way, to think and to watch the storm change the sea as it advanced. As the expanse of calm water below the cliffs became more visible, I picked out a solitary swimmer churning

rapidly for the beach beneath me. Thinking it might be someone who would need assistance, I dropped into one of the ravines that opened out of the cliff face and began making my way
down it, over the rocks and debris washed up by past storms.

I thought of what Freddy had said as I clambered: What is
tautology but logic at its purest? The statement seemed so
sweeping in its innocence, its implicit ignorance of the world,
that I found myself wondering if we had succeeded without
realizing it. Perhaps a genuine Alternate culture would be so
different in orientation that we might fail to recognize it. But
no—it was only Scanlon's own innocence talking. Like Michaelson, he believed there was an order in things, but he was naïve
enough to think it could be comprehended.

At that moment the first heavy drops of water struck laterally
against my back, like soft pebbles tossed by the wind, and a
small flood appeared between my feet, in the V-bottom of the
ravine, reminding me belatedly that the channel had probably
been dug by just such storms as this and that water would soon
be pouring from the ravine to the beach below, as if from a
drain spout. So when I came to the mouth, opening out of the
cliff's face, I pulled myself up onto a rough boulder embedded
in the ravine wall, looking for a way up instead of down.

But it was looking down that I saw Sarah rising from the
shallow water and splashing awkwardly toward the beach,
where Scanlon waited with two large towels draped over his
arms. He tossed one around her shoulders as she drew near, and
then the two of them passed out of my sight, back toward the
cliff face beneath.

For only a second, then, I again considered climbing down,
and in my moment of hesitation the full storm descended. The
rain itself was warm, but the water soaking my clothing and hair
turned cold when the wind hit it. At its peak, the water fell so
heavily that the beach was obscured, but slackened as quickly
as it had begun, settling down after a few minutes to a steady,
quiet, windless shower, reminding me of summer storms in the
city, back home.

I could have moved away then if I'd wanted, but I felt oddly
weary and indecisive, willing for the moment to sit rather than

make the effort to move. The chill wasn't intolerable, and I felt, in that moment, as if I might choose to remain squatting there on my boulder for eternity, my shirt scrunched up against the back of my neck and my hair dripping onto my cheeks. It seemed, in that moment, a safe, unobjectionable thing: simply stasis, no movement or thought or responsibility or hurt. My own culture, and the smaller circles inside it that had had most meaning for me, seemed suddenly unimportant—depressingly so. Something chugged feebly in the professional recesses of my mind, pointing out that what I was feeling was a classic, although mild, form of anomie.

And, as if to underline the point, Sarah came bounding out into the open below, her face and arms opened to catch the warm rain. Perhaps because I was distracted, or perhaps only because I was used to seeing her that way, it was a few seconds before I fully realized that she was naked. Scanlon appeared behind her just then, also without his bathing suit, looking exactly as stiff and foolish and uncomfortable as I would have felt (as I had felt!) in a similar situation. I edged back into the ravine, thinking that he might glance about self-consciously and spot me there.

I had—or thought I had—been prepared for this moment. At any rate, I had fantasized such situations and my most likely responses to them, and it had always seemed to me, in conjecture, that there would be a kind of relief in having things worked out one way or the other—one more problem settled for all time. But with the fantasy come true, my mind trying to fit itself into one of my preconceived responses, I found myself muttering aloud, "Well, that's that, then. Sarah's in the past now. I have to think forward, not back." And it sounded hollow even to me.

For my real response, behind the words, was a hurt, inarticulate awareness of the world having been disrupted in some fundamental way, plus a deep fear, nearly a conviction, that nothing was going to be good for me any more, that life was going to be intolerably difficult. Then, abruptly, I found my entire body trembling with a surge of hatred for Scanlon so intense I thought for a moment I was going to be physically ill.

Sarah was only one of the media by which Scanlon had attacked me, it seemed, working these changes in my life. I felt for a second that I could kill him joyfully—perhaps would—but then it passed and I was left with the earlier mood to withdraw, to choose not to act or to care or to live. Like Job, I thought: Curse God and die.

"Dr. Saricks? Where are you? Are you all right?"

It was Fred-1, calling to me from somewhere above and behind, the rain having stopped, apparently for good. In a moment of wild comedy I realized that they would hear his voice on the beach below and would think he was calling to Sarah. I could no longer see them, but I imagined them suddenly transfixed in mid-stride (or mid-something) like a nymph and satyr chasing each other round an old Greek urn. But then I sighed. After all, Freddy was just an Alternate; maybe they'd pay no attention.

I jumped down from the boulder and squished my way back through the dying rivulet to where I could climb up over the side, covering myself with wet sand.

"Freddy," I told him when I found him, "I have some need of your logic." And we talked for a time about sin and despair and the chaotic universe.

VII

"Whatever you said to him, it won't make any difference to you and me," Sarah told me after Scanlon had gone off and left us alone near the cliff top, where I'd waited for the two of them. Sarah had hung back at first, then joined us when she saw we were going to talk rather than fight. Was it only my imagination, or had she seemed disappointed to find that we were discussing not her but the Project?

"I know," I told her, "but it will make a difference to me. And perhaps more of one for you than you think right now." I glanced down the path Scanlon had taken, hurrying back to his work. "He's going to fail, you know."

"Do you really think that's how it is with me?" she asked.

"That I'm some tribal female, mating with the one who wins? Well, it is a matter of strength, but not that way. You wanted me to be stronger than I am. John is willing to let me be weak and support me in it."

I found that this was no surprise. Under my resentment I could even feel a sense growing that things might have worked out for the best, after all. Though I still intended to have my revenge, as Scanlon, I hoped, would come to realize.

All I had done was point out the implications of Michaelson's reasoning: that the Alternates' universe had to be unbounded because there was no order they could perceive in the chaos of data they had access to—that he was left with choosing between Michaelson's intrinsic order or no order at all.

When he'd gone for the latter, as I'd expected, I suggested that man's uniqueness may lie neither in his ignorance nor his institutions but in his arbitrariness—his ability to *make* order out of chaos, to believe not in what *is* but in what makes sense.

There was really no need to say more; he had taken over, talking eagerly of randomness and model-building, and then he'd gone to "try some new wrinkles," while I posed for myself the questions I hadn't asked him: How can a group of logical minds agree on truths contradicted by the data they have? And, even if they do, how can you get them then to change their minds and accept something they've previously excluded? For, in every living culture, there are those who insist on seeing what is, not what is agreed to, and who insist on forcing it on the rest of us until we finally find a way of making it fit. And how could you get an Alternate to do that? That would be the final sticking place for Scanlon.

"He's used to success," I said aloud. "He's known nothing else, so he'll have to follow this line until he fails at it."

"Will that make you happy, then?" Sarah asked. I'd forgotten she was still there.

"No," I said truthfully, "but it will make him unhappy. And you, too, perhaps. I'll settle for that, I think." I gave a little bark of laughter that sounded unpleasant even to me. "You know," I added, "when he's built an Alternate that knows how to feel vindictive, I may admit he's got something. Perhaps you'll re-

member to tell him that—sometime when you're feeling vindictive."

Sarah turned her back to me then and walked away, and I felt
something touch my cheeks, so I turned back the other way,
toward the island center, thinking: There will never be an Alternate that can weep, not with their fear of moisture. And I
laughed to myself without any joy.